A VERY BAD HABIT

Liza gasped. The warmth of Chad's hands, still on her shoulders, spread through her body and curled into all her secret places. She swayed toward him, and as his mouth came down on hers, her arms rose involuntarily to clasp him to her. His lips were warm and demanding, and she opened herself to them in a wondering response. His hands moved down the length of her back, causing her to arch against him, and when they cupped her breasts, a muted cry of longing escaped her.

"Oh, my dear," he whispered against her mouth, "old habits die hard, don't they?" Old habits! That was what she was to him. A habit in which he indulged.

"Yes," she replied. "But I am determined to break this one." But even as she whirled and ran from the room, she knew it was easier said than done. . . .

LADY LIZA'S LUCK

by

Anne Barbour

A SIGNET BOOK

SIGNET
Published by the Penguin Group
Penguin Books USA Inc., 375 Hudson Street,
New York, New York 10014, U.S.A.
Penguin Books Ltd, 27 Wrights Lane,
London W8 5TZ, England
Penguin Books Australia Ltd, Ringwood,
Victoria, Australia
Penguin Books Canada Ltd, 10 Alcorn Avenue,
Toronto, Ontario, Canada M4V 3B2
Penguin Books (N.Z.) Ltd, 182–190 Wairau Road,
Auckland 10, New Zealand

Penguin Books Ltd, Registered Offices:
Harmondsworth, Middlesex, England

First published by Signet,
an imprint of New American Library,
a division of Penguin Books USA Inc.

First Printing, October, 1993
10 9 8 7 6 5 4 3 2 1

for Delores Ekberg,
whose friendship and support are
so greatly appreciated

Chapter 1

AFTER a period of chill rain, spring had given notice of its arrival in London. On a fine March morning, the sun glistened on neat wrought iron railings and polished brass door handles, and fairly cascaded into the breakfast room of a certain elegant town house in Berkeley Square. Here it gleamed on fine silver and delicate china of Lady Elizabeth Rushlake, seated at the table, coffee cup in hand.

"Mama," she said, breaking the silence that, along with the sunshine, had filled the room for some minutes. "I truly don't mean to offend you, but—"

"Liza." The lady seated across the table spoke severely. She was a small, pretty woman, whose brown hair was barely touched with gray. "You know I have only your interest at heart, and I don't see how you can call it interfering to point out that the way you treated poor Giles last night was positively indefensible."

Liza sighed. It was quite true. She had behaved abominably to Giles Davenport, whose only crime had been to propose marriage to her, again.

"He does get tedious, Mama. He must know by now that I do not wish to marry him, nor am I likely to do so in the future."

"But he is so devoted to you, my dear, and has been for years. After all, he . . ."

" . . . is such a nice young man, and he is so eminently eligible." Smiling, Liza finished the sentence in unison with her mother. "We are in agreement on that," she continued. "I am pleased and grateful to have him for a friend, but I do not want him for a husband."

"Then who *would* you like? For a husband. Honestly, Liza, it is beyond understanding why you have let so many opportunities slip through your fingers. You've certainly had offers enough. You should be a matron by now, with babies in your nursery."

"I have told you, Mama," replied Liza a little rigidly. "I am quite happy as I am."

Letitia, the Dowager Countess of Burnsall gazed at her older daughter in exasperation. "Oh, for Heaven's sake. If you were an impoverished antidote, with no hope of making an eligible *parti*, such a statement might be understandable, but you are one of the loveliest women in London. What was it young Chatsfield called you . . . you know, in that ode he wrote?"

Liza lifted a hand in pained protest. "Please, Mama. Not while I'm eating."

Lady Burnsall chuckled and continued, unheeding. " . . . 'A radiant, golden goddess, with eyes of azure . . .' Well, I forget the rest."

Something very like a snort escaped Liza. "That's what I get for being such a long Meg. At least he didn't refer to me as Junoesque, as did Freddie Dashwood. I draw the line at Junoesque."

Her mother grinned mischievously. "You haven't enough bulk for that epithet. Diana, perhaps, or—"

Liza silenced her with a pleading gesture and rose to move to the window where she gazed at the charming garden laid out at the rear of the house. This morning she was garbed in a serviceable ensemble of gray twilled silk, and her skirts fairly crackled in reflection of her annoyance. Her mother eyed her reproachfully.

"You know your father would not approve of this attitude, my dear. It was his dearest wish to see you creditably established."

Liza's generous mouth curved in a smile of remembrance. "That may be, Mama, but thank Heaven he had enough confidence in me to allow me to maintain my independence." She turned impulsively to her mother. "Don't you see? I'm already creditably established. I'm four and twenty!" She ignored Lady Burnsall's moue of derision. "I have a comfortable home, friends, and you and Charity. What more could I want?"

The dowager uttered a small sound of distress. "A husband, of course."

"Mama, we've had this conversation before. I have no desire to trade my independence for the confines of matrimony—

even for what I hear described these days as a love match. I cannot think of a single man of my acquaintance to whom I would wish to turn over my affairs."

"You did not always feel so," returned her mother tartly. "I recall a time when you sighed and blushed like any other smitten damsel. Of course, that was many years ago. . . ."

"Yes," returned Liza in a flat tone, "that was many years ago. Since then, I have become a good deal wiser."

"Oh, my dear, I am so sorry. I did not mean to bring up—"

She was interrupted by Liza's clear laughter. "Mama, you do not think me wearing the willow, I hope? It all took place so long ago. Indeed, it seems as though the green girl who became so hopelessly enamored of Chad Lockridge was another person."

"Oh—but not hopelessly. He may not have been the man for you, but I could have sworn he returned your affection."

"Mm," replied Liza in a determinedly absent tone. "I suppose he did, after a fashion." She returned to the table for a last swallow of coffee. "I must be off, Mama. I have an appointment with Thomas in half an hour."

She turned and moved to the door, but was forestalled by the breathless entrance of a slim, young woman, her light brown hair flying from its ribboned confines.

"Mama! Liza!" she cried. "You'll never guess. . . . Come see!"

With that, the girl whirled and was gone as quickly as she had come. Liza ruefully reflected that her eighteen-year-old sister, though having emerged from the schoolroom almost two years before, still exhibited the bubbling enthusiasm of an inquisitive puppy. Exchanging glances of amusement, Liza and the youthful dowager followed.

"Charity, what in the world . . . ?" asked Lady Burnsall of her younger daughter as the girl led them to an elegantly appointed morning room.

"Someone is moving in next door!" she replied excitedly, pointing out the window. Following her gaze, the other two ladies observed a rapidly expanding mound of furniture being deposited by two draymen from their cart onto the sidewalk in front of the adjoining residence.

"But," said Liza in astonishment, "I knew nothing of this. Surely Thomas would not have let the place without apprising me." She turned to her mother. "Do you know who the new tenants are?"

Lady Burnsall returned her gaze blankly. "I have no idea. How very odd, to be sure. You do still own the house, do you not?"

"Of course, Mama. It's been vacant for only a month, you know. Have you seen any of the family?" she asked her sister.

Charity allowed a few seconds dramatic pause before answering. Her deep brown eyes sparkled, and the pink of her cheeks matched her blossom-colored sarcenet morning gown. Liza sighed, girding her patience.

"Apparently, dear sister," said Charity, with a gurgle of delight, "our new neighbor is a native of India!"

Again she paused, to savor the satisfactory expressions of astonishment her words had produced. "There is a very large gentleman with an enormous turban directing activities. He must be in the house now—no, there he is, just emerging."

The wondering stare of all three ladies encompassed the turban and its owner, a mahogany-skinned gentleman who strode down the entrance stairs to direct the draymen's activities. As one, their gaze traveled over fierce, bushy eyebrows, a truly magnificent beard, and below that a snowy expanse of tunic, surely large enough to make up three or four beds, the whole culminating in a pair of feet that could only be described as massive, covered in ornately embroidered slippers. When he reached the street, he began haranguing the unfortunate draymen in an incomprehensible tongue.

"Well!" breathed Lady Burnsall.

"Gracious!" said Liza.

"Isn't he marvelous?" sang Charity.

"We'll see about that," Liza replied, striding purposefully to the front door.

She arrived on the street just as the Indian gentleman lifted, effortlessly and with an expression of disdain, a handsome commode that the draymen had been struggling to remove from the cart. He set the commode on the sidewalk and wheeled to hurl what was obviously an obscenity at the hapless navvies, but stopped on observing Liza's approach.

"Good morning," she said, opening negotiations.

The man's face, arranged haphazardly around an imposing nose, spread into a blinding smile, and, placing his hands to-

gether, he made her such a sweeping bow that she almost recoiled.

"Are . . . are you the new tenant?" she asked hesitantly.

She was rewarded with a delighted and totally unintelligible
reply, complete with grandiloquent gestures.

Lady Liza Rushlake seldom found herself at a loss, but after
a few more ineffectual attempts at communication with this
bronzed giant, she was forced to admit defeat. Back in her own
drawing room, she was unable to provide her questioning relatives with any further information.

"Well, we'll find out soon enough," she said drawing on her
gloves of York tan, "for I shall have the whole out of Thomas.
I cannot believe that he would let the place to a family of Indian immigrants, but, on the other hand, I find it quite surprising that as my man of affairs he would lease it to anyone at all
without informing me first."

She glanced up to find her mother's disapproving gaze on
her, and lifted her own brows questioningly.

"Oh," Lady Burnsall said with a small sniff. "I just wondered at your traveling into the City again. It must be the third
time this week."

Liza sighed inwardly. Would her mother never be reconciled to her daughter's unladylike affinity for the hustle and
bustle of London's center? She did not pause in her preparations to leave the house, merely smiling at the dowager.

"I have some plans I'm hatching with Thomas," she said
with what she hoped was a reassuring smile. "I'll be confer-
ring frequently with him over the next few days, and I must do
so, of course, in person. There . . ." She gestured out the window. "Fletching has brought the barouche around. I must fly."

With that, she kissed her mother's cheek, waved to Charity,
and left the room in what she admitted to herself was a craven
rush.

Once in her carriage, she gave herself up to reflection. Why,
she wondered for the hundredth time, was it considered an eccentricity at best, or a brazen flouting of convention at worst,
for a lady to become a useful member of society instead of a
pampered bargaining chip in the marriage mart? Liza well
knew the whispering that went on behind fluttering fans and
gloved hands at her scandalous activities, and it was only her
fierce stubbornness that had allowed her to avoid the interference of several well-meaning male relatives in her affairs.

It had been some years since she had discovered in herself

the need to escape the confines of her life in the Polite World. She felt an unexpected twinge as she realized that this need had made itself felt immediately after she and Chad . . .

Her hands twisted in her lap, and she was shaken by a storm of remembrance. An image of Chad, still shatteringly clear and strong after all these years, seemed to fill the carriage like a physical presence. She had but to close her eyes, and she could feel his touch on her cheek and his mouth on hers. She recalled the moment they had first met, at a London garden party. He had taken her hand and smiled down at her with those incredible green eyes. She was aware of a shocking response to the laughing wickedness displayed there, as though she had just fallen into the clutches of a charming buccaneer. Russet hair, burnished by the afternoon sunlight, fell across his forehead as he bent to press a light kiss on her fingertips—and it was as though someone had lit a flame inside her. Incredible as it seemed on reflection, she had been caught up instantly in the wondrous dream of her first love. She had been so sure that Chad had shared that dream. She had thrown her heart to him, never doubting that he would catch it and hold it forever.

Returning to the present, she drew herself up. No, she thought icily. She had fought too long and hard to attain the self-possession that was her trademark among the *ton*. It was over—had been over and done with six years ago. This was the second time today she had been reminded of him, and it would be the last.

With an effort she turned her thoughts to more pleasant memories. She smiled as she recalled her first sally into 'Change Alley. She had been in her father's company, though why a man would bring his daughter, still a schoolroom miss, into these profane precincts seemed a mystery to his associates. He had brought her to Threadneedle Street, where he had business with one of the directors of the Bank of England, and she had been spellbound at the purposeful flow of men of serious mien, some in conservative garb and others in exotic costumes that spoke of foreign climes.

On the way home she had insisted on an explanation of Papa's business activities that day. He had already taught his inquisitive daughter the concept of stock ownership, and a gleam of pleasure appeared in his eyes as she readily followed his description of the transactions he had made.

Liza had made many subsequent trips to the City in her father's company, and eventually Lord Burnsall had given her money to start on her own carefully monitored program of investments. She was not very cautious and not terribly wise in her first dabblings in the treacherous waters of Commerce. Often she floundered in the shoals, losing her investment and a measure of dignity, but she learned.

Oh, yes, she thought, as her carriage turned into Nicholas Lane and stopped before a venerable building discreetly embellished with a sign that read, "Messrs. Stanhope, Finch, and Harcourt, Investment Brokers." She had learned well, and now when she appeared in Threadneedle Street, she was greeted with respect by everyone from the lowliest clerk to Mr. Mellish himself, the governor of the Board of Directors of the Bank of England.

Before she had ascended the shallow steps of the offices of Stanhope, Finch, and Harcourt, the door swung open and she was greeted by a clerk who, with great ceremony, swept her past a scattering of lesser persons waiting their turns for appointments on uncomfortable-looking wooden benches, and bore her off to the rooms occupied by the junior member of the firm, Thomas Harcourt.

"Liza!" The man who rose from behind the cluttered desk to greet her was of medium height, with comfortably plump features and friendly brown eyes. "Looking lovely as ever, I see. Would you care for tea?"

In response to her nod, he gestured to the clerk and settled her into a chair opposite his desk.

"None of your humbuggery, Thomas," Liza said, laughing. "I know when you start turning me up sweet it means you're about to talk me into something that I may not at all wish to do."

Thomas Harcourt smiled fondly at the young woman before him. They had known each other since adolescence, and though there had been a time when he'd raged against the social conventions that prevented the son of a vicar from presenting his heart and the meager fortune that went with it to the daughter of the Earl of Burnsall, his feeling for her now was one of deep affection.

"Nonsense." He caught her gaze for a moment, then relaxed into a chuckle. "How unfortunate that my methods are as a crystalline brook to you. You are quite right. I have recently unearthed an investment opportunity that I feel is just right for you, but which you will no doubt believe at first to be another South Sea Bubble. First, however . . ." He rose and moved to a wall safe near his desk. Liza sat up with a delighted gasp. "Thomas! Did you get it? Do you actually have it here?"

"Yes. I drove to Aylesbury three days agó and returned yesterday afternoon. It was indeed in the possession of old Lord Wilbraham, just as my sources told me. For some reason he had no idea of its value, possibly because he purchased it for a song from a man who sold it under financial duress. Wilbraham pretended a great reluctance to sell it, but at last . . ."

As he was speaking, he had drawn a package from the cupboard, which was revealed as a small, velvet-swathed shape, which he handed to Liza. She drew from it in slow reverence a small, curiously carved wooden box. Opening the box carefully, she caught her breath as a ray of sunlight streaming through Thomas's window caused a fiery flash to burst from between her fingers.

Cradled in her hands was an astonishing example of the jewelers' craft. It was a pendant, but it could have been called a miniature sculpture, for it was as large as a man's hand and featured a falconer, carved in ivory, standing against an open-worked, scrolled background, with a falcon on his wrist and two hounds at his feet. Surrounding this incredibly crafted marvel, were several rows of rubies, emeralds, and diamonds, and suspended from the whole were three large pearls. An enameled gold loop at the top provided passage for a chain.

"Oh, Thomas," she breathed, "the Queen's pendant."

"Do you plan to tell Chad you have recovered it?"

"Why?" she asked sharply. "Surely it has nothing to do with him."

"Doesn't have . . . Good God, Liza, it was in his family for centuries, and when it vanished it was thought that he—"

"Nonsense. No one credited that ridiculous story. Chad, a thief? He has his flaws, of which I am only too aware, but anyone who knew him would never question his honesty."

"There were those," said Thomas, "who were all too ready to believe ill of him.

"Nonsense," she repeated and was grateful for the entrance of the junior clerk, carrying a tray. She replaced the pendant in its box and returned it to the velvet carrying pouch. She sat back in her chair to accept a cup of steaming tea, sniffing appreciatively at its aroma.

"Mmm, excellent. I do thank you for your efforts, Thomas, successful as your efforts always are. But now, tell me, have you had any luck with Brightsprings?"

She sighed as she read her answer in Thomas's crestfallen expression. "Never mind, my dear, I know there is little you can do if the owner does not wish to sell. Perhaps I am fated never to possess it."

"Well," he interjected, "Brightsprings was your home for your growing-up years, and it's only natural you should wish to make it your own again. I'm sorry I have been unable to secure it for you. I cannot even find out who owns it. It has been leased for some years to the family living there now, but the landlord prefers to remain anonymous—and his representative has become so secretive about his employer's identity that he has ceased to answer my communications."

Observing her friend's discomfort, Liza turned the subject. "Tell me of this South Sea Bubble of yours."

"Mmm, yes," replied Thomas, eyes alight. "There is a new company forming to promote the development of what is being termed a railroad system."

"Railroads?" asked Liza. A frown creased the smooth perfection of her forehead. "I know cars on rails have been used for transport in the mines for a few years, but as far as I know, further expansion of the idea has not met with success."

"Precisely. However a group of forward-thinking investors has been looking into the possibility of laying rail lines between cities and building cars that could be used not only for the transportation of goods, but of passengers as well."

"Thomas, that sounds like the most complete moonshine!"

"I agree, but think of the possibilities if it were all to come to pass. No one is prepared as yet to sink any funds into the project at present, but it is something to think about for the future. If you don't mind, I shall send out a few feelers to the effect that you—or rather, that Mr. R. Lake is considering the possibility of such an investment."

Liza smiled. "People will think that R. Lake, noted financier, has finally taken leave of his senses, but go ahead."

For an hour the two friends discussed Liza's business interests, discreetly conducted under the pseudonym of R. Lake. Many of those who thought themselves her intimates would have been astounded at the complexity and profitability of her dealings, for the Polite World dismissed her unnatural affinity for the world of Finance as merely an amusing eccentricity, acceptable in one of her impeccable breeding and already comfortable fortune. She was not ashamed of her activities, and, since her investments were by and large in small industry, she was not precisely a giant among financiers, but she knew that publication of her true worth would bring her a great deal of unwanted attention. Thus she was content to let her reputation as a mere taker of tentative flights into the exhilarating altitudes of high finance stand unchallenged.

At last Liza gathered up pelisse and reticule and prepared to make her departure. She moved to the door, but whirled suddenly to face her friend again.

"Thomas! I almost forgot. Who is that extremely odd creature to whom you have let my rental property in the Square?"

Thomas seemed taken aback. "Odd creature?" he asked after a moment.

"You have rented the house, have you not?" she inquired.

"Yes, but . . ."

"To an Indian giant, apparently."

For another long moment Thomas simply stared at her. Then, as comprehension flooded his gaze, a slow flush crept over his cheeks. "Ah—that would be Ravi Chand. He is not your new tenant. That is, he is your tenant's major domo. The, um, gentleman who will shortly take up residence is an Englishman through and through. He has recently returned from an extended sojourn in India, and had not thought to make provisions against his arrival here."

"Indeed?" Liza eyed him curiously. Why, Thomas was perspiring as though he'd been running for his life!

"He stopped in to see me a few days ago." Thomas fidgeted with some papers on his desk. "He has been staying at Fenton's Hotel in St. James's Street, and requested me to acquire temporary lodging until he can acquire a more permanent home. He will make an unexceptionable tenant, I assure you. I—I thought," he concluded stiffly, "you would not mind my going ahead without consulting you on this."

"No, of course not," replied Liza soothingly. "You have done so many times in the past. The man is known to you, then? Does he have a large family? I shall call on them as soon as they are settled, for they may not have many acquaintances here if they have been out of the country for long. What is my new tenant's name?"

Again Thomas paused, an odd expression on his face. "Well, as to that, you will find the name a familiar one, for . . ."

They had by now reached the reception area of the building, and an elderly woman, one of those who had been sitting in the waiting area, rose to accost Thomas. It seemed to Liza that he turned to the woman in some relief.

"There you are, Mr. Harcourt." Her voice matched the sharpness of her features. "I have been waiting this hour for your attention, my good man, and watched you bring others in ahead of me." She glared at Liza. "I have important demands on my time, and I insist that you see me at once."

"Mrs. Beddoes!" To Liza's amusement Thomas's voice contained nothing but pleased surprise. "I had no idea you were out here. I had thought our appointment was not until noon, but I must have been mistaken." He turned to Liza and bestowed upon her a barely perceptible wink. "I shall say good-bye, Lady Elizabeth. I'm sure you will not wish me to slight one of my most valued clients."

Liza smiled understandingly, and with a nod to the still simmering Mrs. Beddoes, she swept out of the premises of Messrs. Stanhope, Finch, and Harcourt.

She had a few other small commissions in the City, so that by the time her carriage made its way back to Berkeley Square, the morning was far advanced. As she descended from the barouche, a stylish curricle pulled up to the entrance of the house next to hers, and Liza paused to note it with some interest.

It must be her new tenant, she surmised, and though he was a tall man, all she could see of him as he handed his whip to a diminutive tiger and prepared to dismount was an elegant curly-brimmed beaver hat and the fashionably high collar of a many-caped greatcoat. He was alone. His wife must already be inside the house, making all presentable for her lord.

She moved to intercept the stranger as he made his way toward the entrance of his new home.

"Pardon me, sir," she began. "I beg leave to . . ."

Her sentence floated suspended and uncompleted as she gazed in dismayed astonishment at the handsome face turned abruptly toward her. In a daze she watched recognition flare in his green eyes, and a painfully familiar disdain curve his finely molded mouth.

"Chad!" she gasped, her heart lurching at the sound of his name on her lips.

Chapter 2

"LIZA!" Chad spoke her name in accents no less astonished than hers. For an instant he stood gazing at her, wondering if he were suffering from a hallucination, for her face had been constantly before him since he first stepped onto the dock at Portsmouth.

Dear God, she was even more beautiful than he remembered. The six years since she had turned away from him, her back stiff with anger and contempt, had served merely to strengthen the purity of her features. The long line of her body was as lovely and provocative as ever, and as he stared, he was engulfed in the old sensation of being drawn helplessly into the depths of her incredible eyes. How strange, he had always thought, that so many women should be possessed of blue eyes, but none of such a compelling shade of violet, whose expressive depths could range from sparkling mischief to melting warmth to freezing disdain.

Damn! He chastised himself harshly. He had spent aching months in India ridding himself of her image. He had thrown himself into his work with an almost demoniac fury, and the results, financially and emotionally, had been highly satisfactory. And now look at him—clutching her hand and staring down at her like a gangling looby.

For Liza the rest of the world had melted away at his touch and it was as though she suddenly stood alone with him in a separate universe. How long they remained thus, stunned and oblivious, she could not say, but at last she recalled herself and withdrew her hand, hoping that he did not notice the flush that crept up to warm her cheeks.

She looked about her, almost surprised that Berkeley Square still looked perfectly normal. No trumpets had blown, no cracks appeared in the sidewalk, and horses, carriages, cats,

dogs, and pedestrians perambulated sedately in serene igno-
rance of the shattering event that had just taken place.

She shook her head, adjuring herself not to be foolish, and
turned again to Chad, who still stood staring at her as though
he had been confronted by an apparition from another world.

"Liza," he said again in a softer tone. "I . . . I had scarcely
thought to meet you so soon after . . . that is, this is so . . . so
unexpected."

He had not changed, she thought. At least not out of all
recognition. His features, always rugged, were now almost
harsh. His dark red hair glinted where the Indian sun had
burned it, and clear, sea green eyes blazed against his bronzed
skin. He looked as though he might have spent his entire absence from England adventuring on the high seas.

"Yes," she breathed, willing her pulse to stop its ridiculous
hammering. "Most surprising—but not altogether unexpected.
We are neighbors, you see." She gestured to the doorway of
her own house.

He returned her gaze blankly. "But, I had the place through
Thomas Harcourt. Surely, he would not—" He broke off.
"That is, of all the houses in London to let, it seems strange
that I should end up living next to you."

His tone was curt and unforgiving, and Liza drew a deep
breath. "Having gone to Thomas, the result was perhaps in-
evitable, for I must tell you that not only am I your neighbor,
but your landlady as well."

Chad simply stood for a moment, growing anger apparent in
his stare. "But why would you—" He stopped abruptly.

Liza stiffened. How dare he assume that she had conspired
with her man of affairs, who was friend to them both, to see
him lodged next door to her! "Thomas rented the house to you
without my knowledge, Mr. Lockridge. If you wish to make
other arrangements, I shall be more than happy to cancel any
contract you may have made with him."

A flush crept over Chad's lean cheeks. "I'm sorry. I just assumed that—"

"Quite," finished Liza. "And now, if you will excuse me, I
must go in."

She turned, but was stayed by the appearance of her mother
and her sister, who had apparently been visiting in the immediate neighborhood, for they were on foot.

"Liza," cried Charity, hurrying forward to meet her. "Are

you just now returned from the City?" She turned her gaze with obvious curiosity to the tall gentleman standing in conversation with her sister. "Is this our new neighbor?"

Before Liza could form an answer, Charity's eyes widened in recognition. "Why, it's Chadwick Lockridge, is it not? Look, Mama," she gurgled, "see who has come to live next door to us!"

Lady Burnsall, following at a more sedate pace, lifted her hand to Chad. As he bowed courteously over her fingertips, she exclaimed in a distant voice, "Why, Mr. Lockridge, I had not heard that you have returned to England, from . . . India, was it not?" Over Chad's bend head, she shot a sharp glance at Liza, who stood silently, her bemusement plain.

"Have you had luncheon?" trilled Charity, oblivious to her sister's agonized glare. "Won't you join us?"

Chad looked quickly at Lady Burnsall, who nodded an affable, if not entirely cordial second to the invitation. After a moment's hesitation he accepted with suitable expressions of gratification and the four turned to enter the Rushlake town house.

Over a light luncheon of cold meat and salad, it was Charity's excited chatter and Letitia's more restrained comments that filled the silent void in the dining parlor. The footman may as well have presented Liza with a portion of boiled corset lacings, for she silently pushed the food about her plate. She remained with her head bent, aware of Chad's surreptitious scrutiny. His responses to Letitia's efforts at conversation were at first monosyllabic, but eventually her ladyship's quiet charm had its effect, and his answers to her questions became lengthier.

"No, my lady, many of my friends left the confines of Calcutta during the summer for the cooler mountain area, but my business interests kept my nose to the grindstone. I can't tell you how I look forward to my first summer in England after being away for so long."

"But did you never get off into the jungle?" Charity chimed in excitedly. "Have you ever seen an elephant?"

"To be sure," replied Chad, laughing. "I grew to be friends with the Maharaja of Chatipoor—I met him through a business acquaintance. He had a great fondness for tiger hunts, and I was often invited to accompany him. The elephant, of course, is more or less the required method of travel on such expeditions."

As though from a great distance, Liza heard Charity's crow of laughter as Chad described riding in a swaying howdah atop the great beast's back. She raised her head to catch her mother's speculative gaze upon her and stiffened. Good lord, she was behaving like a smitten schoolgirl! She had long ago bid a tearless farewell to her feelings for Chad, and she had no intention of appearing to have worn the willow for him since their last, painful meeting.

"Do tell us, Mr. Lockridge," she said in a light, bored tone, "about your extraordinary serving man. I had occasion to speak to him this morning."

For the first time since their initial encounter, Chad looked directly at her, and it was as though a current passed between them, sparking a response that Liza refused to acknowledge. His emerald eyes gave nothing away, but his features were lightened by a smile. "You have met Ravi Chand? A most impressive sight, is he not? He has been with me for almost the entire length of my stay in India, and insisted that he accompany me to 'this land of barbarians.'"

"Did I understand Thomas to say that your residence in Berkeley Square is to be of limited duration?" asked Liza, mentally framing some rather penetrating questions to be put to her man of affairs at their next meeting.

Chad's smile died. "Yes," he answered coolly. "I am looking for a house to purchase, and I hope the search will not be a long one."

Charity again chimed in. "What are you looking for, precisely, Mr. Lockridge? Oh, Mama, did you not say that the Pevenseys are selling their house in North Audley Street?"

"But, my dear," replied her mother, "I do not think Mr. Lockridge would be interested in that cavernous old barn. It is hardly the place for a single gentleman. Unless—" She paused abruptly and cast a questioning glance at Chad. "Unless you are planning to, ah . . . that is . . ." She trailed off, and Liza prayed that the earth would rise up and engulf her. As she might have expected, the ground remained disappointingly solid beneath her feet.

"No, ma'am," said Chad in a calm voice. "I have no plans at the moment to marry, but I would be foolish to rule out that eventuality." He did not look at Liza as he spoke, and, having bent her head again, she heard only casual amusement in his tone. Her fingers clenched into fists in her lap.

"I do not wish an overly large place," he continued blandly, "but I have assured my friends in India that when they visit London they may stay with me. Thus, I shall require sufficient rooms for one or two families."

The conversation turned to generalities after that. Liza, with determined courtesy, contributed her mite as her mother made their guest *au courant* with some tidbits of gossip. Chad, in turn, spun more tales of his life in India, at which Charity burbled engagingly. To Liza's annoyance Chad seemed to have made a rapid recovery from the initial awkwardness of their meeting, and now seemed bent on making himself agreeable to her mother and little sister. He and Charity had already established a friendly rapport, and even her mother had thawed rapidly under the charm of his smile.

After what seemed an eternity to Liza, he finally rose to take his leave.

"I know that for a few days," Lady Burnsall said, as the family grouped itself on the stone entryway to bid farewell to their guest, "everything will be at sixes and sevens in your own residence, so if we can be of any assistance, please let us know."

Liza looked up, surprised at the cordiality in her mother's tone. Chad, glancing at Liza's unpromising countenance, bowed smoothly.

"Why, thank you, my lady. I trust you will allow me to return your hospitality at an early date. Ravi Chand is astonishingly efficient, you know, and will no doubt have everything to rights before the cat can lick her ear. He is at this moment choosing furniture, for I brought only a few things with me."

He had just begun to traverse the short distance between the doorways when a dashing phaeton and pair drew up and an equally dashing gentleman leaped down to make his greetings to the ladies still grouped at their door.

"As I live and breathe," the newcomer exclaimed with a laugh, "a welcoming committee! Can I hope that my constant visits have at last made an impression? I cannot tell you how this sets me up in my own esteem."

He was a tall man, slender and lithe. Silvery blond hair waved luxuriantly in fashionable disarrangement above eyes of laughter-lit hazel. As he strode forward to clasp the hands of Liza and her mother, his gaze was checked by the figure who stood nearby, staring in recognition.

"Giles," said Chad. "Giles Daventry."

At this, awareness flared in the newcomer's gaze.

"Lockridge!" he exclaimed, and after a barely perceptible pause, he hurried to clasp Chad's hand in his own. "Grenville told me last night that he had heard you were amongst us once more. I can't tell you how glad I am to see you, old fellow!"

"And I you," responded Chad, smiling as he disengaged himself gently from Giles's vigorous greeting.

"But what is this?" asked Giles in mock severity. "Are you stealing a march on me? Although, perhaps I should have known," he continued archly, "that you would make it your first order of business to visit Lucky Lady Liza."

Liza found herself again wishing for a calamity, with much the same result as her previous prayer.

"Mr. Lockridge's visit," she hastened to reply, "was at my mother's invitation, and very much due to chance."

As soon as she had spoken, she realized that her words had been embarrassingly farouche.

"That is," she continued in some haste, "he is in the process of moving into the residence adjoining ours, and he . . . agreed to join us for luncheon."

"Ah," said Giles with a grin. "Looking to the main chance, as always, Chad."

A certain rigidity crept over Chad's features, but he made no reply.

The silence crept into an awkward pause until Giles, clearing his throat, continued jovially, "If you have no plans for the evening, I'm dining tonight with Johnny Tapworth and George Martingale, and perhaps a few others at White's. Care to join the party? Cards afterwards, of course."

"That sounds most enjoyable, but I'm promised to my Aunt Torrington." Chad noted with amusement Giles's lifted brows.

"Lady Torrington wishes to see you? That is . . . I'm sure it's not surprising—killing the fatted calf, is she?"

"More or less," replied Chad. "I'm not looking forward to a journey all the way out to Twelvetrees, but when she speaks, strong men leap to do her bidding. She seemed most insistent that I visit her, and I must say that, despite her formidable manner, she is quite the most favorite of my relatives."

With that he made his bow and completed the short journey

to his own domicile. In a moment he had disappeared within its doors.

"I had not realized," said Giles, looking thoughtfully after him, "that Lockridge was in his family's good graces. It was my understanding that he left the country under rather a cloud after—" He stopped suddenly, and glanced at Liza. "My dear, I am terribly sorry! I do not know how I came to be so maladroit."

Charity, looking from Giles to Liza, cried impulsively, "What? When he left the country after what?"

Lady Burnsall grasped her daughter's arm ungently. "Never mind, young lady." She turned to Liza. "Were you not engaged to go for a drive in the Park with Giles, my love?"

Liza, her thoughts returning from a great distance, stared blindly for a moment before coming to herself with a start. "Oh, goodness—I had forgotten! Please forgive me, Giles. I spent more time in the City than I had planned, and we lingered over luncheon. Do come in while I change." She gestured at her conservative garb. "I shall only be a moment."

Indeed, scarcely half an hour passed before Liza, now gowned in a charming confection of apricot silk, found herself being handed into Giles's phaeton. Not long after, Giles negotiated his team neatly through one of the Park gates.

Liza studied him in sidelong glances. Why, she wondered, absorbing the regularity of his features and the slender elegance of his bearing, could she not fall in love with this man? Giles was charming and witty and quite singular in his devotion to her. Well, yes, she had heard rumors of a certain dashing opera dancer taken under his wing, but she had learned long ago, to her infinite sorrow, that one should not listen to rumor. Besides, she had nothing to say about his amorous flings.

Giles's birth was excellent, and his fortune, while not vast, was known to be more than respectable. His family owned a prosperous estate in Leicestershire and properties elsewhere, and a wealthy uncle had made Giles his favorite. He had made it clear that his nephew would be remembered most felicitously in his will. No wonder her mother continually edged her older daughter in Giles Daventry's direction.

"Is my cravat askew?"

"W-what?" asked Liza blankly.

"Or, perhaps I have a spot on my lapel." There was a smile

in Giles's voice as he spoke. "There must be some unspeakable flaw in my appearance for you to subject me to such minute scrutiny."

She laughed, flushing. "I was merely thinking how fortunate I am to have you for a friend, my dear."

Giles sighed heavily. "Oh, yes, that's me—good old Daventry, friend to the world, and not a love to call my own," he said, in mock despair.

Liza stiffened. "Giles, you're not . . ."

"No, I am not about to ask for your hand again. I have decided to limit myself to no more than two proposals a week, you see."

Liza chuckled in spite of herself. "Giles, how can you be so absurd and still so . . ."

"Lovable?" he asked in a hopeful tone.

"That is not at all what I meant," she replied severely. "Though I do love you of course, as a dear, dear friend."

Giles delivered himself of another sigh. "Am I supposed to be content with that? I shall not give up, you know, but since I already appear to be in danger of going over my quota, I shan't importune you just at this moment. However, on Tuesday next, you may expect to hear more on the subject. My word, here comes Lady Cardover. Does she not look a positive quiz in that hat?"

The rest of the drive passed in light conversation, as, with the advent of the promenade hour, the Park became increasingly crowded with fashionable equipages.

Bowing pleasantly to friends and acquaintances and maintaining a flow of inconsequential chatter, Liza once again found herself lost in her own thoughts. Again she relived those few moments in Berkeley Square when her hand had touched Chad's and the world had seemed to spin out of its accustomed orbit.

His image settled stubbornly between her and Giles. It was as though she could reach out with her hand and trace the newly acquired lines in his face and the remembered softness of his hair. Her hands clenched in her lap. How could this be happening? In the six years since she had bidden an unpleasant farewell to Chad, she had gone her own way. She had learned to cherish her independence. She was considered a leader of society, and her wide circle of friends included some of the most influential persons in the country.

She bestowed a smiling greeting on two ladies approaching in a town carriage, and sat back against the squabs of the phaeton. How ridiculous she was being! It was merely the shock of seeing him so unexpectedly. Chad Lockridge had no place in her successful, well-ordered life. She would not allow the fact that he was now her neighbor and that they would undoubtedly run into one another frequently at the continual round of social gatherings that made up life in the Polite World to cut up her peace.

She was free of him, she assured herself.

Why then, did the image that still floated at her side suddenly break into a smile of unmistakable irony?

Chapter 3

SOME days later, Chad, just emerged from his bath, stood in his dressing room as Ravi Chand proffered a snowy shirt.

"You will wish to make a grand appearance tonight at the ball, Sahib," his servant pronounced, speaking precisely in his native dialect. "You will wear the Turkish satin waistcoat? With these—what are they?—fobs?"

Chad sighed. Ravi Chand was of inestimable help to him, but as a valet, he left a great deal to be desired.

"No, the figured silk, I think," replied Chad in the same language. "And a single fob—that one there." He pointed to the plainest of the assortment.

Observing Chad's expression, the Indian frowned. "I have displeased you, master. No," he continued as Chad lifted his hand in a gesture of negation. "I am aware that I do not have the talents of a gentleman's gentleman. You spoke of hiring such a one. Have you begun your search?"

"No." Chad grinned. "But I shall make it one of my highest priorities."

He sat down at his dressing table, a freshly starched neckcloth in his hand, ready to arrange it about his throat in a simple, Mathematical tie. He made no move to do so however, as he stared into the mirror, bemused. Before him in the glass, an image formed, with golden hair and eyes of a deep, velvet blue. A warm, full mouth smiled at him in mischievous invitation.

He returned the smile with a grimace. The time had long passed when Lady Liza Rushlake would beckon him with invitation in her eyes. The best he could expect was courteous civility, although she had barely maintained even that at their meeting a few days ago.

He blinked, and his own reflection returned, gazing back at

him sardonically. He wondered if he would meet her tonight. He had seen her only once since that encounter in the Square. They had both left their houses at the same time, and her brief "Good morning" as she entered her carriage might have been issued to an importunate stranger.

He shrugged. He had expected nothing more. Indeed, his own greeting in return had been little short of surly. At least, he thought with some satisfaction, he had beheld her without experiencing the slightest remnant of anger. For so long the mere thought of her had caused acrid swirls of hurt and betrayal to rise in his throat like bile, and the bitter taste of disillusionment had been his constant companion for months after his arrival in India.

He finished wrapping the folds of his neckcloth and tied the ends neatly, and, affixing an emerald tiepin to its pristine folds, he stood to shrug himself into the coat of dark silk, held by Ravi Chand.

By the time Liza's carriage made its way among the throng of vehicles surrounding Mervale House in Park Lane, Lord and Lady Mervale's ball had already been voted a sad crush by their guests.

"Gracious," commented Lady Burnsall as she and her daughters ascended the staircase to the ballroom, "the theaters and clubs must have shut their doors tonight, for all the world and his brother must be here."

As they waited on the stairs for the line to progress, Charity passed the time in comment on the attire of their fellow-guests. "Heavens above," she whispered, "look at Janie Porlock. I'll bet she's damped her petticoats, for you can see every . . . Oh, there's Priscilla Weston. I do think that hairstyle is vastly becoming to her, don't you?" Her voice took on a new note as she continued. "I wonder if her brother, John, is here as well."

Her mother glanced at her sharply. "If he is," she said, "I trust you will not act the hoyden as you did at the Portheby's ball last month. If I had not come upon you in time, you would have allowed that young man three dances in one evening."

"Oh no, Mama." Charity's eyes were wide and guileless. "We were but conversing. Mr. Weston is greatly interested in the science of botany, you know, and he was telling me of some fascinating experiments he has performed with, um, mangel-wurzels, I think he said—they're a kind of sugar beet."

Lady Burnsall uttered an unladylike snort, and Charity continued hastily. "Look over there! What could have possessed Mr. Singletree to appear in public in that perfectly nauseating shade of puce? Do you think he wears corsets? He always creaks so oddly when one converses with him."

Liza listened in amusement, idly watching the jeweled throng about her, greeting friends with a smiling nod or a wave. Her attention was suddenly caught, however, as Charity cried out in delight, "Why, there's Chad!"

Liza whirled to follow her sister's pointing finger. There he was, at the foot of the broad staircase, just beginning his ascent.

"How is it you call him by his first name?" she asked Charity sharply.

"Oh, we are the best of friends. Melanie and Dorothea and I visited him just yesterday, and he showed us some of the ivory carvings he collected while he was abroad." In the face of Liza's disapproving stare, she continued hurriedly. "It was perfectly unexceptionable, you know. Melanie's mother was with us."

She peered at her sister thoughtfully. "Why have you taken him in such dislike, Lizzy?"

At the sound of her childhood nickname on her sister's lips, Liza flushed. To her relief Lady Burnsall tapped her shoulder at that moment to indicate that those in front of them had moved forward enough for the three of them to enter the ballroom.

"Letitia!" Lady Mervale's plump face beamed a welcome. "How splendid to see you tonight. You are in looks, as always."

"And," boomed her husband, standing beside her, "you've brought both your lovely daughters! We'll have the young 'uns buzzing about now, won't we? For bless me, if you don't look like an enchanting honeyfall, m'dear." This to Liza whose clinging undergown of amber satin was lightly covered by a cream-colored net overdress, sprinkled with topaz brilliants. A small topaz tiara nestled in the golden depths of her upswept curls.

"If I do, my lord," she replied, laughing, "it's because you are so adept at turning me up sweet."

She moved aside to make room for others who had come

into the room beside her, and as she did so, she bumped into a masculine figure who had been standing at her elbow.

"Giles!" she cried in pleased surprise. "I did not know you would be here tonight."

He smiled down into her face, his silvery hair catching the candlelight. "Do I not appear, faithfully as the turn of the seasons, at any function that is scheduled to be graced by your appearance? As a reward for my heroic steadfastness, you are now obliged to grant me the first set of country dances."

Liza chuckled. "How can I refuse such a gallant request?" She wrote his name on her card, and that of another gentleman who stepped up to request her hand for a waltz. After that she was besieged by her usual court, and in a few moments her card was nearly full. The orchestra broke into the merry strains of a familiar country dance, and she turned to place her hand on the arm held out by Giles. Before they could move off, however, a deep voice sounded from behind her.

"I see you have one dance unclaimed, Lady Liza."

Liza whirled, her heart in her throat.

"Will you save it for me?" asked Chad pleasantly.

She would have given all she possessed—or most of it, anyway—to have a plausible reason for refusing him, but her brain seemed to have been replaced by a large helping of blanc mange, and she merely goggled at him.

Smiling, he plucked the small pencil from her hand and scrawled his name in the last empty slot. Bowing slightly to Giles, who also seemed at a loss for words, he returned the pencil to Liza's nerveless fingers and stepped aside to allow the couple to join the other dancers.

"B'gad," murmured Giles during one of the rare moments in the dance when they came together. "I'm surprised to see Lockridge here."

Liza lifted her brows questioningly, and he responded somewhat uncomfortably, "Well, after the scandal that followed his departure—you know . . ." he added at Liza's expression of puzzlement, " . . . the Queen's Pendant. One can't help wondering . . ."

"He's still the Duke of Montclair's grandson," she said dryly, "a fact that gains him entree into the highest circles. In any case, I understand the pendant turned up recently," she said, nodding to a passing acquaintance.

"What? The Queen's Pendant found? Where? Who has it?" Giles's eyes were round with surprise.

"Oh, Giles, for Heavens' sake." She smothered a small yawn with her fingertips. "What difference does it make? It was all so long ago, and I'm sure no one paid a whit of attention to the nonsensical tales that were circulated."

"No, of course not," said Giles hastily. "I suppose it was because it was well known his pockets were pretty desperately to let at the time—then disappearing so suddenly—it's no wonder the gabble-mongers had a field day. Oh, I know his father *said* he sold it, but the word was that he merely put that about to cover his son's crime. I mean, that simply kept the scandal going. Been in the family for generations, after all. Gift to one of their ancestors from Queen Elizabeth, wasn't it?"

Liza merely nodded and turned the conversation to another, safely innocuous subject.

As the sprightly strains of the dance died away, Liza discovered to her dismay that she and Giles stood only a few feet from Chad and a young woman whom Liza recognized as Caroline Poole, the beautiful daughter of an obscure baronet. Liza began to move unobtrusively in another direction, but was brought up short by the sound of Caroline's high, sweet voice.

"Why, hello, Lady Liza. How lovely to see you—and what an exquisite gown. It makes you look quite regal."

"Why, thank you, Miss Poole," replied Liza in a dry tone. Though there had been nothing in the young woman's voice to suggest anything other than guileless admiration, somehow her words managed to make Liza feel as large and sturdy as a medieval tower. Miss Poole, on the other hand, was petite and slender and pliant. Her eyes, of a striking cerulean blue, shone wide and disingenuous in her heart-shaped face, and dark hair clustered in feathery curls about a translucent brow and delicately molded cheeks.

Early in her career, thought Liza wryly, Caroline had discovered the word "ethereal" and made it her own. Her gestures were invariably restless and fluttering, and even her apparel enhanced her image of fairylike evanescence. Tonight she wore a simple underdress of azure silk, over which floated a gossamer cloud of tulle. About her throat lay a fragile web of diamonds, matched by a scattering of gems in the inky swirls of her hair.

"My," she breathed, moving her fan gently so that her curls

danced invitingly about her flushed cheeks. "Country dances are so very invigorating, are they not?" She turned to Liza, "My dear, may I present Chadwick Lockridge? He has returned home after—" She stopped, flushing in delicious confusion. "Oh, dear, I had forgotten! Do forgive me—you are already well known to one another, are you not?"

As you are well aware, growled Liza inwardly. Her smile was cool, however, as she replied. "Oh, yes, Mr. Lockridge and I are—acquaintances of long standing."

Chad made no reply, but looking up, Liza caught his glance, and a quick, familiar darkening of his emerald gaze made her breath catch in her throat. To her relief her next partner arrived at that moment to claim her hand, and she whirled away.

The rest of the evening passed in a blur, with isolated incidents thrusting above the surface of her preoccupation from time to time. She had just finished a *bourée* in the arms of a blushing young man in a dashing Hussar uniform, when she saw her mother beckoning to her from the sidelines.

"Liza," whispered Lady Burnsall furiously. "Why haven't you done something about Charity?"

"What?"

"Don't tell me you haven't noticed! She's been in that young Weston boy's pocket all evening long. See?"

Liza followed her mother's glance to a secluded corner at the far end of the room where Charity sat in earnest conversation with a tall, light-haired young man. Liza sighed and began to make her way to the couple. Really, it was too bad of Charity to behave in such a skimble-skamble manner. Because of Lord Burnsall's death two years previously, her Season had been postponed. She had begun brilliantly and already had two highly satisfactory offers to her credit. She had turned down both gentlemen however, and neither Liza nor her mother wished to compel her to a *marriage de convenance*. Her cousin, the present Earl of Burnsall and the titular head of the family, had acquiesced to their wishes, and so Charity remained single and heart-whole. She did not want for admirers, and Liza had for some time hoped that her favor would fall on the young Viscount Wellbourne, who had been most particular in his attentions. While Charity was being allowed extraordinary freedom in choosing a mate, Liza was determined that her little sister would make an advantageous marriage.

So absorbed were the pair that neither noticed Liza's approach until she laid a hand on Charity's shoulder. The girl jumped, and for a moment she simply stared blindly at her sister. The young man leaped awkwardly to his feet.

"Good evening, Lady Liza," he said, flushing to the roots of his hair, "Chari . . . that is, Lady Charity and I were just discussing, er, mangel-wurzels."

"Yes," Charity chimed in eagerly. "Mr. Weston was just telling me of the newest methods of seed improvement. The mangel-wurzel, as you know, is very important to stock production in this country."

Liza was forced to smile inwardly at the girl's enthusiasm, for it was doubtful she would recognize a mangel-wurzel from a mulberry bush.

Liza maintained her usual smiling courtesy, asking John Weston about his latest experiments. After they had chatted for a few moments, she said, "I must beg leave to spirit my little sister away." Turning to Charity, she continued. "Mama wishes for your company for a few minutes."

With another smile and a nod, she placed her hand firmly under her sister's elbow and propelled her away from the hapless Mr. Weston.

"Did you plan to spend the entire evening wrapped in conversation with that young man?" she asked in irritation.

Charity looked at her in some surprise. "But we were simply conversing."

"In case it has escaped your attention, you have been simply conversing with him almost since we arrived. Now, come along. I'll bet your card is not even half full yet, so let's get you out where the young men can see that you are here."

"But I was perfectly happy with John. He is so easy to talk to."

Liza's smile was somewhat brittle. "Charity, have you ever met anyone who is not easy for you to talk to? I wish you would expand your conversational talent to gentlemen who are a little more eligible, however."

At this, Charity's mouth set in a mutinous line. "What's wrong with John? He may not be wealthy, but his birth is unexceptionable—and I like him."

Liza stared at her sister in consternation. She had no idea matters had progressed so far between Charity and the undoubtedly nice but disastrously ineligible John Weston. He sprang from a small estate in Yorkshire and had little aside from his dubious botanical expertise with which to earn his way in the world. She bit back the retort that had formed on her lips. No good could come of setting up Charity's back at this point.

"I like him, too," she said mildly. "John Weston is a very likable young man—as are a number of other gentlemen here this evening. We came to the ball to dance, after all."

As if in answer to her words, a rather stout gentleman in a startling waistcoat of embroidered silk materialized at Charity's shoulder to beg her hand for another country set just forming. With some relief Liza watched her sister glide away on his arm, and turned to find that her own partner for the set was fast approaching.

The first intermission was upon them after that, and when Liza observed Charity safely tucked amid a circle of her friends, she made her way to where Lady Burnsall stood in conversation with Giles and a large gentleman of military bearing. General Sir George Wharburton, Retired, had been one of Letitia's devoted *cicisbée* for as long as Liza could remember. Indeed, after Papa's death, she wondered if Mama would choose him as her second husband.

The dowager's elegantly coiffed head was thrown back in a delighted spurt of laughter at one of the general's witticisms.

The four chatted for a few moments. Then Sir George remarked, "Here comes young Lockridge. Glad to see him back among us."

"Apparently," added Giles, observing the interruption of Chad's progress by a trio of blushing debutantes, "so are all the matchmaking mamas and their daughters. I hear he did quite well for himself in India."

Liza looked up, and her stomach clenched as she realized that Chad must be coming to claim his dance. Really, she reflected wildly, it was no wonder he had caught the attention of the three youthful beauties. His piratical charm was never more evident as his deep brandy-colored hair caught the candlelight and reflected it in coppery highlights. The simple elegance of his evening dress showed to devastating advantage his broad shoulders and muscular thighs. How fortunate it was, she thought rather breathlessly, that she was no longer susceptible to his attraction.

In a moment Chad arrived to join them.

"How goes the house hunt?" asked Giles after Chad had bowed to the ladies and shook hands with the gentlemen.

Chad smiled. "I must admit, I have accomplished little in that direction so far. I have given my agent, Thomas Harcourt, a list of my requirements, but so far nothing has been forthcoming.

"Harcourt?" Giles was suddenly alert. "Isn't that the name of your man of business, Liza?"

"Yes," she replied, an arrested expression on her features. "He is an old friend to whom I introduced Mr. Lockridge many years ago. I have known Thomas since my family moved from Kent to Buckinghamshire, when I was fifteen."

"When your father assumed the title?"

"Yes," she repeated. "Thomas was the vicar's son, and he befriended me at a rather lonely time in my life. I sorely missed Kent, and it seemed as though I had left everything that was important in my life at Brightsprings."

"Mm, yes—Brightsprings," said Giles. "Has Harcourt discovered the identity of its present owner?"

"No," she replied, saddened. "The man must be a recluse, for his agent will not disclose his name, and he has indicated that he is unwilling to so much as see me."

"Well," Chad said reflectively, "Thomas seems to be willing to do almost anything on your behalf. I shouldn't be surprised if he makes the fellow surface eventually."

"Indeed," Giles chimed in, "Liza can consider herself fortunate to have Harcourt as her man of affairs. He has done wonderful things for her."

Chad's smile was questioning.

"Did you not know of her forays into the world of Finance?" continued Giles.

"Oh, really, Giles," snapped Liza, "one would think I had embarked upon a career on the stage." She turned to Chad. "It's just that 'Change Alley entices me, and I like to take a little flutter occasionally."

Chad's brows lifted.

"And quite successfully, too, by all reports." This from Giles, who accompanied his words with a playfully possessive tap on her wrist.

"Yes," said Chad, whose gaze had followed Giles's gesture. His lips curved in what might have been called a smile. "I remember Lady Liza's interest in things monetary."

Liza stiffened at the thrust and her eyes narrowed to slits. "You have a very bad habit of misinterpreting one's motives, Mr. Lockridge," she purred. "Actually, money rather bores me. It is the challenge of financial play that I enjoy."

"Spoken," replied Chad, the smile still in place, "as one who already possesses more money than she knows what to do with."

Liza went rigid, but ignored the thrust.

"At any rate," Giles said after an awkward pause, "it is generally agreed that she has the gods of fortune on her side, for her investments are invariably successful. Lady Liza's Luck, it is called in our circles."

Chad said nothing, and Liza flushed under his gaze. At that moment the orchestra broke into a waltz. Chad bowed and offered his hand to Liza. "I believe this is my dance, Lucky Lady."

A waltz! Of all the dances she might have shared with him, why did it have to be a waltz? Resigned, she lifted her arms, and at the first touch of his hand on her waist, a slow shiver passed through her.

She glanced up into his face. Obviously he remained unaffected by the intimate contact, for his eyes were gazing over the throng of dancers. Slowly, though, his head bent, and he looked directly at her.

"You are wearing the same scent," he said in a colorless tone. "Violets, is it not?"

"You have an excellent memory, Mr. Lockridge."

He cocked his head and smiled amusedly at her. "Do you think, Lady Liza, that since our acquaintanceship is of such long standing, that we might return to Chad and Liza?"

Liza's insides tightened, and she took a deep, infuriated breath. That accomplished, she stared straight into his eyes with studied disinterest. "No, Mr. Lockridge," she replied icily, "I don't believe we might."

The amusement in Chad's eyes did not fade. Sweeping her expertly into a complicated turn, he merely remarked, "Still hostile, I see. I did not realize that our, er, previous acquaintanceship had affected you so profoundly."

By now Liza felt as though she could scarcely breathe, and it took every shred of pride she possessed to force her lips into a cool smile.

"It's not that, Mr. Lockridge. You see, I thought I knew you well—in our previous acquaintanceship—but I was proved to be vastly mistaken. So, now we meet as strangers, and that is how I prefer to conduct our relationship."

His green eyes darkened, as they always did when he became angry or was otherwise stirred by deep emotion, and his arm curved more tightly about Liza's waist.

She choked, and involuntarily pushed herself away. "Tell me," she asked lightly, in a desperate effort to turn the conversation. "What is it that brought you back to England after so many years abroad? A whim, perhaps? Or have you some purpose?"

His voice was a soft growl as he replied. "I came home with a very definite purpose in mind, my lady."

Liza raised eyes to him that were wide and questioning—and a little frightened.

Chapter 4

RETURNING Liza's gaze, Chad knew an unwelcome urge to pull her toward him and bury his face in the golden silk of her hair. Instead he bent upon her the most sardonic smile at his disposal, and continued innocently.

"Why, yes, I have many business interests in this country, and I have left them for too long in the hands of my associates."

"Oh," said Liza in a deflated voice.

"From all reports, things have been going well, but I do think it necessary to bring one's personal attention to one's ventures from time to time, don't you agree?"

"I beg your pardon?" she asked blankly.

"Well, since you are involved in, er, financial dealings yourself, you have surely found this to be true."

The amusement in his tone was so patent that for a moment Liza's hand itched to slap him.

"Ah, but I am only a feeble woman, Mr. Lockridge," she replied, her eyes lowered to hide her anger. "You surely cannot expect that in my dabblings I could reach a true understanding of the real workings of such a masculine bastion as the world of finance. Good evening to you, sir."

The music had stopped, and with what suspiciously resembled a flounce, Liza turned away and marched to the perimeter of the room, where she lost no time in becoming engrossed in conversation with a party of friends.

Chad gazed after her in satisfaction. If she had been laboring under the delusion that his return to England signaled a return of the passion he had once felt for her, it had been his pleasure to set her to rights.

His eyes narrowed as he watched Giles Daventry stroll up to join the group surrounding her. It appeared that the reports he had received in his correspondence with well-meaning friends

during recent months were correct. Lady Liza Rushlake was at
last beginning to succumb to Daventry's blandishments. It was
nothing to him, of course. What in bloody hell did she see in
him, anyway? How could she permit the attentions of a man
who possessed the morals of a shark? Or perhaps she didn't
know of Mr. Daventry's more unsavory dealings. He shrugged
his shoulders. It certainly wasn't up to him to enlighten her.
His gaze followed Daventry's hand as it came up to Liza's
bare shoulder in a light caress, and a knot formed in his stomach.

Turning on his heel, he moved toward the other side of the
ballroom. Perhaps he would treat himself to a second dance
with the lovely Caroline Poole. She, at least, had seemed
pleased to see him returned to the bosom of the Polite
World—as had many other eager young ladies. Or, at least, he
smiled sourly to himself, they were pleased to recognize the
wealth he represented. Thank God he had taken care to conceal from interested eyes the full extent of his worth. If it were
known that he was now one of the wealthiest men in England,
wouldn't that fling the cat among the pigeons?

From her position next to Giles, Liza watched Chad's progression across the room. She saw his burnished head bend
once more over Caroline Poole's dainty figure, and she turned
back to raise her face to Giles.

Liza did not speak to Chad again that night, but she was as
conscious of his presence through the remainder of the
evening as though she were standing in his embrace.

Some hours later Chad emerged from Mervale House and
drew in a lungful of cool night air. Easing his damp shirtfront
away from his body, he reflected that an evening spent at a
London fête equaled in discomfort one spent in the jungles of
the Ganges delta.

He waved aside the lackey who sprang to his feet to summon his carriage. Because the Mervales lived within two
blocks of Berkeley Square, he had elected to dismiss his
coachman for the rest of the evening. He welcomed the opportunity to stretch his legs and to let the nocturnal breeze sluice
away the odor of perspiring bodies and overwhelming per-
fumes that clung to his clothing.

He whistled tunelessly as he reflected on the evening's
events. He could still feel Liza's curves pressed against him in

the waltz they had shared. Her lithe body still fit against him as though it had been designed precisely to fill his hollows and bends, and satin curls brushing against his chin filled him with aching memories of long walks and intimate conversations and kisses stolen in leafy glades.

He smiled ruefully. His mind may have become reconciled to losing her—his body, however, was another matter. His response to her nearness had been immediate and intense.

His musings were interrupted suddenly as he became aware of a disturbance at the periphery of his senses. A shape, large and formless, huddled in the shadow of an alleyway that lay in his path. He did not slow his pace, but took note that the shape had silently separated into four or five smaller, man-size entities. He glanced about quickly and noted with some dismay that the street in which he strode was deserted.

He cursed his carelessness in leaving the house unarmed, but then, one did not ordinarily look for hand-to-hand combat at an evening party, and he had not planned to find himself alone in the dangerous darkness of a London street. He would simply have to rely on skills acquired and honed in the equally hazardous environs of the unsavory streets of Calcutta.

He maintained his attitude of casual stroller, but his muscles tensed and every nerve in his body steeled itself. As he approached the alleyway, the waiting shapes launched themselves, and Chad caught a muttered phrase. "'At's the cove we wants, then." Cudgels were lifted and fists raised, but the assailants found their prey singularly difficult to subdue. One cried out in anguished surprise as a foot thrust with the speed of a striking cobra at a particularly tender portion of his anatomy. Another was caught on the point of his chin by a flashing elbow. A third crumpled as a fist smashed against his temple.

The fourth attacker leaped back out of harm's way, and with an oath, drew a knife from his coat. He plunged forward, but he too, cried out as Chad whirled, and in a silent blur of motion, kicked upward and caused the blade to spin from the man's upraised hand.

By now Chad had begun to hope he might see himself well out of the mêlée, but in the next moment, a glancing blow struck him behind the ear. With a grunt of satisfaction one of the men whom he'd thought disabled bore in to deliver a second assault that drove Chad to the ground.

Now the rest of the group mobilized in a frenzy of kicks and punches, until their victim, rolling himself into a tight ball, suddenly exploded in an unleashing of coiled power that brought him to his feet again.

He whirled once more, this time connecting with bellies, noses, and kneecaps, all to devastating effect. He was beginning to tire, however, as the effect of his injuries drained his stamina. The fourth attacker retrieved his knife and wielded it in a vicious swipe that grazed Chad's arm, and panting in growing weakness, he stumbled backward.

The world was beginning to grow fuzzy when, to Chad's astonishment, a cry of panic rose from one of the assailants. From the surrounding blackness another form materialized at his elbow, launching itself at his attackers. The stranger promptly accounted for two of the would-be assassins, but drew back with a grunt as the knife-wielder lunged once more. Apparently the blade found its mark, for the newcomer staggered and fell back for a moment, only to plunge into the fray with undiminished vigor.

At last the sounds of battle began to draw attention. A window was thrown open, and a questioning voice was heard. At the end of the street light shone from a passerby's lantern. Action on both sides froze for an instant, and in another moment, Chad's assailants had faded again into the shadows, and the two allies found themselves alone in the street.

Chad faced a tall, slender young man, but even as he opened his mouth to question his rescuer, the man slid in an unconscious heap at his feet, blood streaming from a knife wound high on his shoulder. Chad bent dizzily over the stranger, but was brought upright as other onlookers began to stream into the street.

Solicitous hands reached to give assistance, and shocked voices echoed querulously, exclaiming into the night over the dreadful pass things were coming to when a man was attacked in a genteel neighborhood, and only a little after midnight. Chad went on his knees to the motionless figure before him, lifting his head only to ask that someone hail a hackney cab.

Less than fifteen minutes later Chad relinquished the stranger into the arms of Ravi Chand, who, unperturbed, carried him easily to a second-floor guest room. By the time his shabby coat and threadbare shirt had been stripped off, and a makeshift bandage applied to stop his bleeding, the young man's eyes had opened, glittering against the pallor of his face.

"Easy, young fellow," murmured Chad, as the figure beneath the coverlet struggled to a sitting position. The effort sent him instantaneously back against the pillows.

His hair was black as the night that had covered him so successfully just moments before. In startling contrast his eyes were the color of a gray morning. He could not, judged Chad, be much more than twenty or so, but his face was composed of shadowed hollows and sharp planes that gave him a maturity beyond his years. He turned his head slightly to observe his host.

"My thanks to you, sir," he muttered groggily. "I was in sad straits back there."

Chad's brows shot skyward. Despite his decidedly seedy appearance, the man spoke with a certain gentility. A sudden look of awareness crossed his face then, and, pushing himself farther back against the pillows, he glanced about the room.

"Y'got a boman ken here, guv'nor," he growled in rough accents. "Everything slap up to the mark, ain't it?"

Chad frowned at the young man's sudden change in diction. However he said only, "I find it quite comfortable. It is I who must thank you, however, for you saved my life tonight. How did you happen to be in North Audley Street at such an hour, and what possessed you to jump in and—" He stopped abruptly, as the man in the bed moaned and shifted as though in sudden pain. "But," continued Chad hastily, "I think we must get you a doctor."

"No!" The word came sharply and unequivocally. "I don't need no sawbones proddin' at me. If you'll jus' let me rest here for a minute or two, I'll be on my way."

"Very well. I certainly agree that rest is what you need. In the morning I'm sure you'll feel more the thing, and we'll talk then."

The young man snorted. "I'll be gone long afore that."

"I think not," responded Chad mildly. He gestured to Ravi Chand, who picked up the soiled heap of clothing from the floor and bore them off with the air of a man carrying ducal robes.

"Oy!" cried the young stranger weakly. "Them's me mish and steppers. You can't . . ."

"I said, we'll talk in the morning. Sleep now."

Observing that his guest's eyes were already closing in weariness, he left the room, and moved down the corridor to his own, where he spent some hours in thought before settling himself for sleep.

He woke suddenly in the still, dark reaches of the night, brought to consciousness by the awareness of a presence in the room. Chad lay quiet for a moment, readying his strength, and ascertaining the precise position of the intruder. A slight rustling noise in the direction of the wardrobe brought him to his feet and thence to a silent, murderous lunge.

"Aaugh!" A muffled, but anguished cry emerged from the depths of the resultant scuffle. "For God's sakes let loose. I ain't no assassin, you idjit. Leastways, I cert'ny ain't dressed for the part."

Abruptly realizing that the intruder wore nothing but a set of extremely unsavory undergarments, Chad shot to his feet. Lighting a candle, he glared at the figure who remained seated on the floor, clutching his shoulder with one hand and his drawers with the other.

"What the devil . . . ?" began Chad.

"Good God, now lookit what ye've done," said the young man. "I'm bleedin' again. What was ye tryin' t'do? Rip off the rest o' me togs? They ain't much, but yer welcome to 'em. 'Scuse me, please," he added, as he rose and brushed past a gaping Chad. Reaching into a commode, he began opening drawers until he emerged with one of his host's neckcloths, which he hastily wrapped around his shoulder. He sat down on Chad's bed and smiled sunnily.

"I apologize fer disturbin' yer slumber, sir, but I told you I wanted to leave. That darkie giant o' yers took my clothes, so I was just comin' in to borry a set o' yers." He glanced down at his makeshift bandage. "Y'should tell 'im not to use so much starch, by the by. He ain't much of a valet, is he?"

Chad slowly lowered himself into an armchair by the fire and uttered the first words that came to mind. "Ravi Chand is not a valet; he is serving only temporarily in that capacity."

"Don't need t'tell me that, guv. Just look at them boots. Feller must use stove blackin' on them."

Chad surveyed the apparition before him with some interest. "Tell me—what is your name, anyway?"

"Jem. Jem January's me monarch."

"An odd, er, monarch."

"I've heard odder. And what's yours?"

"I'm Chad Lockridge. You're in Berkeley Square, if it's of any interest to you, and you never did tell me what you were doing in North Audley Street earlier this evening, or why you leaped to my rescue."

Jem returned his gaze blandly. "Just happenstance, ye might say. I were standin' about in front of the big house what was 'avin' a party. I watched the swells fer awhile, then moseyed off, jist in time t'see you amble into a side street. Foolhardy thing t'do, if ye don't mind me sayin' so. I thought t'meself, Jemmy, that feller's lookin' fer a cosh on the nob,' so I just sorta wandered after ye. And sure enough, there was a party o' pretties just a'waitin' fer a mark t'come strollin' along."

"And do you make it a practice of, er, standing about in front of big houses? Odd sort of hobby, I should think." Chad's voice was mild, but a certain amusement in his tone made Jem glance sharply at him.

"Well, 'ere's how it is, guv," he said with a disarming air of candor. "I pick up the odd copper now and then by performin' services, when one o' the swells is 'avin' a party. I sweeps the pavement fer a lyedy gettin' inta 'er carriage. Or 'elps a gentleman 'oo's been imbibin' a bit too freely. Like that, don'cher know? The swells gets generous sometimes at the end of an evenin', specially if they's a bit well-to-go, or had a good run at the cards."

"I see." Chad nodded thoughtfully. "Yes, I should imagine at the end of such an evening, your purse would be considerably fattened. Whether the, er, swells are aware of having dispensed such largesse is somewhat problematic, however."

Jem drew himself up with as much dignity as his present circumstances would allow. "I hope you ain't insinuatin' I'm a bung nipper, yer honor. I consider it beneath me to be a-stickin' me fingers in other blokes' pockets."

"Do you, indeed?." Chad stared at Jem for a long, thoughtful moment then, with a smile, he rose and moved to his wardrobe. "Let's see what we have here, then." He pulled out in succession an array of coats, waistcoats, pantaloons, and britches and laid them on the bed for Jem's inspection. After assisting him into a coat of Bath superfine, he stood back to appraise his efforts.

"Mmm," he said. "I'm afraid that won't do. You're not

quite so tall as I, and I'm a good deal broader. You'll look a regular Charlie in my clothes."

"Too true, guv."

"So, I suggest you repair to your quarters and simply wait until Ravi Chand returns your own garments to you—which he will do in the fullness of time, I assure you."

Jem heaved a deep sigh and turned away. Chad watched as the young man removed the coat and held another up for inspection. He slipped it on, and, as his eye caught Chad's, he laughed ruefully, for his appearance in the garment could only be described as grotesque. It occurred to Chad that Jem's slenderness was deceptive, for he seemed to be constructed of honed steel. He moved with an easy grace that suggested the coiled power of a jungle animal, and Chad recalled the ease with which he had dispatched at least three burly assailants before being felled by the knife blade.

He watched Jem through narrowed eyes as the young man ran his fingers over the rest of the assembled garments. "I assure you," he said quietly, observing certain of Jem's barely perceptible motions, "that I do not keep anything of value in my pockets overnight."

"Lord Love ye, guv, just straightenin' things out." This tone indicated nothing but friendly concern. "That man o' yours ain't much good with a sad iron either, is he?" He ostentatiously shook and folded and returned the clothing items to their proper places.

"Do you think you could do better?"

"Sure as spit. I worked in a tailor's shop for a while. There ain't nothin' about a gentleman's togs that I don't know."

"Then, why don't you come to work for me?"

Jem's jaw dropped. "Me? A valet? 'Ave you got rats in your attic? Do I look like a gentleman's gentleman to you?"

"No, you don't," replied Chad, smiling. "I'm only suggesting a temporary situation. As you have pointed out, I'm in rather desperate need of someone to manage my wardrobe, and you seem to have rather fallen into my lap, so to speak."

Jem stared at him, and Chad would have given a great deal to know what thoughts were racing behind those impenetrable gray eyes.

"Yes, but why me?" Jem asked at last. "Employment agencies 'ave valets stacked up like cordwood in their offices. Whyn't ye pick one o' them?"

Because, thought Chad, I daresay none of them speak one moment in pure Eton-educated English, and the next in the rankest gutter cant. Nor, my lad, do I believe you just happened upon my predicament by accident. I think it would behoove me to further our acquaintance.

He shrugged. "Because you're here, I guess. Besides, I owe you something." He rubbed his arm. "I was grazed with that blade, too, you know, and if you hadn't come along, I greatly fear I would have been the primary subject of a murder investigation in the morning."

"You greatly fear, eh?" Jem uttered a bark of laughter. "Why do I get the impression that there ain't much you greatly fear?" He paced for a moment in deep thought, presenting an incongruous picture as his tattered undergarments stirred about him like molting feathers. He turned to Chad. "Orright, I'll do it. Not fer long, mind ye, jist a few days till ye can get a real flunkie t' wait on ye."

The corners of his mouth twitching, Chad assured the young man of his undying gratitude. He saw him from the room, then returned to his bed. Sleep was a long time coming, however, and his windows began to lighten before he finally drifted into a slumber that was laced with dreams of malevolent shapes and flashing knives and voices that whispered, "'At's the cove we wants."

Chapter 5

THE next morning came early for Liza, as well, and as she contemplated the events of the evening before, she was conscious of a dull throbbing behind her eyes. She dressed quickly in somber garb for another trip into the City and descended to the breakfast room. She took her meal alone and was gone before either her mother or her sister made an appearance.

"Thomas, I would like an explanation," were her first words on entering that gentleman's office.

Thomas made no pretense of misunderstanding her. "Ah, your new neighbor," he said with a tentative smile.

"I don't find any humor in the situation at all," she replied pettishly. "How could you do this to me?"

"But Liza, the house was empty, and here was a tenant just perishing to move in. How could I refuse him?" He glanced at her sharply and continued in a more serious vein. "Does it really make any difference where he lives? He is back, and you would have to see him sometime."

"Yes, but . . ."

"Perhaps after you have lived at close quarters with him, you'll discover he's not the villain you have been imagining him these past six years."

"I have never thought of him as a villain," she replied sharply. "It was simply that . . ." She paused, then continued in sudden awareness. "Thomas, did you install Chad in the house next to mine with some idea that we might resume our . . . former relationship?" She took a deep breath. "How could you?"

Thomas rose from his seat and hurried around his desk to where Liza sat rigid with pain and outrage. His brown eyes filled with compassion as he took her hands in his own.

"Liza. When Chad came to me, my immediate response was that here was a perfect opportunity to heal old wounds." He tightened his clasp on her fingers. "It's high time, you know, that you laid the ghost of that relationship to rest. It has haunted you far too long." He continued hurriedly in order to silence the protest he observed in her eyes. "Yes, I know all the world believes that you haven't given so much as a thought to Chad since he sailed off in a fit of pique, but I'm not all the world. I'm your friend."

Liza said nothing, but her eyes were very bright as she stared at him resentfully.

Thomas returned to the chair behind his desk. "I'll say no more on this score," he finished, "but promise me you'll try to look on your new neighbor as simply that. A stranger who has moved in next door. Let the slate be wiped clean, Liza, for people change, you know."

"You ask too much, old friend," said Liza, her voice harsh. "I shall, of course, treat him with civility, but I'm afraid the slate is muddied beyond cleansing. There will be no starting over. I wish he had stayed in India." She paused and with some effort regained her composure. "I did not know you are still his business agent. I understand he has done well for himself in—where was it—Calcutta?"

Thomas smiled warily. "You did not ask, and it is not the sort of information I would be likely to divulge. I never discuss the affairs of one client with another, even those of good friends, so you will understand that as to his success—or lack of same—I'm afraid I can't tell you anything."

Liza stiffened. "Of course I understand. It is what I would expect of you, after all. And I'm not really interested in Mr. Lockridge's successes—or lack of same. I was merely making conversation."

"Quite," responded her man of affairs.

"Now then," she said, changing the subject rather hastily, "tell me about our new School for Girls in Hampstead."

Thomas's eyes lit with enthusiasm. "I believe it will be as successful as your others, Liza. I have found a very good matron, and she had recommended several other women, who have been running schools in their homes, as instructors."

"Excellent." She discussed several other small matters with Thomas before she at last rose to take her leave.

"I suppose you didn't bring a maid with you?" asked Thomas with a frown.

"No, Master Propriety, I did not. I brought my stalwarts, of course." She indicated two sturdy footmen, who could be seen waiting patiently in the corridor. "But I find a maid simply gets in the way."

"You know how people will talk."

"Yes," she answered reflectively, "but, the *ton* puts up with my eccentricities because I am wealthy."

"Oh, yes." Thomas paused, his eyes twinkling. "Everyone has heard of your famous luck. No," he cried, laughing, as Liza's cup rattled in indignation. "Don't eat me!"

"You know very well," she responded in mock severity, "that luck has nothing to do with it. Well, perhaps a little," she admitted after a moment. "But mostly it's been late nights, studying trends and projections and making intelligent decisions," she concluded somewhat pugnaciously.

"Agreed, oh Wizardess of Threadneedle Street," Thomas said, chuckling. "You are one of a very few clients for whom I act as more of a facilitator than a manager. I suspect"—he glanced at her with a grin—"that's why you hired me. You were looking for a man of affairs who wouldn't interfere with your own busy plans."

Liza flushed, but her eyes brimmed with warmth as she laid her hand on Thomas's. "I was looking for an agent whom I knew to be clever, honest, and extremely intelligent. And, to my everlasting good fortune, I found him in one of my oldest and dearest friends—even if he has a regrettable tendency to meddle," she finished with some severity.

"Spare my blushes, you saucy wench." Thomas squeezed her fingers.

Liza bade him a smiling good-bye and made her way to her next stop, walking along Cornhill to the Royal Exchange. Having several appointments here, she slid through the throng of traders, jobbers, and other speculators whose voices joined in the cacophony that drew investors from around the world.

"Liza?" She whirled at the sound of the familiar voice and saw Chad making his way toward her. To her annoyance she experienced a quickening of her pulse at the sight of his muscular figure, and discovered to her irritation that his crooked smile still had the power to made her knees go weak.

"Chad!" Her voice came out in an uncertain croak, and she stood numbly as he approached.

He must have been walking swiftly before their encounter, she thought, for he spoke somewhat breathlessly.

"What on earth are you doing here?" He looked around. "Are you visiting the exchange with a gentleman?"

"No." Her tone was curt. "I am here alone—to conduct business." As she spoke, she nodded to acquaintances and associates passing nearby.

Chad's brows shot upward. "Business?"

"Yes, I came to discover the latest stock quotations."

His expression as he stared blankly at her was almost ludicrous in its puzzlement. "But—what for?" he asked.

"So that I can make some investment decisions, of course." She produced a piece of paper from her reticule and gestured to one of her footmen, standing nearby. "I have jotted a list of stocks that seem promising, and I shall instruct Thomas in the number of shares I wish to purchase."

She handed the paper to Chad, who perused it for some moments in silence. When he raised his head, Liza was pleased to note that his expression had changed to one of unwilling and puzzled respect. She took the list from him and handed it to her messenger, who turned and darted swiftly away.

"I, too, am here to look into further investment possibilities. In fact," he continued slowly, "your list and mine are remarkably similar."

A silence fell between them, and Liza's pulse continued to thunder as he quietly studied her. The pause was brought to an abrupt end as they were jostled by a gentleman hurrying about his business.

"Look," said Chad. "We shall be trampled here; may I offer you a cup of coffee?" He gestured in the direction of a nearby coffee house.

Liza's lips opened to form a brusque refusal, but to her astonishment she heard herself agree. He took her hand and placed it on his arm, and she was immediately conscious of the strength that lay beneath her fingers.

They had moved only a few paces when a gentleman stepped into Liza's path and lifted his hat. He was a fairly young man, with red cheeks, and he was built along the lines of a well-fed bulldog.

"Vy, it's Lady Liza!" said the gentleman in a thick, Germanic accent. "How nize it iss to see you today, my dear. Haf you had a profitable mornink?" he asked, his small eyes twinkling. At Liza's laughing nod he smiled and laid a finger along the side of his nose. "Remember vat I told you uf Horace Pel-

ham. I understant he iss still t'inking uf building anodder
voolen mill in Lancashire. A schmart lady might look in dat
direction to make a liddle money, no?"

With another smile the man turned away, and had soon vanished into the crowd.

"You have picked up some odd acquaintances in your so-
journs into the world of Commerce," Chad said with a smile as
they seated themselves into a booth.

"Oh, that was young Mr. Rothschild—Nathan, his name is."

A startled expression sprang into Chad's eyes. "Nathan
Rothschild, the financier?"

"You've heard of him?" she asked.

"I'm familiar with the name," Chad replied, his eyes narrowed. "We've heard of the family, even in India. He is apparently doing very well for himself in this country as a broker,
though he has been in London for two or three years only. He
and his brothers on the Continent are handling funds for
Wellington's army. How is it you happen to know him?" he
asked curiously.

Liza laughed. "I met him quite by accident several months
ago. By the way, did you know the family name was originally
Meyer? It is only in this generation that they have begun calling themselves Rothschild—which means Red Shield—after
the section of the Frankfurt ghetto in which they lived. Anyway, my carriage was passing through the outskirts of the City
several months ago, and I saw Mr. Rothschild with his wife
and two of his children." She paused before continuing dis-
tastefully. "A group of eight or ten young dandies had them
cornered against a wall. Jew-baiting is apparently a favorite
pastime among a certain sort of young man. I didn't know him
at the time, but I could not pass such a situation by. I stopped,
and my coachman and footmen soon had the cowardly little
band running."

"Good God," interposed Chad. "Were the Rothschilds
harmed?"

"No, but they were frightened. So far the bullies had confined their entertainment to destroying Mr. Rothschild's hat
and subjecting him to some pushing and shoving. Mrs. Rothschild—Hannah, her name is—was trying not to cry, but the
children were screaming in terror."

"What a fortunate thing you stopped. Many would have not,
you know."

"Perhaps . . ."

"But you," continued Chad, his eyes warm, "are not among their number. I well remember the day when you climbed down from my curricle to lecture a passing chimneysweep in no uncertain terms on the thinness of the wretched child forced to act as his climbing boy."

Liza's gaze dropped to her coffee cup, and she went on hastily. "At any rate, Mr. Rothschild apparently feels himself to be under some sort of obligation to me, although I have told him repeatedly that is nonsense, and we have remained on terms of firm, if distant, friendship. He occasionally presents me with bits of information that have come in handy. Now, tell me," she added, "what brings you to the City? I have heard rumors of your success in India. Do you return to us a nabob?"

Chad was silent for a moment before he replied, smiling rather rigidly, "I did fairly well in Calcutta."

Catching his expression, Liza flushed. "I'm sorry," she said, her poise deserting her. "I had no business asking such—"

He flung up his hand. "Liza, let's not start tiptoeing through the pitfalls of our past, er, relationship. Now that I am returned to the bosom of Polite Society, we shall no doubt be seeing each other on a regular basis."

To his surprise she leaned back and smiled coolly. "And of course," she said, "we are now neighbors."

"Yes, indeed. One never knows when I might be obliged to nip next door for a cup of brandy or something. At any rate," he concluded, "it behooves us to forget the past."

"I did so many years ago," she said with a mendacious air of unconcern. "As I'm sure, have you. The two people who spouted romantic nonsense to each other in that mad spring, were foolish beyond reason."

"At any rate," Chad said, somewhat taken aback, "you have carved out a prodigious niche for yourself in Society. Your name is on everyone's lips."

She looked at him, startled. "Well . . . I enjoy going out and about, but I can hardly consider myself a cynosure, even if I should wish for that unenviable position."

"But how could you be anything else?" he said lightly. "You are young and beautiful, possessed of breeding and wealth—and, from all reports, Dame Fortune smiles on you with a positive ferocity."

Liza bristled. "Sometimes I think I really shall scream if I hear the phrase 'Lucky Lady Liza' one more time."

"You fancy yourself a financial wizardess then?" Chad asked in an amused tone.

"Not precisely," she replied in a grim voice, "but I do have my small successes."

He gazed at her thoughtfully. "Well then," he said, "let me propose a wager."

Liza stared at him. "A what?"

"Yes. We shall each start out with, say, a thousand pounds, and whichever of us increases that amount the most within three months will win."

"That's the most ridiculous thing I ever heard," she cried in amazement.

"Are you afraid of losing?"

"No, of course not, but . . ."

"I should think you would welcome the opportunity to make your expertise in fiscal matters known to the Doubting Thomases who consider your success a fluke."

Liza studied him for a moment. His head was cocked to one side, and his green eyes shone pure and limpid as spring rain in a forest. It was an expression she was familiar with, just as she was with every emotion that had ever displayed itself on his brigandlike features, and a sharp awareness came to her that this wager was not an idle whim on Chad's part. He wanted something.

"What did you have in mind?" she asked at last.

"It has come to my attention that you have in your possession a certain piece of jewelry."

She stared at him. *The Queen's Pendant!* The words leaped into her mind as though he had shouted them. Of course! He must have discovered that the pendant had surfaced—perhaps he had been searching for it himself ever since he left England. How in God's name had he known she had purchased it? Was this the reason for his sudden return to England? She smiled coldly within herself. How it must have galled him to discover on his arrival that his quarry had been snapped up from under his nose by his spurned love.

The thoughts tumbled in her mind like pebbles skittering in the wake of a speeding carriage. How pleased he must have been at Thomas's transparent suggestion that he lease the house next to hers. Now, he no doubt felt he could renew their acquaintance to his advantage. Why had he simply not offered to purchase the pendant from her? It must be beyond his means. Did he think her such a green girl that he could wrest it away from her by means of a trifling wager?

She rose from the table, controlling with difficulty the trembling rage that surged within her. Her voice was steady as she picked up her reticule from the table. "I collect you are speaking of the Queen's Pendant." She did not wait for his nod as she continued swiftly. "Yes, I do own it. It is quite costly, and I fear I do not wish to risk it in such a manner, sir."

She turned to leave, but was stayed by his hand on her arm. Even in her agitation, she was aware of the throb of response that shot through her at his touch.

"But, my dear," he said lazily, "you have not heard what I offer as my part of the bargain. You see, I, too, recently came into possession of a rather valuable item. I am the present owner of Brightsprings."

"Brightsprings!" So astonished was she to hear the word on his lips that it took several seconds for the meaning of his statement to penetrate her brain. "What are you talking about?"

"I own Brightsprings," he repeated. "Your old home. Your heart's desire."

"But that's impossible! The present owner is a recluse—no one even knows his name. You can't . . ." She trailed off, reading the truth in his eyes.

"I purchased it three years ago from the man to whom your father sold it when he moved his family to Buckinghamshire."

A slow finger of anger began to curl in Liza's stomach. "But why did you not tell me? Why didn't you respond to Thomas's inquiries?" *Is this to be your revenge, Chad?*

Chad refused to acknowledge the question that fairly blazed in her eyes. He knew a moment of discomfort, but maintained his aspect of disinterested calm.

"I simply considered it an investment," he drawled. "I had no desire to engage in any more brangles with you. Now, happily, I find it is the perfect bargaining chip. How convenient, don't you think, that each of us has something the other wants?—something of a change from our last encounter."

She wanted to hit him. She ached with the desire to pick up her coffee cup and dash its contents in his face. It would have given her pleasure to claw his eyes from his face. She railed silently at the Fates, who had put her once again in his power. But, this was different, wasn't it? Long ago it was his love that had bound her to him with a thousand gossamer strands—and she had welcomed her imprisonment. Now, all she felt was rage and helplessness.

She gathered the last shreds of her control and sat down at the table. Clenching her hands in her lap, she spoke in a color-less voice. "Yes, most convenient. But why a wager? Why not a simple exchange—for I should imagine the worth of the items to be comparable?"

"Ah, but that would destroy the challenge." A smile stretched across his teeth, and Liza was reminded of a preying wolf. "Besides," he continued, "I plan to win the wager, thus I shall finish the contest in possession of both the pendant and Brightsprings."

From somewhere she produced a brittle smile of her own. "You are very confident, Chad Lockridge, but then you always were—as well as being ever so watchful for the main chance. I will accept your wager. I suggest we allow Thomas to handle the details."

Without another word she rose again, turned, and walked away, her carriage as rigid as a church steeple, leaving Chad to stare after her.

Some minutes later Chad faced an astonished Thomas Har-court across that gentleman's desk.

"You . . . *you* own Brightsprings?" Thomas spluttered. "But . . . but . . ."

"I hope you won't take it too badly amiss, old fellow," said Chad, "that just this once I used another agent for my affairs. I could not, after all, ask you to participate in what would surely be a conflict of interest."

"Humbug!" snorted Thomas. "You wanted to present Liza with a *fait accompli* at the moment of your choosing, calcu-lated for maximum effect."

"There is that," agreed Chad, unruffled.

Thomas hesitated a moment before continuing. "Does it re-ally matter to you so much to get her at a disadvantage? Was that the purpose of your return, to somehow have her at your mercy?"

"Good God!" Chad rose to his feet, stung. "Is that what you . . . ?" He paced the width of Thomas's office, then turned to face him. "I suppose that's what it looks like to her, as well?"

Thomas said nothing, merely eyeing him expressionlessly.

Chad threw himself back into his chair. "I—I wouldn't hurt her, you know."

"You already did that."

At this Chad straightened abruptly. "Did I indeed? It wasn't I, you know, who called our betrothal quits before it had even begun."

"Odd," murmured Thomas. "I heard otherwise."

"Did she tell you—that she accused me of—that she thought me a . . ."

"Fortune hunter?" Thomas interposed sharply. "No. That little item could have been gleaned from any gossip-monger in town. As a matter of fact," he continued, as Chad's lips whitened, "Liza told me nothing. It was merely my privilege to watch her turn, almost in a breath, from a bright, laughing girl caught in the magic of her first love, into a brittle, worldly, not very happy young woman."

Chad's lips tightened. "She seems happy enough now. She has all of London at her feet—to say nothing of Giles Daventry about her neck."

Thomas frowned. "You've heard of that connection then? He's been dogging her steps for years, even before you and she met, but up until the last few months, she gave him little encouragement."

"She appears to be giving him plenty now," mumbled Chad sourly. He shook himself. "Be assured that Lady Liza's *affaires de coeur*, have nothing to do with me. Now about this wager . . ."

Chapter 6

"Now about this wager," said Liza to Thomas. She was seated in the chair vacated by Chad not an hour earlier. "It is the most perfidious piece of work imaginable, but if it is the only way I shall acquire Brightsprings, I might as well bite the bullet."

"It seems fairly straightforward," replied Thomas. "You will each invest one thousand pounds in any manner you see fit. I will make the transactions for you and keep a record of the gains and/or losses for you both. At the end of three months—that would be the twenty-third of June—whichever one of you has realized the greatest profit from his or her investments will win."

"Very well." She smiled gleefully. "I have the perfect place to start. I wish you to institute an inquiry into land for sale in the area of a village called Tittlesfield in Lancashire."

She outlined in detail the information she had received from Nathan Rothschild. "He told me some time ago that Horace Pelham is planning to build a mill near there on some land he owns. It is not a large piece, however, and he will require more for his employee housing. I ran into Mr. Rothschild today, and he says that apparently Mr. Pelham is going ahead with his plans."

"Yes, I see," said Thomas, nodding. "Property thereabouts probably sells for a song right now. If you could snap up some acreage, it will be worth a great deal to Pelham later on. Excellent, Liza—I'll get right on it."

Declining an offer of tea, Liza bade Thomas farewell and thoughtfully made her way back to her home.

What had been Chad's motive in making this outrageous wager? She very much doubted that it was, as he had said, a way to scoop in both prizes. She did not wonder that winning the Queen's Pendant meant a great deal to him. She could well imagine the need he must feel to get it back into his family—particularly given the manner in which the family had lost it. For the first time in years she allowed herself to ponder on the humiliation Chad must have felt so long ago when all the world had turned against him. He was branded a fortune hunter and a thief all within a few months. What rage he must have felt at this injustice.

She had not, heretofore, examined her own motives in searching for the pendant. At the first whisper that it was in the hands of the reclusive Lord Wilbraham, she had made it her first priority to acquire it. Now, for the first time she asked herself—why?

Surely she was not so petty that she would use it to hurt Chad. Was she? She frowned. She was not a vindictive witch, after all. Besides, Chad meant nothing to her. She was no longer interested in his pain or his joy. He could purchase a mansion on Park Lane, marry that beauteous ninnyhammer, Caroline Poole, and live happily or miserably for the rest of his life, and it mattered not a whit to her—not a single, solitary whit. She had purchased the pendant, she assured herself, purely as an investment. Lord Wilbraham had been persuaded to sell it for a fraction of its worth, and if and when she decided to sell it herself (for she had no doubt she would win the wager), it would be for a handsome profit.

Having talked herself into a comfortable feeling of self-satisfaction, she turned her thoughts to the soiree she would be attending that night. There would probably be no dancing, she thought, so perhaps she would wear the Italian crepe with the very narrow skirt. She knew it to be one of her most becoming ensembles, and she wondered idly if Chad would be there.

Not that she cared.

Her carriage had by now stopped at her front door, and once inside the house, she went directly to her room. She changed from her "banker-lady rig-out" into a morning gown of pomona green sarcenet, with a beguiling frill about the neckline and a treble-flounced skirt.

Seating herself at a small, tambour-topped writing desk, she addressed herself to some correspondence too long delayed. Reaching for a sheet of writing paper, she began an industrious mending of her pen. Once that was accomplished, she sat, nibbling on the feather end of her quill for some minutes, staring out the window that overlooked the Square.

Thus it was that she happened to observe, with some astonishment, Chad Lockridge emerge from Gunter's pastry shop with Charity. Arm in arm, obviously in great harmony with each other, they strolled along the south side of the Square, past the great expanse of Landsdowne House to the front door of Rushlake House.

Liza could not see Charity enter the house, of course, nor could she see if Chad entered with her, and she certainly was not going to crane her neck so she could do so. She removed her nose from the windowpane and hastened downstairs.

To her surprise she found Chad cozily ensconced in the drawing room between Charity and Lady Burnsall. All three looked up as she entered the room.

"Liza!" exclaimed Charity. "See who has come to visit us."

Really, this was the outside of enough! First he presented her with a proposition that amounted to little short of blackmail, and now he was trying to ingratiate himself with her family. To what purpose? she wondered frantically. And how was it that he was already on a first-name basis with the two persons who might have been expected to consider him persona most particularly non grata in the Rushlake household. One would never know to look at the charming group arranged on the damask settee that one of them had broken the heart of the nearest and dearest of the other two.

"How nice," she said in a tone of repressive courtesy.

"What a good thing you have come down, Liza," said Letitia, "for I must take Charity off. We are promised to Great-Aunt Candida for a visit this morning, and we must call on Lady Gerard as well, to see her new granddaughter. You may keep Chad entertained. Perhaps he would care to stay for lunch."

Nodding delightedly to Chad, her ladyship swept out of the room with her younger daughter in tow.

Silence reigned in the sunny little drawing room.

"One hates to be rude," said Chad at last, his green eyes sparkling with mischief, "and I know you will be shatteringly disappointed, but I must decline your kind invitation to lunch. I have commitments elsewhere, I fear."

"What invitation would that be?" replied Liza through clenched teeth.

"Why, did you not . . . ?" Chad's voice was full of innocent surprise. "Ah, I must have been mistaken. In that case I shall take my leave of you, dear lady."

He picked up his curly-crowned beaver hat and made as though to depart.

"One moment, if you please, Mr. Lockridge."

Chad's brows rose in surprise, but he seated himself again on the settee. Liza chose a cherry-striped silk armchair some distance from him. She sat on its edge, hands clasped on her knees, and forced herself to meet his gaze.

"I must ask you, sir, what your intentions are toward my little sister."

This time, Chad's brows shot skyward. "I beg your pardon?"

"You escorted her home a few moments ago from Gunter's."

Once again, amusement glinted in Chad's eyes. "I do beg your pardon, Lady Liza. I had no idea that treating a young lady to an ice at Gunter's could be construed as an impropriety."

"No, of course it is not. It's just that . . . I have noticed that you and she seem to be on remarkably close terms, and I am concerned."

The expression of glee on Chad's face became more pronounced. "In addition to my other iniquities, do you consider me a seducer of very young ladies of quality?"

"I am happy to say," snapped Liza, "that I am completely unfamiliar with the catalogue of your iniquities. It is Charity with whom I an concerned, although I am not surprised that such an emotion is a cause for mirth on your part."

Abruptly his sardonic smile faded. He rose from the settee and took a chair close to the one in which Liza was seated. "Please accept my apologies, Liza," he said rigidly. "I have no wish to cause you concern." His intense emerald gaze, as always, made her breath catch in her throat. "You seem to think I am engaged in some sort of vendetta against you, and such is not at all the case."

He reached to cover her hands with one of his, and the warmth of his fingers spread through her like a burst of sunlight on a cold day.

"That is most gratifying, Mr. Lockridge." She was pleased that her voice remained cool. "However, you have not answered my question."

Chad abruptly released her hands. "I do confess to an interest in Charity," he said, and Liza felt suddenly cold. "I never missed not having a younger sister—or even a niece—but now, having made her acquaintance, I find her a delight." He shot a glance at Liza. "I promise you, she regards me in the light of an uncle. In fact, her conversation at Gunter's revolved around a certain young man named John, er, Weston, I believe."

She felt as though a large, unbearable weight had been lifted from her breast, and she exhaled the breath she had been holding for what seemed like hours.

"John Weston." She sighed. "I might have known. That young man is becoming a real problem. Well, he is totally unsuitable," she continued, in answer to the question in his eyes. "He's nice enough, but quite ineligible." She hesitated. "Do you believe she has given her heart to him? I should not wish you to betray a confidence, of course," she finished hastily.

"Well," replied Chad in some caution, "I don't know about her heart, but thoughts of him seem to fill her head. I am not acquainted with the fellow, but he seems to represent a combination of Sir Galahad, Socrates, and the Archangel Gabriel."

Liza laughed ruefully. "Indeed, I can only hope that as she comes to see him more, she will realize that he is quite ordinary."

"If she does not continue to see him with the eyes of love." Chad's eyes fixed upon hers, until she dropped her own.

"Yes," she murmured, "for love indeed blinds, does it not?"

"Perhaps," he answered shortly. "But why have you such an objection to him?"

"I have no objection to him. I simply would not choose him for Charity. She can look where she may for a husband, and I would have her wed someone who will care for her and give her the life she deserves."

"And young Weston does not measure up to your grand dreams."

Liza looked up into eyes that had turned once more to opaque bottle bottoms.

"My dreams are not—" she began indignantly. She halted abruptly, angry with herself for rising to his bait. "I do not propose to discuss my sister with you, Mr. Lockridge," she finished with great dignity, and, rising, began to move toward the door. "And now, if you will excuse me, I have matters to which I must attend."

But he was not to be dismissed. He rose also, but ambled casually across the room in her wake. He smiled down at her. "I wonder if you would grant me a viewing of the Queen's Pendant before I leave."

"The pendant?" she repeated stupidly.

"Or perhaps you do not keep it here in your home?"

"Oh, yes—of course. Yes," she said again, cursing her own idiocy.

She beckoned him to follow her to the small room at the back of the house, used by her as a study. There she led him to a cupboard, which she unlocked to produce the small velvet packet. Opening it, she removed the Queen's Pendant from its resting place in the little wooden box and placed it in his out-stretched palm.

For a long moment he simply stared at it, and Liza took the opportunity to study him covertly. Strange, she mused, how his nearness caused the years to fall away. She breathed in the familiar soap and leather scent of him and, as always, it filled her senses. How, she wondered for the thousandth time, could things have gone so wrong between them? How could he have believed her so willing to listen to the malevolent whispers that had spread about him. Worse, how could he have believed her eager to marry for wealth and a title? How . . . ?

"What?" She lifted her head, suddenly aware he was speaking to her.

"I was just saying—poor Father. It cost him such pain to part with this—and for all its craftsmanship, it is so very ugly. I should imagine the Queen was only too glad to be rid of it. She probably had it as a gift from some importunate ambassador."

"Yes," she answered a little breathlessly. "I suppose that is the way with heirlooms. Fashions change, but sentiment never dies."

He paused in the act of returning the pendant to her. His hand curved around hers, and she was conscious of the jewels' warmth in her palm.

"No, sentiment never dies," whispered Chad, a dazed look in his eyes as he bent his head toward hers.

She stood motionless, spellbound by the unspoken message

she found in his gaze. Time seemed to slow, and her pulse drummed thickly in her ears.

The discreet cough that sounded near the doorway thundered in the room like a pistol shot, and she whirled toward its source. A footman stood there, diffidently waiting to be noticed. Chad straightened abruptly, like a man suddenly awakened from a disturbing dream.

"What is it?" asked Liza. The footman came forward, bearing a note in his gloved hand.

Liza replaced the pendant in the cupboard, which she locked swiftly before turning to receive the note.

"Why," she exclaimed as she examined the direction scrawled on the outside of the missive, "it's from Giles!"

"Ah, yes, Giles," said Chad expressionlessly. Liza's expression of delighted surprise created a singularly unpleasant sensation in his interior. Bad enough that she was familiar enough with Daventry's handwriting to recognize it on the outside of what was no doubt a *billet-doux*, but she needn't look as though it were the answer to her maidenly prayers. And right after that moment of communion between the two of them. Had she felt nothing just then? For him it had been as though his very essence were being pulled into the azure pools of her eyes.

"How lovely!" trilled Liza. "He says he has arranged for a party to go to Richmond this afternoon, and requests my company. What fun!"

Chad clenched his fists, but he commented serenely. "Seems a little early in the year for a ramble in the Park, but I do hope you will enjoy yourself. As for me . . ." He made a graceful bow. " . . . as I said, I must be on my way. No, no, don't bother—I can see myself out."

With that he turned on his heel and left the room.

Liza stared after him.

Several hours later she found herself reflecting ruefully on Chad's prediction. She glanced at skies of an ominous gray and shivered in her linen spencer. She was forced to admit that, despite her fatuous expressions of anticipation to Chad— good Lord, had she really thought to make him jealous?—she was not having a good time.

None of the persons included in Giles's outing were very well known to her. The gentlemen were a lively lot, ripe for any jollification, and the ladies were only too ready to join in the fun. Once the picnic luncheon had been spread, there had been a great deal of teasing and squealing and not a few pursuits into the surrounding copses and bowers.

Giles had remained at her side during most of the expedition, and they had conversed amiably. A few moments ago, however, two damsels had joined them, and as the conversation had taken a more feminine turn, Giles drifted away to join a group of gentlemen involved in a discussion of cock fighting, loudly disputing the merits of the color red over the color gray.

"I do hope it won't rain and spoil our fun," remarked one of the young ladies left in Liza's company, a Miss Wyvern. "I think it was so very nice of Mr. Daventry to invite us."

"My mother did not want me to come at first," chimed in the second girl, a Miss Chiltenham. "Mr. Daventry talked her around, though, promising that there would be two married, older couples in the group." She cast a dubious look at one of these, Mr. and Mrs. George Taverner. At the moment Mrs. T. was engaged in a raucous flirtation with a laughing young bachelor, while her husband devoted his attention to the brandy decanter he had appropriated shortly after their arrival.

"Well," said Miss Wyvern, simpering, "my mama said that Lady Liza Rushlake's presence would certainly lend sufficient respectability to any outing."

Liza thanked her in a faint voice and turned the subject by noting the daffodils that were just beginning to bloom against the deep green of a nearby copse.

As they turned to look, their gaze was arrested by the emergence from the woods of two other members of their party, a lissome miss and a gentleman, both in considerable disarray.

"Why, look," cried Miss Chiltenham, pointing her finger excitedly, "it's Freddie Fallgarth and that dreadful Jane Bridgemore."

"And just this morning," said Miss Wyvern, her fat curls atremble, "Jane was telling me about how awful it was that Sarah Rand was making up to Freddie. Butter wouldn't have melted in her mouth!"

The two young women then embarked on a gratifying exposé of Miss Bridgemore's character and morals, and after a few moments, Liza turned and walked quietly away.

She strolled toward the woods just vacated by the dreadful

Jane and her partner, musing on the foibles of youth, and paused beside a clump of young oak trees. It had been a day not unlike this one that Chad had kissed her for the first time. They had come on a picnic in the Park with friends, and had stolen away at the first opportunity. She had lost her heart to him weeks before, of course, but this was the first time they had escaped the surveillance of chaperons and tattle-mongers to retreat into their own world. Had it not been for Chad's own return to sanity, she would surely have been compromised beyond hope. For in his arms she had experienced her first, wondrous foray into the magical landscape of love. She had melted against him, astonished and delighted at the response the touch of his lips had brought forth from her.

She pressed her fingers to her heated cheeks. How absurd she was being! She was no longer the green girl whose flesh had turned to fire at Chad's touch. And yet . . . Her response to his touch just this afternoon had been distressingly vivid. What had possessed her to . . . ?

She became suddenly aware of voices floating toward her on the afternoon breeze. Two more gentlemen from the picnic expedition were sauntering toward her, and her attention was caught as she heard Chad's name. As they approached, Liza remained still and unseen, sheltered by the oaks.

"S'truth, Percy. The feller's nothing more than a common criminal."

"Don't see how you can say that, old man," responded Percy, a willowy youth with light hair and close-set eyes. "You meet him everywhere, y' know. Got pots of money, one hears."

"That's just m' point. He stole it all. Was speakin' to a feller just last night. Said his cousin has a friend who just returned from a visit to India. Says it was common knowledge that Lockridge got his start by siphoning off the profits of the business where he was employed."

"No!"

"Yes! After that he simply raked in the ducats using shady practices. Why I hear he's even involved in the slave trade!"

"Well," reflected Percy after an astonished gasp, "I suppose one shouldn't be surprised. After all, didn't he leave home under rather a cloud several years ago? And I've heard . . ."

Their voices trailed off as they moved away from Liza, and for several moments she remained where she stood, transfixed.

Her fingers curled into fists, and she fairly shook with rage. She wanted to call after the two, to scream a denial of all they had said. How dare they—a pair of brainless twits whose sole preoccupation was with the cut of their clothes—how *dare* they malign a man whose boots they were not fit to polish.

Where could they have heard such calumny, she wondered frantically. Who could be spreading such filth about Chad? Shady dealings! The slave trade! Dear God, if such lies were given circulation—and if they were believed—he would be ruined.

She paced in agitation, her brain fairly humming with outrage and speculation. It was happening all over again! The same vicious rumors that had driven him from England so long ago were being stirred again. Who—"

"Here you are, Liza!" It was Giles, laughing and out of breath as he flung an arm about her shoulders. "I've been searching for you everywhere. Why did you—why, what is it, my dear?" he asked, concern apparent in his voice as he observed her pallor and the tears that glittered in her eyes.

"It . . . it's nothing, Giles. I was just . . ." She turned, suddenly and faced him. "Giles, have you heard any—talk about Chad since his return?"

Giles's returning gaze was shuttered. "No, of course not—that is, there is always talk, but nothing one would regard. Why?"

Liza hesitated a moment, then in an anguished burst, she recounted the conversation she had just overheard. She gestured toward one of the young men standing in conversation not far away. Giles's mouth hardened as she concluded.

"That's Charlie Summersby. I can well believe it of him. Young snake never has anything good to say about anyone." He turned once more to Liza. "You know, I never was one of Chad Lockridge's intimates, and Lord knows—" he bent a twisted smile on her—"I have no reason to love him, but I do consider him my friend. Come."

To Liza's astonishment he grasped her hand and pulled her with him. He tapped Summersby on the shoulder.

"A word with you, Charlie," he murmured. The young man swiveled to face him, and Giles gripped his arm to force him a few paces away from his friends.

"I understand," he said, his face very close to Summersby's, "that you have been discussing a friend of mine—Chad Lockridge."

Summersby's eyes widened. "What if I have?" he mumbled defensively.

"Just where did you get the information you were bruiting about so freely?"

"Ah . . ." The young man looked down at the ground. "I . . . I don't know. Boodles. Yes, I was there last night with a group of friends and his name came up."

"And did any of your friends offer conclusive proof of the allegations made against Mr. Lockridge?"

"No, but . . ."

"Then in the future," said Giles in a very soft voice, "I suggest you cease spreading what can only be termed the most scurrilous of gossip. Indeed, you have this afternoon provided Mr. Lockridge grounds for suit, should he choose to so dignify your pathetic squealings."

Charlie Summersby whitened, then flushed scarlet. He did not answer, but backed away from Giles as though he had been struck. He uttered an unintelligible croak, then stumbled away.

Liza turned to Giles, her eyes shining. "Oh, that was well done of you."

He smiled ruefully. "I trust that will put a spoke in Charlie's malicious little proclivity for scandal mongering, but I hope I have not done more harm than good. It is possible," he continued, noting her quizzical expression, "that by expressing myself so vehemently, I may have simply brought more attention to bear on all the unfortunate prattle."

"All the unfortunate . . . Giles, you *have* heard something. Are there truly stories circulating about Chad?"

Giles shifted uncomfortably. "I didn't want to tell you, my dear, but, yes, I have heard some—unsettling rumors."

"Oh! How can people be so wicked?"

"Does it matter so much to you what people say about Chad Lockridge?" His question was uttered casually, but his gaze was penetrating, and Liza flushed.

"I—no, of course—that is, I dislike seeing anyone falsely accused. Please, Giles," she continued, feeling an urgent need to turn the subject, "let us go back to the others."

Nothing more was said regarding Chad for the rest of the afternoon, and when they returned to London, Liza bade Giles a smiling farewell at her doorstep, grateful for his understanding.

It was not so easy to put the incident from her mind however, and, finding the house empty, she went into the cheerful morning room where she settled herself in a damask chair overlooking the Square. She stared blindly at the bustle of late afternoon traffic.

She could not believe it was beginning all over again—the lies, the rumors, the innuendo that had ruined Chad's young life and created a cataclysmic crack in her own. For the first time in many years her eyes brimmed with tears. She blinked. No. She had not cried since the day she had discovered that Chad did not love her, and she was not going to start now. Still, regret coursed through, almost as sharply as it had those many years ago.

She shrugged and prepared to rise. It had all happened so long ago. If only Chad had stayed in India! Now, here he was, embroiled all over again in what appeared to be a mysterious campaign to ruin his reputation—again.

She shook herself. Perhaps she was being foolish. One overheard conversation did not a campaign make. Perhaps the words were the result of a fit of pique on someone's part—an isolated incident. She turned to leave the room, but her attention was drawn again to the window as a carriage drew up before the house.

In a moment Charity stepped from the vehicle. She had evidently just come home from an expedition with friends, for several bonneted heads could be seen inside the carriage. Why, what in the world was wrong with Charity? She had bounced down from the carriage, her cheeks fiery and her eyes snapping. She ran into the house without so much as a wave to her companions.

Liza hurried to meet her sister in the hall, arriving just in time to watch Charity snatch her bonnet from her head and fling it onto the little table below the hall mirror with cyclonic force.

"Charity," began Liza, "what on earth . . . ?"

Charity whirled. "Liza! What a dreadful thing! I have just discovered that Sally Jewett is the most hateful cat in the world." She took a deep breath. "I am afraid I just slapped her."

Chapter 7

"WHAT did you say?" gasped Liza.

"She was saying perfectly awful things about Chad!"

Liza drew her sister into the morning room and directed her to a damask-covered wing chair by the window.

"What happened?" she asked tersely.

"I was telling Sally and Dorothea Welles—and Trixie Satherswaite was with us, too—about Chad taking me to Gunter's for an ice this morning. They were all simply consumed with envy, of course, especially Sally, for only yesterday he sent regrets for her mama's Venetian breakfast. Chad is quite the social success of the Season, you know," she added with a proprietary air, as though she spoke of one of her family.

"Yes, yes," replied Liza with some impatience. "Just tell me what Sally said about . . ."

Charity stiffened. "She tossed her head in that superior manner of hers and said that she had heard—'from a reliable source', if you please—that Chad is nothing more than a common thief, having embezzled funds from his employer in India some years ago. Can you imagine?" Her cheeks flushed with indignation, and she pounded an arm of the wing chair as though the hapless Miss Jewett lay beneath her small fist. "And then, if you would believe, she said that the reason Chad left England in the first place was because his father caught him stealing a valuable family heirloom, which he then sold to pay for his passage to India."

Charity shot a glance at Liza before continuing. "Sally capped it all by claiming that, far from having made a fortune in India, his head is barely above water, and the *on dit* was that he had hoped to recoup his fortune by marrying you. That," she finished, her eyes lowered, "was when I slapped her."

Liza had been pacing the floor during Charity's recital, but at its conclusion, she hastened to her chair and sank to her knees to clasp her sister's hands impulsively. "Oh, my dear, I should chastise you for such unladylike behavior, but I must say, I would have been tempted toward the same action myself."

Liza rose and took a nearby chair. She frowned. "However, I fear Sally was merely repeating rumors that are apparently making their rounds all over town."

Charity gasped. "But, how can that . . . ?"

"I don't know, but it happened six years ago, too."

Her sister sat still for a moment, than looked at her straightly. "Was that why you broke off your relationship with him?"

Liza recoiled slightly. "I did not . . ." she began, her face pale. She stopped and looked down at her hands for some moments before returning Charity's gaze.

"It was Chad who broke off our relationship."

Liza heard her own words with surprise, for she had never uttered them aloud before. She was additionally startled to observe an expression of compassion cross her sister's face, imparting a new maturity to the flighty girl with whom she was so affectionately familiar.

"And yes," she continued haltingly, "it was because of a tapestry of lying innuendo, such as the words you heard today."

Charity said nothing, but watched her expectantly.

"It started," began Liza, "with a conversation similar to the one you just held with Sally Jewett."

She closed her eyes and felt a rising nausea as she recalled her disbelief the first time, those many years ago, she had been the recipient of a sly confidence from a distant acquaintance. "But, Lady Liza, I speak only as a friend. You and your dear mama and papa are but newly arrived in the metropolis, and are no doubt unaware of the pitfalls that lie in wait for the unwary. As one concerned with your welfare, I hate to see you encouraging the attentions of one such as Chadwick Lockridge. He is in desperate financial straits, you know, and one hears . . ."

Liza bent a bitter smile on Charity. "The woman went on at some length, pointing out in the kindest manner possible, that Mr. Lockridge had been heard boasting to his friends that his fortunes would soon be seeing a marked improvement, now that he had caught the fancy of the wealthy Lady Liza Rush-lake.

"I was wholly outraged, and I rushed to tell Chad, to warn him of the calumnies being perpetrated against him. I thought he would fight against them, but he refused to do so. He said that his character was known to his friends, and they were all that mattered.

"In the coming weeks others brought whispers of warning for me, and soon even Mama and Papa eyed Chad askance when he came to call. I never discussed the ugliness again with Chad. It seemed the only person with whom I could speak of Chad in my unhappiness was Giles, for only he, among all my friends, disbelieved the awful things people were saying about Chad.

"Chad's visits became less frequent, and the time we did spend together was laced with awkward silences and forced declarations of devotion. Soon the cloud of doubt that hung over Chad's life permeated my own like a poisonous fog."

"But," interposed Charity, who had sat perched on the edge of her chair during this recital, her eyes fixed on Liza's with painful intensity. "But, still you planned to marry, did you not?"

"Oh yes. In fact, I blithely planned for the night I was sure all would be made right. Chad had been invited, against Papa and Mama's judgment, to dinner in celebration of the promotion he expected to receive that day. He worked in the office of the Exchequer, you know. This was to be the evening when, his future assured, Chad would ask Papa for my hand.

"When Chad arrived that night, however, it was to tell me that the promotion had been given to another. Apparently his employer had come to the conclusion that he was no longer to be trusted. I asked if he had defended himself to his superior, and he said that would have been pointless."

Liza choked. "I was so caught up in my own pain, I failed to perceive his, and I rushed on, unheeding. 'Dear God, how can you just accept this? Don't you care that we may never marry now? Why, you have never denied the lies even to me!'

"Chad whirled on me. He grasped my shoulders, and in a voice I had never heard before, he rasped, 'I do beg your pardon, Lady Liza. Please accept my assurances that I am neither a liar, nor a thief. Nor am I, most particularly, a fortune hunter. Is that what concerns you?'

"Stung, I cried out. 'I never meant . . .'

" 'As for our not marrying, perhaps that is for the best if my lack of position in the world—and my evil reputation—is so distressing to you.'

"I was furious, and I fairly screamed at him. 'How could you think that? I was talking about my father. You know he . . .'

" 'I well know what your father thinks of me. I have seen the contempt of late in his eyes, and now I see it in yours.'

" 'Then you are reading something that is not there,' I cried. By now, I had allowed my anger to fan into a royal rage. 'I have defended you for weeks now, since you will not speak out for yourself. And, I might add, I've lost some good friends in doing so. If you think . . .'

" 'I cannot tell you how your words warm my heart, my lady. I had no idea you found it necessary to take my part against the world,' Chad said.

" 'Well,' I retorted not caring anymore how I was hurting him 'somebody had to, since you would not—and now, see what has come of it all! But, of course,' I continued, heaping coals on the conflagration, 'you have said it would be just as well if we did not marry, after all. I begin to believe you are right!' "

Charity uttered a soft gasp as Liza paused for a moment, unable to go on. At last she continued in a low voice, "I waited for the response I was sure would come. But Chad merely stood there, staring at me as though I had struck him.

"When he said nothing, I cried out, desperate to goad him into replying, 'Perhaps I should have listened to my friends! How stupid I have been. All this time, I thought it was my irresistible self you loved. How lowering it has been to discover it was merely my famous fortune that attracted you to me!' "

"Oh, Liza! How could you?" Charity's voice was choked.

"The minute the words were out of my mouth," Liza continued, "I would have given anything to have them back. I knew I had gone too far, but I felt that now, surely, he would assure me that his love for me was pure and steadfast. It had been so long, you see, since he had told me that he loved me, and I . . . I needed to hear it.

"His eyes widened, and I felt as though I were being

drenched in an icy green shower. Unable to bear his gaze, I turned to stare into the fireplace. The silence seemed to scream at me, but after a very, very long pause he said, very softly, 'Yes, it appears that you should have listened to your friends, Lady Liza, but how fortunate for you that you have now discovered the true state of your heart. Fortunate for us both, I might add, for it seems as though I, too, have just been saved from making a grievous mistake. Please give my regrets to your parents.'

"Stunned, I tried to form my thoughts into words. I whirled and lifted a hand to him, but he was gone. The next moment I heard the front door close.

"I thought he would return, of course, but he did not. In a few days, I sent a note to him in which I asked his forgiveness for my unthinking words and requested that he come to see me. It was then I discovered that he had left the country. It was only after many months that I learned he had gone to India. He had not even cared enough for me to try for a reconciliation."

Liza sat back in her chair, drained. Charity merely stared at her. At last she said quietly, "And you never wrote to him to explain . . . ?" she trailed off.

"Explain what? It was he who left. I had tried to assure him of my devotion, and he turned my words against me. I have my pride, after all."

"Yes, you certainly do, Liza," replied her sister. "I hope it has provided a satisfactory substitute for Chad's love."

Liza could only stare at her.

It was several days before Liza again saw Chad. She emerged early one morning from her front door, garbed in another austere City ensemble, this one of a muddy green bombazine, and found that not only was her own carriage drawn up to the curb, but Cad's curricle was parked there as well.

She nodded to Chad, who was also just leaving his home, and smiled as his amused gaze swept over her dark green ensemble.

"Another invasion of the profane precincts of Mammon?" he asked sardonically.

"Yes, I go to meet with Thomas."

Chad hesitated a moment, then approached her. "I have an appointment with him as well. Shall we travel together?"

Liza searched her mind frantically for an excuse to refuse

him. She was finding that proximity to this russet-haired buc-caneer was detrimental in the extreme to her peace of mind. What fell from her lips, however, was, "Why, that would be very nice. Shall we take my carriage? I prefer to ride in an en-closed vehicle when I go visiting with Mammon."

A few minutes later, seated side by side, they made their way through the streets of Mayfair and on, beyond St. James's, sweeping past the Palace into Pall Mall. Every cell in her body seemed to be aware of Chad's presence just a hand's breadth away. She pressed against the side of the carriage, feeling that it had unaccountably shrunk several sizes. It was also uncom-fortably warm. She smoothed her gloves of Irish tan and tried to think of an innocuous topic of conversation. When Chad spoke, the sound of his voice was loud in her ear, and she jerked convulsively.

"What?" she asked blankly.

"I said, how was your expedition to Richmond?"

"Expedi . . . oh . . . yes," she replied, realizing that she must sound perfectly demented. She shot him a sidelong glance, wondering if the malevolent whisperings promulgated by Charlie Summersby had reached his ears, but his expression was bland. She affixed a smile to her face and said casually, "I'm afraid you were right. It was too early in the year for such an outing. It was chilly and damp and began to rain just as we left the Park. It's a wonder we didn't all come down with an ague."

Chad nodded. "Spring is such an unpredictable time of year, after all."

"Yes, I suppose that's true," she responded uncertainly, re-lieved to note that the carriage had swung into Nicholas Lane and drawn to a stop outside the offices of Stanhope, Harcourt, and Finch.

Liza's appointment with Thomas was of short duration, as was Chad's. She had waited for him for only a few moments in another office before she heard masculine voices announc-ing their presence in the corridor. She joined them as they completed their conversation.

"Did I hear you mention Macclesfield?" she asked.

"Yes," replied Chad. "I'm thinking of building a silk spin-ning mill there. Are you familiar with the area?"

"Not very, although I know it is a silk center." She turned to Thomas. "Did you tell Chad of my own interest in the silk industry? But, no," she continued, answering her own question with a laugh. "It would never do for you to reveal my doings to another."

"Are you indeed a mill owner?" he asked in surprise.

"In a very small way. I do not own a mill, but I have an interest in two or three weaving firms in Spitalfields. I set up several families with Jacquard looms, which I purchased in France. The operations are quite small—almost what you would call a cottage industry. They produce figured silk, and some lovely ribbon."

The two bade good-bye to Thomas and left the office building. As they moved toward Liza's carriage, she asked idly, "How is it you are interested in silk production?"

"I own five *filatures* in India. Those are factories situated where the silkworms are raised. The silk thread is taken from the cocoons in these factories and shipped to other places—such as England—for the later stages of manufacture. I cannot see how it would be other than profitable to own a mill here, thus providing my own outlet for the produce of my plants in Madras. I would like to build from scratch, however, so that my employees may be housed in humane conditions on the property."

Liza stared at him for some moments.

"I had no idea," she said slowly, "that your commercial interests were so varied."

Chad bundled her hurriedly into the carriage. Conversation was desultory on the way home, and when the vehicle reached Berkeley Square, she bade him the briefest of farewells before hurrying into her house.

Later that afternoon, as he ascended the stairs of Gentleman Jackson's Saloon in Bond Street, Chad found himself mentally reviewing, again, his expedition with the charming Lady Liza Rushlake. As always, time had seemed to abandon its usual function when he was in her company. He grinned, recalling her animated smile glowing from beneath that dreadful bonnet. How absurd she was to imagine that encasing herself in that ghastly bombazine affair could diminish her loveliness by so much as a degree. Tendrils of golden hair had escaped her severe coiffure, and it had been all he could do to keep his fingers from tracing their line along the soft curve of her cheek.

Damn! He scowled, furious with himself for once again allowing the old feelings to surge within him. He should have known better than to suggest they share a carriage into the City.

"Chad! Thought you'd never get here!"

Chad lifted his eyes. "Jamie!" He smiled at the young man awaiting him at the head of the stairs. "Sorry to be late—got held up. Is Fairburn here?"

"In the changing room. He said he couldn't wait anymore—he's been saying all morning that this will be the day he finally pops a hit over Jackson's guard."

Laughing, Chad followed his friend James, Lord Whissenham, into the precincts regarded as holy by the Fancy. The rest of the afternoon passed swiftly in the bruising activity of the ring. Later, panting and perspiring, he and his friends made their way back to the changing rooms, exchanging friendly badinage. Chad paused as he entered the room, nodding to a gentleman just leaving.

"Selwyn! Good to see you, old fellow—I didn't notice your arrival."

To his astonishment the gentleman continued on his way, brushing past Chad as though he had not spoken.

He turned to Jamie, following behind him, a question in his eyes. "What the devil . . . ?" he began. Then, to his further surprise, Jamie dropped his eyes without answering.

"Jamie?" asked Chad in gathering anger.

Jamie exchanged glances with Stephen Fairburn, who had joined them. Fairburn had evidently witnessed the cut direct offered to Chad, for he, too, looked away in discomfort.

"Will one of you please tell me what is going on?" Chad spoke quietly, but there was steel in his voice.

Stephen Fairburn sighed heavily, and with another glance at Jamie, put a hand on Chad's arm. "Can't discuss it here, old man."

A few minutes later, under Chad's purposeful direction, the three men sat at a table in a small ale house in Clifford Street, not far from Jackson's Saloon.

"All right, out with it," he ordered uncompromisingly. "Tell me precisely why a man I've known since Eton has suddenly declined to recognize me."

There was a moment's silence before Jamie blurted out, "It's started again, Chad."

"The rumors," finished Fairburn, as Chad raised his brows.

"Good God," responded Chad. His stomach tightened, and he experienced a prickling sensation across his shoulders as though tiny stilettos were dancing on the back of his neck. "You mean . . . ?"

"Yes," said Jamie in a weary voice. "The same sort of rot as . . . as last time. It's the same sort of persons who are spreading it—and the same sort who believe it—jumped-up nobodies who don't even know you."

"That's right," Fairburn chimed in. "Those who know you realize the stories are pure balderdash."

"Such as Selwyn?" asked Chad with a painful smile.

"Oh, Selwyn," said Jamie with a shrug. "He's never liked you since you stood up to him and Assheton Minor back in the third form. You can't have forgotten what a nasty little pair of bullies they were!"

Chad's smile broadened with warmth. "As I recall the incident, I was on the losing end of a very bad situation until you two stalwarts showed up." He took a long, thoughtful pull at his tankard of ale. "What, specifically, sort of rot is it this time? Surely, I cannot be accused this time of fortune hunting?"

"No," agreed Jamie morosely. "This time they're saying you're a thief. Yes, I know," he added hurriedly as Chad opened his mouth, "six years ago it was said you stole the Queen's Pendant, but your father's explaining that he had sold it put somewhat of a crimp in that story—at least for those who believed him."

"Now," interposed Fairburn, "it is being put about that you stole from your employer in India."

"Sir Wilfred Bascombe?" This time Chad's mobile brows fairly shot skyward.

"Yes, if that's the name of the first person who hired you in Calcutta."

Chad nodded.

"Well, it seems Sir, er, Wilfred was forced to let you go because you stole vast quantities of cash and merchandise from him. He didn't prosecute because he had no proof, but he knew what you had done."

"I see," murmured Chad. "And I suppose what small success I achieved abroad is all due to more larceny on my part."

"Precisely." This from Jamie. "The rumors have included everything from piracy to the slave trade."

"Good God," said Chad again.

"It's said no decent Englishman in all of India will give you the time of day."

This time Chad was rendered speechless. "But that's preposterous!" he said finally. "How in God's name do such things get started?"

"Have you considered, old man," began Fairburn tentatively, "that the rumors are a deliberate effort on someone's part to discredit you?"

"Yes, I have," growled Chad. He shook his head at their questioning expressions. "Just a hunch. What I don't understand," he continued musingly, "is why start a rumor that can be so easily disproved? I mean, anyone in correspondence with a friend or relative in India could soon discover that I have an excellent reputation there, if I do say so as shouldn't."

"Y-yes," responded Fairburn after a moment. "But that would take time. Perhaps your enemy is working on a timetable. Last time, his—or her—smarmy little campaign cost you your promotion at the Exchequer. Was it scheduled to do so?"

Chad stared at him, unblinking. "Yes," he said slowly. "A campaign—but one designed to cost me much more than a promotion, I think. And this time . . ." He rose suddenly. "Gentlemen, I must leave you. I thank you for your efforts on my behalf." He hesitated. "When I left England six years ago, I thought myself damned near friendless. It seems I was mistaken, and for that, well, mere thanks are not enough, but it's all I can offer you at the moment."

"Gudgeon," mumbled Lord Whissenham.

"Cawker!" blurted Mr. Fairburn, reddening.

Grinning, Chad raised a hand in farewell and hurriedly left the little tap room.

Chapter 8

MECHANICALLY Chad threaded his curricle through the bustling traffic of St. James's and Mayfair, his mind busy with speculation and discovery. Good Lord, how could he have been so stupid—so incredibly green? He followed his thoughts along a tortuous route that took him back through the years to the moment when he realized that his life was crumbling, blasted by innuendo.

When the whispers had first reached him, he was shocked and disbelieving. Later, rage and humiliation were added to the catalogue. Even when his worst fears had materialized, and Liza turned against him, it was at fate he had railed. Raw as he was in the way of the world, he was still aware of the power of fickle rumor. An idle falsehood, a titillating lie murmured behind a hand, the whispers drifting across one's path like strands of gossamer, until suddenly the threads became a web. He had seen others caught, their lives left in ruins by a single, careless morsel of gossip that had taken on a life of its own. He had always assumed his own destiny had fallen victim to a similar fate, never seeing the pattern that was all too clear now.

And Liza. He closed his eyes, and the pattern shifted once again like the disordered pieces of a mosaic. Lord, what a fool he had been! He was outraged and bitterly disappointed that he had lost the promotion, but somehow he had believed it would make no difference to Liza. His Liza, whose sapphire eyes and artless beauty had captivated his heart, and whose wit and intelligence and open-hearted passion had stolen his soul.

For so long she had declared her belief in him, passionately denying the rumors. But he watched, sickened, as that trust had faltered. Her belief in him had died, he reasoned, and so had her love. Why else had she turned her back on him that night?

But now it was all too apparent that Liza had not simply been listening to gossip. The poison had been ladled into her ear, cleverly, with malice and precision. Perhaps he had been too harsh with her, for, in her innocence, could she be blamed for drawing away from him?

There was no doubt in Chad's mind now that his destruction had been meticulously planned. And there was very little doubt as to the identity of the plot's perpetrator. Now, it seemed, his enemy was preparing a second campaign.

As Chad pulled up to his own doorway, his mouth curved upward. How very fortunate that he was no longer an inexperienced youth, without power or influence.

He remained in a thoughtful mood for the rest of the day, and, later that evening, Jem January was forced to call his attention twice before he made his way to his room to dress for dinner.

To Chad's surprise Jem had fit into his household with scarcely a ripple. The young man had made it his first order of business to put himself on good terms with Ravi Chand, and it was not long before the two could be heard conversing genially in a thick mixture of Pidgin English and thieves' cant.

Best of all, thought Chad, was the discovery that Jem's claim to sartorial familiarity was not an idle boast. His master's boots became objects of glossy splendor, and his neck-cloths were minor works of art in their pristine magnificence. Coats and pantaloons appeared as if by magic in freshly pressed perfection.

Chad accepted a reverently proferred waistcoat. "Thank you, Jem, but tonight's party will be a small one. I don't think I'll require the embroidered satin. Something a little more subdued, I think."

Jem shook his head. "P'raps ye might want t' consider riggin' yerself out in a more imposin' fashion this evening."

Surprised, Chad turned to face the young man. "What is this? Do you think I must, er, pad my status?"

"No," replied his newly acquired servant, "but . . ." He paused, shifting awkwardly.

"But, what, Jem?" His gaze sharpened. "What is all this in aid of?"

Jem shifted uncomfortably. "Nothin'. Nothin' atall. Only, well, I mentioned to a few o' me pals that I'm now in yer employ. Werry impressed they all were, too. Howsomever—

they're all coves as what knows what o'clock it is—keeps their ogles and hearin' cheats open, y'know—and as I was conversin' with them, I heard some odd bits an' pieces, if you take my meanin'."

"Bits and pieces? As in rumors?"

"Well, yes, ye might call 'em that. Mind, I didn't b'lieve none of 'em, but there it is."

Chad smiled warily. "And why would you not believe them? You don't know me very well, after all."

Jem stared at him for some moments. "Guv'nor," he said at last, "I've been bangin' about the streets o' Lunnon fer a goodly number of years, and I'm still alive."

Chad merely raised his brows questioningly. Jem rubbed his nose.

"What I mean is, a feller don't last long if he don't learn to size up a cove in pretty short order. I learned a long time ago to tell the difference between a right 'un and a Captain Sharp, or even a rum go. I reckon you'll do."

Chad felt oddly touched by these words, and after a moment's thought, reached for the bell pull that hung near his dressing table. In remarkably short order Ravi Chand loomed in his master's doorway. Chad motioned him to be seated on a small settee near the fire, and gestured to Jem to join him. Seating himself in a nearby armchair, he spoke musingly.

"Ravi Chand, Jem has just told me a tale I find interesting. It seems he has heard some most distressing rumors about your illustrious master."

Ravi Chand cast the newly minted valet a sidelong glance before returning his attention to Chad. After a moment's hesitation, he replied, "Are they the same sort of ruinous gossip that resulted in your journey to India?"

Jem turned an astonished gaze upon the Indian.

" 'Ere now, you never told me you could natter in the King's English. Ye sound like a reg'lar swell!"

Ravi Chand smiled benignly, his teeth a white banner against his mahogany skin. "I have found that the English do not expect to hear their language spoken correctly by foreigners—though why they continue to use that label in a land where they, themselves, are the interlopers has been of some puzzlement to me. In fact they seem to find such a circumstance unsettling. On the other hand, they apparently derive a great deal of childish amusement from the speech imperfections that result when these persons unsuccessfully attempt their language. Being a magnanimous soul, I merely endeavor to live up to expectations."

Jem made no reply, but simply gaped at Ravi Chand as though the giant had sprouted an extra head until Chad commented in the most dulcet of tones, "I'm sure you will agree, Mr. January, that language usage—or misuse—can serve a variety of purposes."

Jem straightened in his seat and returned Chad's grin with a stony stare.

"I wonder," continued Chad musingly, "if you and perhaps one or two of your, er, pals, would perform a certain service for me."

"Sure as spit, if ye can come up with the possibles. I hope it ain't anything terrible illegal. Ye don't want anybody put t' bed with a shovel, do ye?"

"No, nothing like that, and yes, I'll pay well. What I would like you and your cohorts to do is to watch a certain gentleman of my acquaintance. His name is Giles Daventry."

At this an arrested expression crossed Jem's angular features. He turned away to place the refused waistcoat in the wardrobe.

"This Daventry feller's creatin' a problem for ye, is he?" he asked, his eyes still on the offending garment.

"I'm not quite sure, but I strongly suspect he is not foremost among my well-wishers. As for the rumors, I shall be forced to take countermeasures, it seems, but for now, I merely wish to ascertain their source. Ravi Chand, I'm sure, will provide you with any assistance you might require of him."

The bronzed giant rose and gave Jem a smile of acquiescence, and the valet chuckled. "Ye're a mite conspicuous for sneakin' about, but I can see where ye might come in handy in a tight spot."

He watched as Ravi Chand strode majestically from the room, and then went to the wardrobe to procure a second waistcoat for Chad's approval. Receiving the nod, he eased the garment over his master's shoulders. Finished with his ministrations, he stood back to admire the finished product.

"There y'are, sir. As prime a go as ever toddled on the strut."

Chad bestowed a modest smile on his minion, and, collecting hat, gloves, and walking stick, exited his chambers.

*   *   *

Some days after his conversation with Jem January, Chad stood with Lady Charity Rushlake in the center of Picadilly's celebrated Egyptian Hall, gazing in considerable gloom at an array of ancient sarcophagi lining one wall of the cavernous room.

"How did I let you talk me into this?" he said, glowering.

"But I have been anxious to see the exhibition," replied Charity sunnily. "Everyone has been talking of nothing else, you know—and I thought, since you are interested in artifacts, you might like to see it, too." She took his arm, propelling him toward the stairway that rose from the center of the main floor. "I know you will enjoy it prodigiously."

Chad paused, eyeing the young girl in suspicion.

"Since when have you developed an interest in ancient objets d' art, young lady?"

"Why, since it became the fashion to do so, of course," she replied with an engaging chuckle. She tugged at his sleeve, urging him up the stairway. "Do come along, please."

Several paces behind, her maid, Peggy, toiled wearily after them, and when they reached the upper floor, she sank gratefully onto a nearby bench at her mistress's direction.

"There," continued Charity, pointing to several small clay objects displayed on a nearby shelf. "The catalogue says these are cartouches. It appears they were rather like nameplates used for the pharaohs." As she spoke, Chad noted that her eyes darted about the room as though she were looking for someone.

Her restless perusal halted abruptly, and a flood of pink rose to her cheeks. "Oh!" she cried artlessly. "It's John Weston. I wonder what he can be doing here?" Relinquishing her hold on Chad's coat, she fairly danced across the chamber to the young man standing diffidently to one side.

Chad expelled an exasperated grunt. So that was it! The little minx had set him up as cleverly as any Captain Sharp snaring his prey. Apparently his role for the afternoon was to play gooseberry to this ingenious pair of lovers. Sighing, he followed in her wake, and as he approached them, she turned with a radiant smile.

"Chad, do you know Mr. Weston?" She performed the introductions and added, "Mr. Weston is interested in crop improvements. We have enjoyed several most enlightening conversations together on the subject."

She cast a hopeful glance at Chad, who smiled determinedly and expressed his gratification at meeting Mr. Weston.

John Weston blushed and stammered something unintelligible, after which an awkward silence descended on the three.

"If you would like to look at the exhibition, Chad," said Charity with a guileless stare, "you needn't wait for us. I am feeling rather fatigued and would like to sit for a moment. I am sure J . . . Mr. Weston will bear me company."

John's color deepened. "Oh, yes. That is, it would be my pleasure, Lady Charity."

"That will not be necessary," returned Chad smoothly. "I spy a bench over there that will hold us all nicely."

A mutinous flush sprang to Charity's cheeks, and her eyes flashed. "I suppose you think I brought you here on purpose," she said to Chad. "I suppose you think John and I arranged an assignation here."

John raised a protesting hand. "Here, I say, Charity. That is no way to talk to Mr. Lockridge."

"Actually," replied Chad, ignoring him. "My guess is that you arranged the assignation with little regard to Mr. Weston's feelings in the matter." He turned to John. "I would think twice, if I were you, about furthering your acquaintance with young Miss Machiavelli, here. She is bound to plunge you into all sorts of unpleasantness."

"Well!" gasped Charity. She opened her mouth to deliver a stinging retort, but closed it immediately as Chad favored her with the look that had reduced many a junior clerk to stammering incoherence. "And if you think, my girl, that I will be suborned into your plots and schemes, you are very much mistaken. I shall give you five minutes in which you may discuss agricultural matters with Mr. Weston to your heart's content, and then I shall take you home."

"Chad!" The word came out in a wail, as John stood by, seeming uncertain as to whether he should pat Charity's hand or take umbrage or both.

"We don't want to behave in an underhanded fashion," he finally said, and Chad was impressed despite himself with the young man's youthful dignity and forthrightness, "but it is so difficult to see one another. Lady Burnsall and Charity's sister,

Lady Elizabeth have not precisely barred me from the house, but . . ."

"But, they are so disapproving and discouraging. Merely because John is not a viscount or is not wealthy. It's not fair," she cried in the age-old plaint of youth.

Chad was forced to smile. "I know," he said gently. "I was once young—and in love—and I have an excellent memory. And I do," he added, "sympathize with your plight. However I cannot be a party to what you will have to admit is a blatant deception perpetrated on your sister and your mother."

"Yes, but . . ." cried Charity.

"Oh, but you see . . ." said John in some anguish.

"A deception," repeated Chad firmly. He turned to Charity. "You must know I cannot go along with a project that will cause your sister pain. I may not agree with her stand on this matter, but it is she and your mother who hold your future in their hands by right."

Charity pressed her lips together. She did not respond, but behind her sparkling eyes, her thoughts could be plainly read.

"However," continued Chad, his hand uplifted, "I am not impervious to your sad plight. I promise I'll do what I can to persuade Liza to look on Mr. Weston more favorably."

With that Charity had to be content. In what he considered to be a magnanimous gesture, Chad invited the two for tea and cakes at a nearby pastry shop, and the rest of the afternoon passed in amity. Chad directed most of his comments to the youthful agronomist, listening in flattering attention to that gentleman's descriptions of his work.

"For," he said earnestly, "England's population is increasing, and the land available for producing food is decreasing. I believe it is imperative that we strive to improve our crop yields through seed selection and other improvements."

To Chad's amusement Charity sat perched on the edge of her chair, absorbing John's words in rapt attention.

"You see?" she said to Chad, without changing the adoring focus of her gaze. "I told you he is brilliant."

"I begin to think you may be right," he replied musingly. "Tell me," he said, directing his words to John, "about these mangel-wurzels of yours."

Returning to Berkeley Square with Charity an hour or two later, Chad again took up the thread of his earlier discourse with her.

"I meant what I said, my dear." He smiled into her troubled brown eyes. "I will not be a participant in your schemes, and I wish you would promise me that you will inveigle no one else into them, either."

Charity's expression was unreadable as she gazed back at him. "Chad, I love John." She spoke simply, but with heart-breaking certainty.

"I see. You are thinking of marriage, then?"

She dropped her eyes and twisted the cords of her reticule.

"He has not asked me. In fact"—she raised her head—"he has not declared himself at all. But I know he returns my feelings. It is only his blasted nobility of soul that prevents him from speaking his heart."

Chad found it necessary to cough peremptorily.

"For," Charity continued, "he feels that because his birth is barely respectable, and because he has no money and no expectations, that he is unworthy of me. Have you ever heard such nonsense?"

"Never," he replied unsteadily.

She stared at him for a long moment, then broke into an unwilling smile. "Yes, I see what you mean. I suppose I can't blame Liza for fretting, but, don't you see? John is . . . is wonderful. And he's terribly clever. Some of his experiments have been very successful. His parents own an estate in Yorkshire, and they have been growing a new strain of flax there for the past two years."

Chad wrinkled his forehead. "Flax is not considered a primary crop in this country—too susceptible to overgrowth by weeds, and not particularly useful as a feed grain."

"Oh, but John has developed a strain that is resistant to destruction by weeds—and it is exceptionally nourishing. He tells me it's very good for young calves."

Chad's brows flew up. "Well," he replied thoughtfully. "That is something. I wonder if . . ." But they had drawn up before Rushlake House, and he did not finish his thought aloud. Handing the reins of his curricle to his tiger, he descended from the vehicle to assist his guest.

"Will you come in?" asked Charity "Or, perhaps, since it is getting so late, you would care to stay to dinner?"

Chad grinned. "I think perhaps your sister would have something to say to that. Besides," he continued hastily, "I have some rather special plans for the evening. I can't quite

see my way to thanking you for a lovely afternoon, but I will
say that you've given me food for thought."

Having seen Charity to her door, he bowed and doffed his
hat with a flourish before moving on to his own house.

Chapter 9

INSIDE her home Charity relegated her bonnet and pelisse into the care of her maid, and had just begun to ascend the stairs to her room when Liza emerged from her study in the back of the house to join her.

"I had no idea it was so late," remarked Liza, referring to the small watch pinned to her gown. "It's time to dress for dinner already." She wound an arm about Charity's waist as they climbed the stairs. "Did you enjoy your outing with Chad? What was it—the Egyptian Hall?"

Charity flushed. "Yes, it was very pleasant." She halted, debating whether or not to confess her perfidy to her older sister, but was spared the necessity when Liza interposed. "Do remember, you will be dining alone tonight. Mama and I are off to Carlton House, you know."

"Ooh, I wish I could go with you! I've never seen the inside of the Regent's residence."

"For which you should thank God, fasting," replied her sister acidly. "It is sure to be an impossible squeeze, with at least four ladies swooning because of the excessive heat and two or three others following suit simply because they find the exalted company overwhelming."

Later that evening, as she strolled with Lady Burnsall through one of the glittering corridors of Carlton House, Liza realized the truth of her words. The gathering tonight was not one of the Regent's more democratic crushes, where men of birth and power brushed shoulders with others of lowlier status, invited because their royal host had found them charming, or witty, or in a position to do him a favor. This evening's festivities were a signal that the Season was officially open. It was meant to be the first of the many grand entertainments of the year. As such, the prince's soiree would be attended only by the most flawless jewels of the Polite World.

Liza smiled inwardly. Her position in the *ton* was lofty enough to have secured her an invitation on her own merit, but she felt that her presence this evening was probably due to the fact that her father had for years been one of the prince's favored cronies.

She glanced appreciatively at her surroundings. They had just entered the Crimson Drawing Room, with its welter of red velvet carpets adorned with the insignia of the Garter. The chamber was cluttered with priceless objets d'art glittering in the light of hundreds of candles that were, in turn, reflected in the crystal lustres of three huge chandeliers. She felt as though she had been caught inside an overstuffed jewel box.

"And wait till you see the new addition he's built onto the conservatory," said a voice at her elbow. She turned to find Giles smiling down at her.

She greeted him amiably, and turned to present him to her mother, who was deep in conversation with her attentive swain, General Sir George Wharburton. "With whom did you come?" asked Liza.

"My brother-in-law, Farnsworth," he replied with a grin. "Ordinarily, I wouldn't subject myself to one of Prinny's crushes—even were I to be invited, but Farnsworth felt he needed reinforcements to face the Regent this evening, since he advised him badly at the Kettering mill. Poor Prinny lost an appalling amount, I hear."

"And is your sister here as well?"

"Sukie? No, she's expecting to be confined at any moment with their fourth child, you know. You're looking exceptionally lovely tonight, Liza. You quite take the shine out of every other woman here—even the painted beauties on the ceiling, if you don't mind my saying so."

"Of course, I don't mind," she bubbled, glancing upward. "Even though I scarcely feel equipped to compete with Venus and her court."

In point of fact she had dressed with special care tonight in honor of the occasion, and knew that in her undergown of azure *gros de Naples* silk, over which floated a tunic of silver net, she was looking her best.

"I declare," chimed in Lady Burnsall, who had drawn herself and the general into the conversation, "every hearth in the place is blazing." She fanned herself vigorously. "George, if you don't escort me to one of the gardens immediately, I believe I shall perish."

"Ah," responded her escort with a roguish tap on her gloved fingers, "I was rather hoping you'd come all over faint, my dear, so that I might be obliged to carry you out in my arms."

"Not in front of the children, George," her ladyship returned with a laugh. Liza watched, smiling, as the two made their way through the throng and out of sight.

"Have they made a match of it, then?" asked Giles.

"They are very fond of each other," Liza responded. "Whether it will culminate in marriage, of course, is another matter."

"Do you not mind? I mean, your father passed away only two years ago. I would have thought . . ."

"Oh no. I am very happy for her. For both of them. Mama and Papa were supremely happy together, and, though I'm sure she does not feel for Sir George the once-in-a-lifetime love she shared with Papa, she holds Sir George in a great deal of affection. I am pleased that she finds comfort and enjoyment in his companionship."

"Ah," replied Giles musingly. "You feel then—Good God!"

Liza glanced up at him, startled, and followed his gaze to the end of the corridor to where a tall gentleman stood conversing, candle-glow glinting in coppery reflections from his hair.

"Chad!" She barely whispered the word, but his head lifted, and he turned to gaze directly into her eyes. Instantly the talk around her seemed to hush, and she knew the achingly familiar sensation of being alone with him in a crowded room. She felt in his gaze an intense awareness of her presence, but after an instant, he turned away again to the group with whom he was speaking.

"What do you suppose he's doing here?"

Liza swung back to Giles, but it was a moment before she absorbed his words. "Doing here?" she asked blankly.

"Or more correctly, how did he obtain an invitation?" Giles craned to see past the other guests.

"Really, Giles. You speak as though he were a social outcast."

"Well, no, but one would hardly think he'd be welcomed with open arms at Prinny's hearth, so to speak. That is," he amended hastily, "I had not wanted to tell you, Liza, but the rumors about him are becoming quite virulent. I trust Chad will not find himself on the wrong end of some rather scathing snubs tonight."

Liza's stomach churned, and she said in some irritation, "I'm sure Chad can take care of himself."

"Oh, but—" Giles halted abruptly and seemed to come to himself. "Of course. I had not meant to suggest that the whole of London has turned against him. I just hope . . ." he added, then trailed off in frowning uncertainty. "I just hope his friends won't show him their backs as they did before."

Liza made no response, but turned to greet another acquaintance who had come up behind them. When she looked again, Chad was no longer in sight.

A few moments later the prince himself hove into view, creating an expectant flurry. Like a corpulent bubble floating on a tide of silks and jewels, he bobbed among his subjects, pausing to exchange a pleasantry here, to kiss a hand there. Finally he came to rest before Liza, and his appreciative gaze swept from the jewels sparkling in her curls to the embroidered sweep of her flounced hemline.

"Lady Elizabeth!" he exclaimed, brushing her fingertips with pouting lips. A creaking sound accompanied this effort, and Liza could barely stop herself from wrinkling her nose at the heavy scent of cologne that wafted from his person.

"You are looking charming, as ever." The prurient gleam in the royal gaze was only too apparent, and Liza flushed as she bobbed a small curtsy.

"It has been too long since you graced our presence, Lady Liza. We have not seen you since—by gad, I believe it has not been since the victory celebrations last summer."

"Your memory serves you correctly, Your Highness," Liza responded smoothly. "I was honored with an invitation to the fête you held here last July."

"Ah," he cried eagerly. "Did you enjoy that? I thought it rather splendid."

"Indeed, sire, it was—magnificent." Liza recalled the impossible crush of hundreds of guests squeezed into a hall especially constructed for the occasion by John Nash. "The muslin tent was an inspiration, so light and airy, and—festive." She omitted to mention that the masses of flowers banked to conceal the orchestra playing in the center of the room had nearly overpowered everyone with their scent.

"Well," chuckled the Regent, "we had a great deal to celebrate. The Battle of Toulouse, you know, was one of our finest moments." His pomaded curls quivered as he lifted his eyes to the ceiling where the goddess of love disported with her handmaidens. "We were aware as we led our troops up the awesome slopes of Mont Rave that this would be the decisive battle of the Peninsular War. Ah, so many gallant lads lost their lives there." His eyes glazed in reverent memory, and Liza stiffened. Had she heard him aright? He spoke as though it were he himself who had led the charge, when all the world knew he had never set foot in Spain—at least for military purposes.

Returning to the present with an effort, the Regent shook himself, sending a seismic ripple over the sequins that adorned his coat and the avalanche of glittering orders that fell across his breast. He bowed once more over Liza's hand. "We are pleased that you have deigned to grace our little affair this evening." With a playful squeeze he bestowed a lingering kiss on her fingers. When he straightened, he nodded briefly to Giles, upon whom he had stared unrecognizingly a few moments earlier, and resumed his course through the crowded room.

Liza and Giles exchanged amused glances.

"Whew!" Giles shook his head in disbelief. "It appears that Prinny will be joining his papa in the royal loony bin. Leading a charge up Mont Rave, indeed."

"Hush, you wretch," replied Liza, smothering a laugh, "before you're brought up on a charge of treason."

Other friends approached then, and Liza drew away from Giles, swept away on the current formed in the Regent's wake.

It was not until some hours later, as the assembled multitude was preparing to go into dinner, that Liza saw Chad again. She had given Giles permission to take her in, so she was once more in his company as the crowd moved through the Oval Salon with its oriental statuary and terra cotta figurines. This time she heard his voice before he actually came into view, and was startled to hear a feminine voice trill in response to his pleasantry. She observed with an unexpected pang that he was with Caroline Poole. Was he her escort? she wondered. Perhaps it was through her that he had obtained an invitation tonight, for it was well known that her father was one of Prinny's intimates.

Liza backed determinedly away from the sound of his deep baritone, but Giles, with equal determination, moved her forward.

"Lockridge," he cried in pleased accents.

Chad whirled, and, greeting Giles, he bent over Liza's gloved hand. Caroline expressed her delight at encountering them.

"Though I wish they would announce dinner soon, for I am positively famished, to say nothing of melting in this dreadful heat, as I'm sure everyone else is. How charming you look tonight, Lady Liza." Her eyes flew to the sapphires lying against Liza's throat, and behind her china-blue gaze, Liza could almost hear the calculation of their worth clicking into place. Smiling, she murmured a compliment in return, for Caroline, she had to admit, was undeniably luscious in a robe of mulberry satin adorned with silk rosebuds.

"I'm surprised," said Giles after a moment, "that you two are speaking to each other." His glance flicked between Chad and Liza, each of whom bent a questioning glance on him. "I should think you would be at daggers drawn after making a wager fraught with such possibilities for enmity."

Chad swiveled to Liza, his expression closed, and Liza turned on Giles. "What are you talking about?" she asked in a tone of forced amusement.

Giles wagged a playful finger at her. "Now, now, my child. I have my sources. I am not aware precisely what the stakes are, but I've heard they are quite astonishing."

Liza shot a glance at Chad, whose bored smile failed to reach his eyes. "I'm surprised her ladyship did not divulge that information to you," he said disdainfully. Before Liza could open her mouth to dispute Chad's assumption that it was she who had told Giles about the wager, he continued. "She has a certain property in her possession, the Queen's Pendant—perhaps you've heard of it."

Giles's pale eyes widened, and he whirled to face Liza. "You did not tell me you had the pendant!" Liza's brows lifted at the vehemence in his voice, but the next moment he smiled. "Forgive me. Of course you have no reason to confide your dealings to me. It's just that . . . we spoke of it the other night and you said nothing."

"No, I did not," said Liza sharply. "As you say, my dealings are my own, and I do not choose to have them aired for all the world to see." She glared at Chad, who, to her further fury, smiled disbelievingly.

"But this is so terribly exciting!" exclaimed Caroline prettily. "What pendant? And what did you stake against it, Chad?"

Indulgently Chad explained the terms of the bet, while Liza listened in growing anger. She had considered the wager a private matter between her and Chad, and she experienced a wave of distress at his careless revelation of their bargain.

"So, you are the mysterious owner of Brightsprings," said Giles, his eyes glittering oddly. "And here poor Liza has been mourning its loss for years. Trying for a spot of revenge, old man?"

Before Chad could reply, he was bumped from behind by a sturdy matron, who turned to apologize. Upon beholding Chad, however, her face stiffened in surprise and, bowing slightly, she turned away again without speaking.

"Why, that was Lady Moorhaven," cried Caroline. "Whatever is the matter with her? You'd think you had never met each other, but we attended her soiree together not a fortnight ago."

"Yes," murmured Chad. "I seem to be causing a general plague of forgetfulness in this town lately."

Giles exchanged a meaningful glance with Liza before saying awkwardly to Chad, "I say, old fellow, I'm most dreadfully sorry—that is, I'd heard—but I didn't realize . . ." He broke off, expelling a sigh. "Look here, is there anything I can do? If you'd like to leave before you have to face any more unpleasantness, I'll be happy to . . ."

"Leave?" Caroline fairly squealed. "What are you talking about?" She swung to Chad. "What is he talking about? What was the matter with Lady Moorhaven? What unpleasantness?"

"Good Lord, my wretched tongue," said Giles before Chad could reply. "I assumed you had heard the rumors. I should not have said anything."

Caroline stepped away from Chad, and when she spoke, her blue eyes were cold. "What rumors? Is there something I should know, Chad?"

Liza's clear voice cut into the conversation. "Good Heavens, Miss Poole, there are always rumors," she said coolly. "I can't imagine anyone's putting any credence in any of them. Why, did you hear the latest? It concerns the Duke of Albemarle and the Countess of Worthing, if you can imagine anything so ludicrous. They are both over eighty, I believe."

Liza was astonished at the perfect calm she was able to portray, for within seconds she had gone from wishing to strike Chad Lockridge with a blunt instrument to experiencing a burning desire to scratch out the eyes of first Lady Moorhaven and then the wretched Miss Poole for causing him pain. At the moment she felt she might simply explode.

"You are very right, Lady Liza." There was a smile in his voice as he spoke, but it vanished when he turned to Giles. "I thank you for your concern, old fellow, but I'm bearing up. Rumor, like luck, is a fickle mistress. I should keep that in mind if I were you," he concluded softly.

"I wish somebody would tell me what this is all about," said Caroline in a complaining voice. "Oh good," she continued before anyone could answer her. "Here comes His Highness. Perhaps we're going in to dinner at last."

As the prince made his way into the room, the crowd parted before him, so that by the time he neared the small group, there was a clear path between them. The Regent beamed at Liza, then his gaze fell on Chad, and his eyes widened in recognition.

"Lockridge!" he called and started to move forward.

Liza's stomach clenched. How was it that Chad was known to the prince? Had rumors of Chad's disgrace reached the Regent? Was he approaching for the purpose of ordering Chad to leave the gathering?

"Lockridge, old fellow!" The prince turned the full power of his admittedly charming smile on Chad. "Been looking for you all evening."

Out of the corner of her eye, Liza observed Giles's jaw drop.

Chad made a leg and murmured a respectful greeting.

"I understand you're expecting visitors," remarked the prince.

"Yes, sire. I believe you know Sir Wilfred Bascombe. He hired me when I first arrived in Calcutta, and we've remained friends ever since. He and Lady Bascombe will be here next week for an extended visit."

"Well, the three of you must join me for a little gathering

I'm planning for later this month. Nothing elaborate, you understand—just a few old friends." He clamped a well-padded arm across Chad's shoulder. "Come along, then, Lockridge. I told them to seat you near me at dinner, for there is a matter I have been wishing to discuss with you." He bowed genially to Liza and Caroline as he drew Chad away into the milling throng. "I know you have friends at the Bourse," he continued, his voice growing fainter with distance, "and I've been hearing some interesting rumors . . ."

When they could no longer hear him, the others turned to each other, speechless, and Liza was surprised to note an expression of distinct displeasure writ large on Giles's face.

Chapter 10

"Do you mean to tell me," gasped Charity, her brown eyes alight, "that Chad—*our* Chad—is on terms with the Prince Regent?"

"Apparently," replied Liza with a laugh. "From dinnertime on, the prince would scarcely let him out of his sight. And Lady Moorhaven, who had given him the cut direct earlier in the evening, became affability itself."

Charity gave her rich chuckle. The sisters were seated in Liza's high-perch phaeton, tooling smartly through the Park. Promenade hour was well advanced, thus their progress was impeded by greetings from friends and acquaintances disporting themselves on horseback, on foot, and in every type of fashionable vehicle.

Both the Rushlake ladies, agreed these personages, were in excellent looks this afternoon, and put the fresh beauty of spring to shame with their vibrant loveliness. Charity was dressed in a delicate shade of her favorite pink that brought a matching color to her cheeks, while Liza wore an elegant carriage dress of twilled primrose silk that clung to her lissome curves.

Liza became aware of a sharp intake of breath from the girl beside her, and, following Charity's gaze, saw John Weston approaching in a modest curricle, his sister Priscilla beside him. Liza stiffened as he bowed and raised his hat to Liza, then bent a warm look on Charity.

"Good afternoon, Mr. Weston," breathed Charity. "Miss Weston."

"Good afternoon," responded brother and sister in unison.

Liza nodded, unspeaking, a very faint smile curving her lips. John looked as though he might have pulled up, but Liza, the discouraging smile still in place, trotted past him with a flourish.

"Really, Liza!" Charity swiveled to face her sister. "That was terribly rude."

Liza lifted her brows.

"John wished to stop and converse with us," continued Charity indignantly, "and you just swished right by him. And Priscilla, of course."

"But we scarcely know Mr. Weston," said Liza in a voice of sweet reason. "Surely a smile was sufficient greeting."

"Liza," Charity spoke through gritted teeth. "Why are you so beastly to him?"

The look of surprise Liza bestowed on her sister was quite genuine. "But I am always cordial to him."

"You are cordial to everyone, even encroaching mushrooms who solicit your hand for a dance, but with such persons you bestow a smile of such brilliance and utter disinterest that they slink off feeling lower than a cellar drainpipe. And that's how you treated John just now. And," she continued, a militant sparkle in her eyes, "I won't have it!"

"Charity!" Liza stared at her sister. "Are you telling me that you are seriously interested in John Weston?"

Charity had not meant to tell her any such thing, at least not at present, but at this, her lips clamped into a thin line, and the spark in her eye became more pronounced.

"Yes, I am very interested in John Weston. He is so far superior to any of the fops to whom you've been endeavoring to marry me off for the past year, that I am amazed you cannot perceive his worth and . . . and his strength of character, his intelligence, and . . ."

"Charity!" cried Liza again. She gazed at the girl in consternation, observing her flushed cheeks and trembling curls, and the agitated rise and fall of her breast. "I had no idea! My dear, this won't do. You have birth and breeding and beauty and a more than respectable fortune. You cannot be thinking of throwing it all away on—"

"If you say one more word," stormed Charity, "I shall get down and walk home!"

Glancing about her, Liza observed that they were gathering curious glances from passersby. She took a deep breath and faced Charity again.

"My dear, I have no wish to get into a brangle with you in the middle of Hyde Park. Nor is it my desire to denigrate someone for whom you seem to have developed a tendre. In any case, the subject will be better pursued when we get home."

So saying, she lifted a gloved hand in greeting to a passing acquaintance. Charity flung herself against the squabs of the phaeton and glowered for several minutes before she, too, became aware of the spectacle she was presenting. Her innate good sense came to her rescue, and, possibly realizing that a fit of the sulks would serve no purpose, she straightened.

"Look, Liza," she said mildly, "isn't that Lord Miniver waving to you? And isn't that Cassie Frederick with him?"

Liza smiled in appreciation of Charity's *volte face*. "Yes, it appears Cassie's mama is seeing success in her efforts to snabble his lordship for her daughter. He looks quite smitten."

"And look, there's Chad," said Charity. "My word, who is that stunning creature with him?"

Liza's grip on her reins tightened involuntarily, and the next few moments were spent correcting the confusion caused in her spirited team by this action.

"Her name is Caroline Poole," she said finally. Her father is Sir Henry Poole. You've met her, surely. She was at the Mervale's ball. In fact," she added somewhat acridly, "she seems to turn up at an astounding number of functions."

"Oh yes, I remember her now. My, she seems to have Chad completely entranced."

"Oh?" Liza managed to keep her tone casual, but her fingers again clutched her reins. Resolutely she turned her gaze elsewhere, and in doing so found herself staring up into the pale eyes of Giles Daventry, who, astride a mettlesome black, had pulled abreast of them.

"Hello," he said breezily. "It seems as though all the world has come out to take the air this afternoon."

Liza returned his greeting with cordiality, but in truth, she felt oddly uncomfortable with her old friend. It had seemed to her that last night Giles actually relished the idea of Chad's fall from favor in the Polite World and had been more than a little chagrined at his effusive welcome by the Prince Regent.

Surely, she thought, Giles could not be so mean-spirited as to wish ill to Chad. He surely could not view Chad as a rival for her affections.

Her thoughts must have been visible behind her eyes, for Giles laughed uncomfortably. "Am I in your black books this morning, lovely Lady Liza?"

Startled, Liza shot a glance at Charity, who had turned away, oblivious, chattering to one of her friends.

She said coolly, "What makes you think that? Just because you chose to air my affairs to the world?" Her eyes narrowed. "Precisely how did you become aware of the wager between Chad and me?"

Giles laughed boyishly. "How does anyone come across anything in this town? I expect some diligent scandal-monger whispered it in my ear." His hazel eyes bored into hers. "I do apologize, however, for bringing it up at a moment when you obviously did not wish it discussed. It was most maladroit of me."

"Yes, it was," replied Liza, but her smile removed much of the sting that might otherwise have accompanied her words. "I'd appreciate it in the future if you'd leave me out of your gossipy gleanings."

"I shall do so, my dear."

And I am not your dear, Giles. The words popped into her mind, and she was surprised at the anger that had propelled them there. Contrite, she bent an even warmer smile on him and laid her hand on his sleeve.

"The wager, after all, is merely a business deal."

"Of course. And look," he said, as his gaze shifted to a point just behind her. "Speak of the devil." He nodded and tipped his hat as Chad swept up in his curricle, the triumphant Miss Poole clinging to his arm.

To Liza's combined relief and displeasure, Chad did not stop, but merely tipped his hat and murmured a greeting as they continued on their course.

"Well, well," murmured Giles, watching their retreating vehicle, "it would seem that Miss Poole is the current front runner in the great Lockridge leg-shackle stakes."

Charity had by now concluded her conversation with her friend and turned back to catch these words. Her mouth rounded in surprise. "Chad?" she squeaked. "Getting married? To that silly widgeon?"

"Oh, are you acquainted with Miss Poole?" asked Giles.

"No, of course not," snapped Charity. "That is, we have met, but I do not know her well. What I meant was—well, just look at the way she's hanging onto Chad, for all the world as though he were a prize pig she just captured at the Bartholomew Fair."

"The analogy may not be too far off," drawled Giles, his eyes twinkling in amusement.

"Really, Giles," Liza responded in annoyance. She kept her emotions tightly in check as she spoke, for the sight of Chad bent over Caroline Poole, his eyes laughing into hers, had sent a shock of such pain through her that she nearly cried aloud. It was over, then. Really over. Nothing at all remained of the love he had proclaimed for her six years ago. Her brain had told her this many years before, but somehow her heart had clung to a foolish belief that, fragile and tattered as it was, a bond lay between them.

How wrong she had been.

Giles cast a sharp glance at her, but his smile was bland. "Don't forget you are promised to me for the opera tonight, my dear. I have booked seats for your mother and Lady Charity as well, of course. Catalani is singing the role of Clara in *The Duenna*, and all the world will be there. Perhaps afterwards we might go to Grillon's for a light supper."

Liza's immediate reaction was to concoct a polite refusal, but before she could open her mouth to issue her regrets, a second, stronger reaction spread through her. "All the world" would undoubtedly include Chad and, very possibly, Caroline Poole. Her absence would inevitably lead Chad to conclude she had chosen to sit home and mope. Was she going to give him that satisfaction?

She bestowed a brilliant smile on Giles. "I shall look forward to it." With a regal nod she slapped her reins smartly against the backs of her matched team, and the phaeton moved off.

Charity remained silent for several moments after they resumed the progression. "Do you think," she said at last, "that Chad is really serious about Miss Poole?"

"I neither know nor care," replied Liza briskly as she guided her vehicle through the Stanhope gate and onto Park Lane.

Charity eyed her speculatively, then cast her eyes to where her fingers lay twined in her lap. "I expect that everyone will be buzzing at the opera tonight about them."

"I suppose they will." Liza's tone was off-hand. "It certainly matters not a whit to me what or who the gossip-mongers will choose as a topic."

Meeting Charity's gaze, she abruptly turned her attention to her driving.

*   *   *

As it happened, the conversation that hummed through the theater that night concerned an entirely different subject, for London had been stunned that afternoon by the news that Bonaparte had escaped his island prison and was said to have sailed directly for France.

"I heard," said Cassie Stipplethwaite to Charity with a delicious shudder, "that the Corsican monster is gathering an army of thousands as he marches toward Paris."

Miss Stipplethwaite had stopped in Giles's box during the first interval in order to enjoy a few minutes' gossip with Charity. Her mother was chatting quietly in a corner with Lady Burnsall, and Giles had gone to procure refreshments. This left Liza with little to do beyond contribute an occasional smile of agreement and look over the throng of theatergoers.

Despite herself her gaze kept drifting to a certain box almost directly opposite hers. There, as expected, sat Chad, beaming in enjoyment at Miss Poole, whose somewhat less than musical trill floated about the theater like the echoes of one of the theater's more unfortunate vocal performances. Catching Liza's eye, he nodded briefly, then returned to his fatuous scrutiny of Miss Poole's charms, which were, considered Liza, indecently exposed in an insipid gown of pale mauve. Really, it fairly turned the girl's complexion to mud.

She turned determinedly away. "I hardly think Napoleon will have reached Paris yet, Miss Stipplethwaite," she said, picking up the thread of the conversation taking place behind her. "I believe he will have to overcome considerable opposition before he can consider himself once more emperor of all he surveys."

"But, it is so frightening, don't you think?" exclaimed the young girl, her eyes round as pennies. "Why, who knows? If the monster has his way, we shall all be murdered in our beds!"

"I think not," Liza replied with a laugh. "I'll grant you, the situation is serious, but it is early days to look for an invasion."

Giles returned at this point with lemonade and ratafia. Casting one last surreptitious glance at the charming scene across the theater, Liza allowed her lips to curve in an intimate smile as she took a glass of wine from Giles's hand. When he slid a hand across her shoulder, she leaned into the caress, murmur-

ing her thanks over her shoulder in a manner that would indicate to anyone who happened to be watching that Lady Liza
Rushlake was completely enthralled in the company of her escort.

Thus the evening limped along in fits and starts, and when
she finally arrived home, she bade Giles a brief good night and
climbed the stairs to her chamber, completely exhausted. Dismissing her maid, she stood for a moment at a long window
overlooking the small but exquisite rear garden of her town
house. March was preparing to give way to April, and the
night was unusually warm and heavy with the promise of a
burgeoning spring. The moon shone palely on early blossoms
casting their scent into the air, and Liza, on an impulse, moved
silently from the room.

She hastened downstairs and slid through the French doors
opening into the garden from her study. Meditatively she trod
the graveled paths for a few moments before settling herself
on a stone bench beneath an ornamental cherry tree. She
leaned back and, inhaling deeply, gave herself up to the peace
and beauty surrounding her. It took only a few moments, however, for her to come to the unfortunate conclusion that the
magic of the night seemed to be having little effect on her per-
sistent melancholy. She stretched her fingers out to the surrounding fragrance as though it were a physical presence she
might draw to her for comfort, and she was swept by an aching
sadness, a yearning for she knew not what. She almost wished
she could cry the tears that seemed to have permanently settled
in a thickening tightness at the back of her throat.

How absurd she was being. She had allowed herself to be
swept into a maidenly flutter over a man she didn't care tuppence about—a man, moreover, who felt nothing for her beyond a slight condescension. And now, Lady Elizabeth
Rushlake, darling of the *ton* and one of the most marriageable
females in all of England, was sitting in her own garden in the
middle of the night, moping like a disheartened gnome. What
a perfectly ludicrous situation.

"Don't you know about the dangers of the night air?"

At the sound of the voice floating to her from some distance
away, Liza started, bumping her head on a low hanging branch
of the cherry tree.

She whirled and looked up to see a shadowed figure standing at a window on the second floor of the house next door.

"Chad!"

"Is there a gate between our gardens?"

"No," Liza began. Then, to her consternation, she heard herself continue. "That is, yes, but it's rather overgrown."

Good God, what possessed her to say that? Perhaps the tales of madness in the full moon were true. When she looked again, the figure had vanished. In a few moments a rustling noise brought her to the wall between the gardens, and in another instant Chad appeared in a vine-trimmed aperture.

"This is . . . this is most improper." *Lord, what a stupid, missish thing to say.*

"You used not to be so concerned with propriety."

She could hear the laughter in his voice, and could only be relieved that the darkness hid the blush she knew must be staining her cheeks. She was intensely aware of his nearness, and stepped back so suddenly she nearly lost her balance. She sank back upon the bench she had left at his approach.

Chad joined her there. Liza was sure he must be able to hear the thundering of her heart and searched frantically in her mind for a suitably neutral topic of conversation.

"Did you hear the news—about Bonaparte?" She spoke through dry lips.

"Yes. I wonder whose heads will roll for the blunder?"

"I don't know. I haven't even heard how he escaped."

"As I understand it he simply gathered up a group of his supporters and sailed away. One gathers the security arrangements surrounding the deposed emperor left much to be desired."

"I expect Wellington will be called upon again to deal with him."

"I expect he will, and did you know that in the moonlight your hair takes on a glint of polished silver?"

Liza jumped. "We were discussing Napoleon."

"Yes, and I think we've about exhausted the subject. I would much rather talk about us." He had edged closer to her so that now she could feel the warmth of his breath on her cheek. She moved toward the end of the bench.

"That subject will be exhausted even more quickly, for there is no 'us' anymore."

"I'm sure Giles Daventry would applaud that statement."

"Giles?" she replied frigidly. "What has he to do with anything."

"Nothing, except that the odds are shortening at White's on whether you're going to accept his suit."

Liza stiffened in outrage. "And just how much have you put on that prospect?" She gave a short laugh. "Is this how you propose to win our wager?"

"No," he replied calmly, "I'd win precious little on that flutter. As I said, the odds are becoming negligible. After your performance tonight, they will be all but nonexistent."

"My performance?" She stood abruptly, her anger almost palpable.

Chad also rose to his feet. "You were leering at him like a lightskirt, and you allowed him to fondle you as though you were a collector's item he is preparing to buy for his curio cabinet."

Liza unthinkingly lifted her arm to strike him, but he grasped her wrist. She stared at him, panting in her fury.

"What about you and Caroline Poole?" she spat. "You were practically disrobing her in front of all the world. Not that you had very far to go, for her gown was a disgrace. Tell me, Mr. Lockridge, what are they saying at White's about a union between you and the luscious Miss Poole?"

For a moment Chad was still, and in the darkness Liza could feel his gaze boring into hers. She attempted to pull back, but she was still held in his grasp. Suddenly he sighed.

"Liza, I'm sorry. I did not come out here to brangle with you."

"Then what did you come out here for?"

The instant the words slipped out, she could have bitten her tongue. Chad said nothing, and in the electric stillness that hung between them, Liza caught her breath. In the next moment Chad released her only to coil one arm around her waist and to bury the other hand in the disordered curls on the nape of her neck. She gave an inarticulate cry of protest as he pulled her to him. She was silent then, and an involuntary response shuddered through her as his mouth came down on hers, urgent and demanding.

Without volition her arms rose to twine about him, and she pressed the length of her body against him. His lips left hers for an instant to press feathery kisses against her eyes, cheeks, and temples until she was robbed of breath and will. When his mouth came down again, she welcomed it in an open response.

Drawing Liza down beside him on the bench, he drew her against him and spoke against her hair.

"Oh, God." The sound was almost a groan. "Oh, Liza, you thorn in my flesh."

At this Liza experienced an abrupt return to sanity. She wrenched herself from Chad's arms, feeling as though she had just been slapped. She rose from the bench, and with an incoherent cry, she fled into the house, leaving Chad to stare after her.

Chapter 11

"AND on Thursday," said Jem January, "Mr. Daventry spent most of the afternoon at Limmers', in the company of one Charles Summersby."

"Summersby?" replied Chad. "I'm not familiar with the name."

The two were in Chad's study on the ground floor of the rented town house. Chad gazed in amusement at his valet, who sat sprawled with casual elegance in a chair opposite Chad's desk. If it were not for the fact that he was garbed in the sober ensemble of a gentleman's gentleman, one would have thought him a guest dropped in for a chat and a glass of wine. His speech had miraculously improved over the gutter dialect in evidence when he first took up residence in Berkeley Square. He credited the transformation to a natural talent for mimicry.

"Summersby," said Jem, referring to a tattered notebook he held in his hands, "is a vicious little snerp who clings like a limpet to the edge of the Polite World. He rigs himself out like the veriest tulip, and somehow manages to maintain reasonably respectable lodgings in Jermyn Street, but he is a thoroughly bad man. Or at least he would be if he weren't such a coward. He specializes in fleecing well-breeched young sprigs from the country, but word has it he'll do anything for a price, as long as it doesn't involve violence. He's an inveterate tattlemonger, which apparently makes him attractive to some of Society's less discriminating hostesses."

"A tattlemonger, you say," commented Chad thoughtfully. He leaned both elbows on the desk and steepled his fingers. "Mm. Anything else?"

"Daventry appears to number several of Mr. Summersby's ilk among his acquaintances, and it is believed he has recently been setting them to various unsavory tasks in return for such favors as a roll of flimsies, or an introduction to a pigeon ripe for plucking. Lately—" Jem paused, frowning. "He's been receiving some most peculiar visitors at odd hours of the night."

"Peculiar? How so?"

"Some are servants who work in houses all over town. Others work in minor positions in the City—mainly in financial institutions. I have their names here," he indicated the notebook.

Chad sat back in his chair. "Most curious." He nodded in agreement. His green gaze narrowed as it swept over Jem. "Your information seems extremely thorough. I wonder how you came by it."

Jem's returning glance was shuttered. "I have my sources, sir."

"Quite a network of them, it would seem. How did you manage to put this web together so quickly? Or perhaps it has been in place for some time?"

He was rewarded with a blank stare of such unsullied innocence that Chad almost laughed aloud.

"It occurs to me," he continued, "that your familiarity with Giles Daventry and his style of life borders on the encyclopedic. I do not believe the wealth of information you have provided me could have been culled just within the past few days."

Jem rose unhurriedly and slipped the little book into his waistcoat pocket. He glanced at the ormolu clock on the mantlepiece and said, "Look at the time, sir. You must be up and dressing for the Woodcross musicale."

With that, he turned and opened the door, waiting with brows lifted in a supercilious manner that could have graced any butler in Mayfair. Chad hesitated, then, deciding not to press the issue, strode through the door, nodding peremptorily as he did so.

When he reached his chambers, he rang for hot water and strolled aimlessly to the window overlooking his back garden and that of the Rushlakes. His thoughts, as they had done so often recently, flew to the moment, some evenings ago, when he had looked down to see Liza, sitting in the moonlight, pale and still as a carved statue.

What a fool he had been, galloping down for an interlude of moonlit dalliance. What had he hoped to accomplish? He must have known how he would react to her nearness. The scent-drenched beauty of the garden had assaulted his senses, and her nearness had completed the conquest. The memory of the feel of her against him, the softness of her mouth under his, even now created an ache in him.

And she had responded, hadn't she? For just an instant, she had melted against him, all warm, womanly softness before she had drawn back. In the silver luminescence that surrounded them, the angry blaze had been plain in her magnificent eyes.

He shrugged, what else could he have expected? He had already been aware that her anger and contempt had not diminished in the time since she had turned away from him. And it was just as well. He had no intention of falling victim to her loveliness again.

In the house next door, Liza had already begun her preparations for the evening's festivities at the home of Lord and Lady Woodcross. Gazing gloomily at the gown of sea-green crape laid out for her, she listened to the sounds of preparation in the rest of the household. Tonight, Lord and Lady Woodcross were to give their annual musicale. Lady W always entertained in bursts of grandeur, sparing no effort to out-decorate, out-feed and out-entertain every other hostess in Mayfair. The cream of the Polite World would be in attendance. Thus, much time and energy had gone into what the ladies of Rushlake House would wear. After endless discussions and many trips to merciers, linen-drapers, and modistes, the critical decisions had been made.

Liza's preparations had been minimal, for she had seemingly lost her zest for the social occasions that regularly burst over London's West End like small explosions of fireworks at a children's party. Her maid, Prescott, however, would have none of her indifference. "If you think, my lady," she had said with a sniff, "that I will allow you to set foot out of this house with your skirts in a twist and your hair looking like you'd just come through a bush backward, you're very much mistaken. I have my reputation to uphold, after all."

Liza sighed in resignation and, tossing her long silk gloves on the bed, sat down at her dressing table to submit to Prescott's ministrations. She stared balefully at her reflection.

The past fortnight had passed in a dismal blur. When she had reached her room again after those shattering moments in the garden with Chad, she had flung herself across her bed and had spent the next hour staring, dry-eyed, at the ceiling. What a beast he was! She had opened herself to him, letting down all her defenses, and instead of murmuring words of tenderness into her ear, he had complained of her influence over him.

Grief had turned to anger as she contemplated his words. What the devil did he mean, "a thorn in his flesh"? It sounded like some sort of unpleasant affliction. There was evidently something about her that aroused passion in him—she might be pleased at that if it were not for the fact that it was surely an emotion that could be called forth by any clever Cyprian. And when it came to her, it was certainly not an emotion he welcomed.

She allowed Prescott to assist her into the sea-green crape and sat passively while that young woman occupied herself communing with her mistress's hair, combing and curling it into a fantasy of tumbled ringlets, swept into a Clytie knot atop her head. A few tendrils escaped to frame her cheeks in a golden tracery. Clasping a necklace of emeralds and diamonds about her throat, Liza rose from her dressing table.

Downstairs, she found her mother and her sister awaiting her. Lady Burnsall fairly glowed in a silver-shot silk gown of midnight blue that clung to her still youthful curves from just under her bosom to a sweep of vandyked hemline embroidered in silver acorns.

Charity was a floating bonbon in a peach sarsenet underdress over which lay a tunic of cream-colored gauze sprinkled with brilliants. In the silky wavelets of her brown hair, lay a wreath of roses.

Lady Burnsall fanned herself briskly. "Gracious, it seems that summer is upon us already. I've never seen it so warm in April! Come along, girls," she continued, shepherding her daughters toward the front door. "We're already on the borderline between fashionably late and downright rude."

"Well," said Charity, gathering up her fan and gloves, "I guess we can be thankful for Lady W's addiction to fresh air. You can be sure she will have every window and door in the house open on an evening such as this."

Such proved to be the case, as the Rushlake party discovered as soon as they entered the Woodcross ballroom.

"Ugh!" exclaimed Charity, fishing a moth from her decollatege. She raised her eyes to the chandelier, from which drifted a veritable rain of singed creatures of the night. "Well," she continued philosophically, "at least it's too early for mayflies. I can't bear them—nasty big buzzing creatures."

The ladies turned to greet their host and hostess and then drifted away along separate paths. Instinctively, Liza glanced about the room, but Chad was not in evidence. She turned as Giles Daventry materialized in front of her.

"I thought you must have removed to the country," he said pleasantly. "I have not seen you for this age."

She returned his smile. "I have not been out and about much—nothing beyond the obligatory calls and a few dinners with friends."

"And, of course, your interests in the City."

She nodded with another smile but refrained from commenting on the nature of those interests.

"Well," continued Giles playfully, "it is simply not to be tolerated that you remove the sun of your presence from our lives. I must consider it my civic duty to see that you come out of your self-imposed exile so that we may all bask once more in the radiance of your smile."

"Coming it too strong, Giles," she said in a dry tone. "Let us move along with the crowd into that salon down the corridor. I believe we're to be treated to a poetry reading."

Stricken, Giles placed his hand on his heart. "For you, my angel, anything, but do you really intend to subject me to an hour's unremitting boredom? Did you know the poet in question is Roddy Pemberton?"

"No!" she gurgled in reply. "Who but Lady Woodcross would have the nerve to inflict her nephew's execrable verse on an unsuspecting public? However, my friend, duty calls. Come along—onward and upward."

She strode toward the small salon that was their goal and with a sigh, Giles followed.

The poetic interlude proved to be as painful as Giles had predicted, and it was with dazed relief that the audience returned over an hour later to the great ballroom where they found an increased crowd of guests milling in aimless conversation.

Once again, Liza surveyed the throng, and this time she spotted Chad immediately. As before, his head lifted as though she had called his name, and his gaze searched quickly until he found her. Her breath quickened as she felt herself pierced by an emerald shaft. He started to move toward her; then, as his glance shifted to Giles, he merely nodded and turned away.

She felt suddenly desolate and moved a little apart from Giles. Looking up, she saw John Weston in her path gazing ahead of him with such naked tenderness in his eyes that Liza felt her own go moist. She turned her head, knowing already who it was that had claimed the young man's attention. Yes, there was Charity in the center of a giggling group of her contemporaries. As though John had reached out a hand to touch her, she turned to meet his glance. A delicate flush spread over her cheeks, and she dropped her eyes. Chad's face rose up again before Liza with a breathtaking clarity, and she moved restlessly about the ballroom. This was, she thought to herself with bitter amusement, turning out to be quite an evening for the expression of inchoate desires and unrequited yearnings.

The conversation was still of Napoleon and his daring escape. News of his progress was scanty, but the initial fear that the Corsican would immediately draw to him a vast, invincible army seemed to be fading. Indeed, talk now was of Wellington and the short work he would undoubtedly make of the puny little emperor. Liza found both views as puerile as they were irritating.

Liza accepted the company of a middle-aged baronet for the buffet supper. She smiled at him and charmed him until he declared he had quite lost his heart. She laughed with friends and regaled them with her wit until they vowed they had none of them seen Lady Liza in such spirits. Later, she sank gratefully into a cherry-silk striped settee in yet another salon and prepared to have her ears assaulted by the latest fashion in Italian sopranos. To her dismay, Chad entered the salon a few moments later, accompanied by Caroline Poole, who chose a chair near her own. Liza greeted Caroline distantly and turned her attention to the singer beginning her first aria. For the rest of the concert Liza resolutely kept her gaze on the corpulent coloratura.

After only a few eons, the diva warbled her last note, and Liza rose with some alacrity, bidding a hurried farewell to the lady with whom she had shared the cherry-striped settee. Avoiding Caroline's attempt to draw her attention, she moved toward the room's exit.

"All right, Liza," came a voice from behind her. "You've

done your guestly duty. Now, it's time for a soupçon of real amusement. I challenge you to a game of piquet."

"Oh—Giles," she answered absently. "I wondered where you had got to." Beyond Giles' shoulder, she saw Chad's hand come to Caroline's bare shoulder to guide her through the press of escaping concert attendees. She bestowed a blinding smile on Giles.

"My heart's dearest wish," Liza said, brushing his hand with her gloved fingertips. A sudden smokiness in her amethyst eyes made Giles pause, and his gaze sharpened. He said nothing, but drew her closer to him, going so far as to lift her hair to place a light kiss on the nape of her neck. Blushing, she pulled away and looked up to find Chad's contemptuous gaze on her. Turning abruptly, she followed Giles into Lady Crosswood's drawing room.

"So how goes the wager?" he asked casually as he dealt the cards.

"The—oh, the wager between Chad and me? I think I'm doing quite well. I've increased my portion most satisfactorily."

"And Chad?"

She shrugged her shoulders. "I have no idea. Thomas would not tell me—even if I were to ask—and Chad certainly won't. Not," she grinned mischievously, "that I wouldn't give a great deal to know."

"Mmm." Giles picked up his cards and perused them with apparent interest. "One hears that he is doing fairly well."

"Giles! How could you possibly know anything of Chad's dealings."

"I don't, really. I only repeat what I've heard."

"What do you mean, 'doing fairly well'?"

Giles paused before answering, meditatively selecting a discard. "I understand he has invested heavily in the Consols."

A frown creased her forehead. "That seems odd. Surely he cannot expect to see a large short-term gain from government securities."

"Perhaps that's why he's doing only fairly well. Although," he continued, "it sounds as though he's doing much worse in his other endeavors. Did you hear about his new silk factory?"

Liza shook her head in wordless apprehension.

"Burned to the ground yesterday. And it wasn't even completed yet."

Liza simply gaped at him. "But that's terrible!" she gasped. "That will represent a staggering loss to him."

Why had Chad said nothing of this to her? There was no reason he should have, of course, but her heart sank. She knew he had invested heavily in the factory and its environs. Dear Lord, such a setback could easily ruin him.

Giles watched the play of emotion on Liza's mobile features and mused aloud. "One hears he was gathering investors into some sort of scheme for laying gas lines north of here. I suppose he will now have lost their confidence."

Liza's brows snapped together. "One seems to have heard a great deal lately. Have you been snooping, Giles?"

A flush spread over Giles' cheeks, and Liza caught an odd glitter in his eyes for an instant, before he bowed his head. "I cannot deny a certain interest in his activities, Liza. When his name comes up, I—I find myself paying attention."

Liza fluttered her fan in agitated swoops. "I fail to see why you should take any interest in Chad Lockridge."

Giles smiled, but said nothing, instead returning to the contemplation of his hand of cards. Liza found that her mind was preoccupied now with the news of Chad's appalling financial reverses, destroying her ability to concentrate on the game. She brushed away an insect of indeterminate species that buzzed about her ears.

"Really, one might as well be sitting out of doors. I know the rooms would be unbearably hot with everything closed up, but it does seem as though Lady Woodcross could have reached some sort of compromise. One or two open windows per floor would surely suffice. At any rate"— she rose from the table—"it's time for the piano recital. I understand Lady Woodcross prevailed on young Mr. Gruber to play for us, and I hear he's very good."

Giles accompanied her from the room, and they parted on the edge of the ballroom. As Liza made her way through the crowded hall, she was surprised to see Charity in animated conversation with Chad. The two were just reentering the house from the outside, and from the expression on Chad's face, they had not been indulging in casual pleasantries. His mouth was set grimly as Charity faced him, her eyes huge and pleading.

Now what? thought Liza. She turned to follow the pair with

her gaze, but they were soon lost in the throng still circulating in the great ballroom.

She continued on toward Lady Woodcross's gold salon, and reaching her destination, she sank into a convenient armchair.

The celebrated pianist arrived, played with great skill, and left to unanimous acclaim without Liza having heard a note. She sat motionless, unable to peel her mind away from Chad and his financial difficulties and the memory of his disdainful stare at the intimate kiss she had allowed Giles—and in such a public place. What must he think of her?

It was only after the audience had filed out of the room that Liza's thoughts began to take a different turn. She had done nothing wrong, after all. And what did it matter what Chad thought, anyway? He was nothing to her. His opinion mattered not a whit. Let him think what he wished.

Strengthened by these salutary resolutions, she rose from her chair and strode from the room.

Reaching the ballroom, she encountered her mother, chatting amiably with a group of friends. She beckoned to Liza, who joined them with a smile, and several minutes were whiled away in a comfortable exchange of gossip. A surreptitious glance around the ballroom revealed no sign of Chad, and with a surge of relief, Liza prayed that he had departed the musicale.

She was listening in rather bored amusement to a mildly scandalous tale delivered by one of her mother's elderly friends when she felt a diffident pressure on her back, accompanied by a softly spoken, "Pardon, please."

She turned to observe in some surprise, that John Weston was trying to make his way through the little group to a small corridor that led away to a series of closed rooms.

Recalling her acrimonious discussion with Charity a few days earlier, she greeted the young man with more warmth than he was accustomed to from her, and he blinked.

Liza peered into the darkness of the hall. "Where are you off to, Mr. Weston? If you are looking for the card room, it's over the other way. And I understand charades are being got up in a small salon down the corridor just to the left of the statue of Adonis."

"Uh, no." Wondering, Liza observed the blush that rose to suffuse his square features. "That is—I'm looking for— I mean . . ."

His disjointed explanation was interrupted by an odd, muted sound that rose from behind one of the closed doors lining the dark corridor. It was immediately followed by more of the same, uttered in a high, feminine voice, accompanied by various clattering noises indicating somewhat spirited activity taking place in the room beyond.

John paled visibly, and as the others gathered nearby looked at one another in surprise, he hastened into the corridor. Liza was on his heels; thus, when he flung open the door from which the sounds had emanated, she had a clear view of the cause of the commotion. The chamber, lined with bookshelves, was furnished with comfortable leather chairs and couches. And on one of these couches lay Charity, flung full length. Her clothing was in disarray, and her hair flowed about her shoulders, unbound. Atop her, lay Chad Lockridge.

Chapter 12

THERE was a moment's appalled silence. Chad leaped to his feet, and, staring back at the group still frozen in the doorway, blurted the word, "Bat."

Liza and her mother, after one anguished glance at Charity, gaped at each other, then at John, whose brown eyes blazed darkly against his white face. A confused babble broke out among those behind the three.

"Bat," repeated Chad in a louder voice, as Charity struggled from the couch, ineffectually trying to twist her hair into its previous conformation. He pointed to where draperies fluttered in the night breeze at the window. "A bat flew in," he continued, his voice strained. "Charity was frightened, and I tried to catch it. We ran into each other and stumbled over the back of the couch."

Another silence, almost palpably disbelieving, greeted this statement.

"I see no bat." The words came in a puzzled quaver from old Mrs. Tremont, who stood at the back of the group, vainly trying to see what was going on.

Chad looked about him. "I must suppose it . . . left," he said weakly.

Charity flew to where young Mr. Weston stood, still white and silent and unmoving. "Oh, John," she wailed, "it was just huge, and it flapped and swooped at me. I was so frightened!" She flung her arms around him, but after a moment, when he did not respond, she moved back to look at him uncertainly.

At this moment Liza stepped in. She grasped Charity's arm and drew her over to Lady Burnsall, all the while uttering soothing words of comfort in a clear voice. "You poor dear, how dreadful for you. Bats are such nasty things. I believe I saw it flying out the window as we came in. There, there," she continued, glancing meaningfully at her mother.

Lady Burnsall immediately took up the thread. "Come along, dearest, we shall go upstairs and have one of the maids do your hair. Would you like a glass of wine?" Placing a tender arm about her daughter, she kept up a steady murmur as she led the sobbing girl from the room. The others in the group, avid with curiosity, followed, leaving Liza and John and Chad alone in the room.

John had not spoken, nor had he moved since his entrance to the room. Chad said nothing, but he watched Liza warily as he straightened his cravat.

"Chad!" The word came from Liza in a vibrant whisper. "How could you?"

Chad returned her outraged stare with one of his own. "How could I what?" he snapped.

"You have utterly compromised Charity!"

"Nonsense. I was merely talking to her when the bat flew in and the silly little chit flew apart in all directions at once."

Liza was consumed by a desire to run across the room and pummel him with her fists. "You don't seriously imagine that any of those people," she raged, gesturing with a trembling finger in the general direction of the corridor, "believed your bat story for an instant, do you? The two of you were alone in a secluded room, for Heavens' sake, and to call your position compromising would be the depth of understatement. What in God's name possessed you to seek a rendezvous with her here?"

"I would very much like an answer to that question myself, Mr. Lockridge." After a startled glance at John Weston, who had at last broken his silence, the two turned back to each other as though he had not spoken. Chad stood unmoving. His eyes had darkened to the color of very old sea ice.

"Are you calling me a liar, Lady Elizabeth?" he said quietly.

"What I believe makes no difference—" she began.

Chad raised his hand in a curt gesture. "As for my being in the room alone with Charity, I believe your question might be better directed to Mr. Weston."

Liza swung back to face John Weston, whose face had turned as bright red as it had been pale a few moments before. "I . . . I don't understand," he said in a high voice.

"Do you not?" asked Chad harshly. "Perhaps I should tell you," he said to Liza, "that your conniving little sister inveigled me for a stroll on the terrace a little over an hour ago. She then proposed that I enter the card room with her just before the pianist was scheduled to perform. She would give no reason for this unorthodox request, and the fact that she nearly burst into tears when I demurred, made me suspicious.

"She left me then, to converse with friends, but as the time drew near for the pianist to make his appearance, she approached me again and all but dragged me bodily into the card room. As she did so, she made a point of catching her mother's eye. Lady Burnsall smiled, apparently satisfied that her daughter was safely occupied for some time to come. Charity looked around the ballroom for some minutes, searching, I believe, for you, but you were nowhere in sight.

"We began a game of piquet, and after about five minutes, her crafty little ladyship spilled a glass of wine on her skirt and jumped up, declaring she must go and repair herself. She scampered from the room, and I followed at a discreet distance. She did not head for the ladies' cloak room, but nipped into the corridor leading to this room, which is where I found her a few moments later. I could only assume she was here for an assignation with Mr. Weston."

John made a sound that was ignored by Liza. She faced Chad, her eyes blazing. "Why did you not come to me immediately?" she cried.

"But how did I know where I might find you?" he asked silkily. "In what secluded room might I have found you with *your* lover?"

Liza gasped, but Chad continued before she could give utterance to the words that were seething almost visibly on her lips. "Besides, almost immediately after I had entered the room, that wretched bat flew in. I have told you the rest."

"Might I ask, Mr. Lockridge"—John Weston's words, though softly spoken, seemed loud in the silence that followed Chad's explanation—"why, when you saw Charity moving toward this room, you did not simply go to the gold salon and apprise Lady Burnsall of your suspicions?"

"Because I did not want to immerse her in any more hot water than was necess—" He stopped short, and an expression of astonished disdain crossed his features. "Are you accusing me of having designs on that young chit's virtue?" he asked incredulously. He advanced on the young man in what could only be called a threatening manner.

John remained where he stood. "I am merely saying that the

situation looks dashed havey-cavey from any direction in which you look at it." It was by now clearly apparent that John Weston was a very angry young man. "I have noticed that Lady Charity takes an inordinate pleasure in your company, and you in hers. As for your bat story, I can only say that it is hard to believe that one small, flying rodent could cause Lady Charity's clothing to become disgracefully tumbled about and her hair to cascade about her shoulders."

Chad snorted. "Then you know absolutely nothing about women, you young twit."

Liza swung on John. "Do you mean to tell me that you believe Charity could act so wantonly? How can a man who professes to love a woman be convinced so easily of her perfidy?" She shot a glance at Chad, who eyed her with lifted brows. "And how—" she continued, only to be interrupted by the opening of the library door.

Charity ran in, closely followed by her mother. Her coiffure had been repaired to some extent, and her gown was now arranged with propriety about her person, but her eyes were wide and anguished.

"Ah, you're all still here," she said breathlessly. Her eyes flew to John, who on seeing her had reverted to his former attitude of pale disapproval.

Charity halted abruptly. "John?"

When he did not reply, she moved to him and laid her hand on his arm. "John, what is it?"

Chad rose lazily from the corner of a desk on which he had seated himself. "Your swain," he informed Charity, "is apparently convinced that he interrupted a moment of passion between us. He has no faith in my character, your virtue, or the destructive powers of the average bat."

Charity bent a look of astonishment on John. "Surely you don't believe that Chad and I . . . that we . . ." She broke off in an outraged gasp as he continued to stare woodenly at her.

"I see," she said after a moment in a shaking voice. "You believe me to be a . . . a trollop who would meet a man in secret and allow him to . . . to *maul* me!" She moved to stand directly in front of him. "But, then you are right, aren't you? At least, partially so—for I did agree to meet you here secretly. You may rest assured, John Weston, that I shall never do so again," she concluded, her brown eyes glittering with unshed tears.

Liza turned to Chad. She felt ready to choke on the surge of emotion that had assaulted her the moment she had stepped inside the library to find Chad and Charity apparently in the final scene of a cunningly planned seduction. In her heart she believed the bat story, no matter how flimsily it rang in the ears, for she knew Chad to be an honorable man. She was also perfectly aware that Charity was not the sort of young woman who would give her heart to one man and allow another to fondle her. She was, thought Liza dismally, the sort of young woman who, having decided where her future lay, would not hesitate to flout convention. Charity, decided Liza, could very well have arranged an assignation with John.

Still, she was in no mood to absolve Chad from blame. His high-handedness was inexcusable, as were his foul aspersions on her own behavior. As if he had not been making a perfect cake of himself all evening with Caroline Poole! No, this entire imbroglio was all Chad's fault, and she was furious with him.

For Chad the evening had been one of almost unalloyed irritation. He had not wanted to come to the Woodcross musicale. He bowed to no man in his enjoyment of a song or two after dinner, but a musicale, with its interminable piano thumpings and violin scrapings, with the odd poet sandwiched in between was beyond his endurance. Caroline, however, had been adamant. And that was another thing. Somehow, he seemed to have been assigned to the position of chief admirer to Miss Poole, and if he were not extremely careful, his next post would be that of devoted husband. Caroline was lovely, and as charming as she could hold together. She was a pleasant evening's companion, provided one could keep up a steady stream of compliments and mindless gossip, but he had no desire to find himself leg-shackled to her.

Liza, on the other hand, gave every indication of having let her heart slip into Giles Daventry's greedy fingers. Every time she drifted into Chad's field of vision, she was in the company of that smarmy scoundrel, allowing him to pet her and leer at her as though she were Haymarket ware. Well, he wished her joy of her prize.

Liza faced Chad with her fingers curled into rakes. In his gaze she perceived arrogance and contempt, and she fairly exploded in her rage. "You have compromised my sister, Chad

Lockridge. You and your conceit and your complete lack of scruples and . . . and your interference have ruined her life."

"Don't be ridiculous," snapped Chad, his brows drawing together.

"Perhaps," continued Liza, unheeding, "since you have been out of the country, carving out your ambitious designs, you are unaware of the customs dictating the lives of those who live in the higher ranks of society here in England. Charity was discovered in disgraceful abandon in your arms. Alone. Without benefit of chaperon. You saw the reaction of John Weston. There is not a man in the country who will now even consider asking her to be his bride."

During this diatribe Chad had not moved, but remained staring at her, meeting her outraged glare with shafts of pure emerald animosity. When she finally ceased speaking, breathless, he stepped forward to grip her by both shoulders.

"Then I shall be that man," he said. Releasing her, he turned to Charity, who had ceased her lamentation, and, with her mother, stood watching the scene unfolding before them. His smile was the grin of a buccaneer standing on a burning deck, and in his voice could be heard the clash of burnished blades. "Lady Charity, will you do me the honor of becoming my wife?"

Liza's gasp was audible, and Charity simply gaped at him. With a crisp rustle of silk, Lady Burnsall moved to face Chad. "Mr. Lockridge, what sort of monstrous joke are you attempting?"

The freebooter's smile became more pronounced. "I am perfectly serious," he replied. "Despite the vehement, and totally unfounded accusations of your older daughter, I am not a barbarian. I am quite conversant with the prevailing social mores, absurd as they may be. Thus I realize that the only course in this situation for a gentleman of honor, such as myself, is to ask for the hand of the, er, injured damsel. How about it, Charity?"

For a long moment Charity remained absolutely still, and Liza was struck by the incongruity of the scene. The only sound to be heard in the room was the humming of nocturnal insects and the distant buzz of conversation emanating from the ballroom. It was as though they stood in an alien enclave.

Charity stared for a long moment at Chad, then her glance flicked to John, who said nothing. Drawing a deep breath, she

turned again to Chad. "Thank you, Mr. Lockridge. I would be
most happy to accept your offer."

John, after a single indrawn breath, turned on his heel and
left the room. Charity immediately erupted in a desolate burst
of tears, and Lady Burnsall rushed to her side, handkerchief at
the ready.

Liza stared at Chad, unbelieving, and she noted that his expression was one of complete startlement. Charity's acceptance of his offer was evidently as much a surprise to him as it
was to the rest of the assemblage.

The next few moments were chaotic. Lady Burnsall alter-
nated between soothing Charity and railing at Chad, whose attention was centered not on his betrothed but on Liza, who in
turn, for reasons known only to herself, professed herself delighted with this turn of events.

"I think," said Chad at last, "that it would behoove all of us
to quit this house. There is a side entrance that can be reached
at the end of the corridor. I shall have your carriage brought
round there."

"That's very kind of you, Mr. Lockridge," said Liza. "I
hope we shall have the pleasure of your company on the morrow. We must begin making wedding plans."

If she had hoped to discommode him by this statement, she
was very much disappointed. Pausing only to cast her an insouciant grin, Chad hurried from the room. She did not see
him again that evening, and on the short return journey to
Rushlake House, Liza raged silently at his despicable behavior. Her only consolation was derived in picturing the discussion that must be taking place at that very moment between
Chad and Caroline Poole.

Arriving home, she saw a subdued Charity off to her bed,
and settled down for an uncomfortable discussion with her
mother in that lady's bedchamber.

"What are we to do, Mama?" was her first question. "We
cannot allow news of this ridiculous betrothal to become
spread about. On the other hand, if it becomes known that she
was caught in a compromising situation with Chad, a betrothal
is essential."

"I believe," said the dowager countess, nodding gloomily,
"the first thing we must do is insert an announcement of Charity's betrothal to Chad in the *Morning Post.*"

"What!" The words, spoken aloud, made Liza almost physically ill. "You cannot mean to let Charity wed Chad."

Her mother blinked at this abrupt about face.

"I do not see that there is much choice," she replied with asperity. "After this evening's debacle, it is of prime importance that she become betrothed. After that, I do not see how she can avoid marrying him."

"Perhaps she can cry off—decide they will not suit—later, when the dust settles." Liza found that she was having difficulty forming coherent sentences.

"Such an act would reflect badly on each of them. Charity will appear to be the most arrant flirt, and Chad will look quite badly used."

To this Liza could make no answer. She knew too well the scorn society heaped on a maiden perceived to be a jilt. The man on the receiving end of the maiden's rejection invariably appeared rather as a figure of fun. She sighed.

"Very well, Mama. We will apprise Charity of all this in the morning, though I'm not sure she will not dig in her heels at the idea. She must already be regretting her quick acceptance of Chad's . . . of Chad's perfectly ridiculous offer."

When she retired to her chamber for the evening, however, her thoughts centered not on her wayward sister, but on her sister's betrothed. What had possessed Chad to offer for Charity? In his proposal he had spoken only of a gentleman's honor. Liza's lip curled. It had been her observation that gentlemen used that word merely as a convenient tool to gain their own ends. But what ends? He had stated clearly that his interest in her was strictly avuncular, and his behavior toward her had borne out his words.

She sighed. She would never be able to fathom Chad Lockridge and his motives. She was sure of only one thing, that when Charity had a chance to review her acceptance, she would be only too anxious to find a way out of her betrothal.

Unable to discover a path away from the wretched entanglement, she thumped her pillow and at last, fell into a restless sleep.

The next day, however, saw no improvement in her mood. To her astonishment, when Charity came down to breakfast, she burbled a bright, brittle good morning to the two ladies already seated at the table.

"My gracious," she continued, a smile almost painful in its intensity pasted to her lips, "I'm simply starved this morning."

So saying, she sat down to a cup of coffee and a piece of toast, which she began crumbling in her fingers.

Liza and Lady Burnsall exchanged glances, and the dowager cleared her throat.

"Charity, dear," she began. "We were just discussing last night."

"Last night?" asked Charity, as though the events of the previous evening had erased themselves from her memory. "Oh, yes, of course. Chad. What a darling he is, don't you think?"

Liza gave a noticeable start, and her lips tightened. Charity looked at her in concern.

"You don't mind, do you, Liza?" she queried in innocent concern. "That is, you said you feel nothing for him anymore, so I shouldn't imagine . . ."

Liza ground her teeth in irritation.

"No, I feel nothing for him, but—good Lord, you are not going to pretend that you wish for a . . . a union with him?"

"But why not?" asked Charity, her eyes round and guileless.

"Because," snapped Liza impatiently, "he is not the proper husband for you."

Charity tossed her head.

"On the contrary, I think he will be the perfect husband. He is handsome and wealthy and charming, and we are . . . are very fond of one another."

Lady Burnsall clicked her tongue in exasperation. "Gracious, Charity, you sound as though you were choosing a partner for the waltz. Your sister and I have been looking for a way of dissolving the betrothal."

"But why?"

"Well—because you feel nothing beyond a sort of sisterly affection for him—and I am sure you have not deluded yourself that he offered for you out of love."

Charity flushed. "I'm sure that love will come in time."

"But why do you wish to marry on such a basis?" Liza asked with a shake of her head. "Do you not want to wed a man for whom you have already formed a tendre?"

Charity dropped her eyes to her plate, where her toast lay in an artistic arrangement of crumbs.

"I shall never love any man again," she whispered almost

inaudibly. Her mother and her sister looked at each other once more.

"Oh, my dear," said Lady Burnsall. "You may think your heart broken this morning, but I assure you, you have suffered only a mild contusion."

Charity stiffened. "I assure you, Mama," she said frigidly, "my heart is not even bruised. I merely think it is the height of foolishness to base a marriage on . . . on the whim of one's emotions. Much better to spend one's life with a person one respects and whose company one enjoys, don't you agree? Now, if you'll excuse me, I have some correspondence to attend to."

With that she rose from the table and sailed from the room, much in the manner of a queen exiting an audience.

"Oh, dear." Mother and daughter breathed the phrase in unison.

"This is much worse than I thought," continued Lady Burnsall.

"I'm sure that with time . . ." Liza trailed off uneasily.

"Yes, of course, but . . ."

"Indeed. But what if . . ."

Breakfast concluded in a gloomy silence. As the two ladies rose from the table, a footman entered the room and presented a note to Lady Burnsall on a silver salver.

"It's from Chad!" she exclaimed, rapidly perusing the missive. "He asks permission to call on us this afternoon to discuss his betrothal to Charity." She lifted her eyes to Liza. "He wishes to make wedding plans."

Chapter 13

"IT was good of you to see me, ladies."

Chad sat stiffly on a brocade settee in the morning room at Rushlake House, his shoulders brushing against Charity, who huddled next to him. Liza and her mother sat in close proximity in matching armchairs.

Chad sighed. Liza had not said above two words to him since he had entered the house some minutes earlier. Occasionally he felt her glance on him, a look that could have penetrated granite. He was left with the unavoidable impression that Lady Liza Rushlake was unhappy with him. And how could he blame her? Dear God, how had he managed to embroil himself in such a disaster?

How could he have let himself be maneuvered into this absurd situation? Charity, of course, had . . . He shook himself. No, he had no one to thank for this fiasco except himself. He had no moral responsibility to make amends for the chaos created by one flying mouse, and he was not at all sure that he had a social one, either. It occurred to him that a lady of Liza's deserved reputation for quick-wittedness might have come up with some other solution to the problem of her sister's supposed ruination. It was almost as though she were determined that he should take Charity as a bride, and was merely using last night's social contretemps as an excuse. Why else had she been so quick to agree to his hastily uttered solution? And why did this reasoning cause such a profound depression within him? Further, what was he going to do now? What was he going to do about Charity?

He shot a sidelong glance at the young miss in question, who was apparently absorbed in the plaiting of the fringe on her shawl. He had received the shock of his life when she had actually taken him up on what he had spoken as only a token offer. He would be willing to stake his life on the fact that the willful young chit had no wish to marry him. She had obviously accepted him out of hurt and mortification, without any thought as to the pit into which she was plunging them. He looked up as Lady Burnsall cleared her throat delicately.

"About the, er, wedding," she began. "It is our feeling that we should insert a notice in the *Morning Post* at once, for the gossip-mongers will be busy already, and word of last evening's, er, incident will already be making the rounds."

Charity's eyes filled, and her expression was stricken, but the next moment, she straightened.

"Yes, certainly," said Chad after a pause. "That would seem to be the proper thing to do. And shall we include a date?"

"As to that," said her mother carefully, "I believe it would be best just to announce the betrothal. After we have worked out the . . . the details, then perhaps we can begin thinking about a date."

Charity opened her mouth as though she would say something, but sank back instead into the silence that curled around the morning room like a fog.

A spark of hope kindled in Chad's breast. "That, too, seems reasonable," he said.

Liza glanced around at the others sitting stiffly in their places. Lord, she thought dismally, it's as though we were discussing a death in the family rather than a wedding. How had things come to such a pass? The last person in the world to whom she wished to see her little sister joined in marriage was Chad Lockridge. Charity didn't love him, nor, she was willing to swear, did Chad harbor any feelings for Charity beyond a mild affection.

Last night a betrothal between the two seemed the only answer. She paused in her introspection, uncomfortably aware of a niggling unpleasantness lurking in a dark corner of her mind. She forced herself to examine it, and was horrified to discover that part of her self-righteous demand last night for Chad's immediate redress had taken root in a malicious determination to teach him a good lesson. But why was he in need of punishment? The words thrust themselves painfully into her consciousness, and the answer came just as uncomfortably. Because he had made her feel guilty. And because he persisted in making a cake of himself over Caroline Poole.

She turned these ideas over in appalled silence. What kind of a person was she that she could push two people into an action that would surely ruin their lives in a mindless effort to soothe her own petty hurts? Further, why had she felt such pain at Chad's reading of Giles's unwanted attentions? Besides which, surely she didn't care about his ridiculous infatuation with Miss Poole.

Did she?

Liza closed her eyes, then opened them to glance surreptitiously at Chad, who was chatting amiably with Charity and their mother. The afternoon sun, slanting through the long windows bordering the Square, had turned the careless russet waves of his hair to molten gold as his eyes shone in jeweled laughter.

Yes, she was forced to admit. She did care that Chad appeared to be on the point of becoming betrothed to Caroline. She cared that he thought she was in some sort of wanton liaison with Giles. In short it appeared that despite all her protestations to the contrary, she cared a great deal about Chad Lockridge.

She caught her breath, unwilling to face this horrific thought. Hurriedly she buttoned it into the murky little nook from which it had escaped and, affixing a bright smile to her lips, joined the others in conversation. She turned to Chad.

"I have been meaning to ask you about your silk mill. I heard it was destroyed by fire." She hesitated, and continued with an intensity that startled and dismayed her. "I'm so sorry, Chad. I fear it must represent a complete disaster for you."

"Where did you hear about that?" asked Chad, his eyes narrowed.

"Why, I believe it was—yes, Giles mentioned it to me last night at—" she hesitated, furious at the blush she knew had flared in her cheeks "—the Woodcross soiree. Why?" she asked as Chad frowned slightly.

"No reason," he said thoughtfully, "except that word of the fire did not reach me until this morning."

"Oh." Liza felt at a loss. "Perhaps he learned of it from a friend arriving from the north."

"Yes, that must be it. No, the burning of the mill was a setback, but it does not represent a disaster. It was not yet finished, you know, and it was insured—but I thank you for your concern."

Selkirk, with the instinct present in all good butlers, entered at that moment with champagne. After toasts all around, Chad asked Charity if she would like to take a turn about the Square with him, and she accepted with grave dignity.

"They make a handsome couple, do they not?" remarked Lady Burnsall, watching them from the window a few minutes later.

Annoyed, Liza faced her mother. "No, they do not. They are grossly unsuited for one another."

"Do you think so?" Lady Burnsall remained silent for a moment, then sighed. "Yes, you are quite right. Look at them. He is teasing her as though she were a prattling child, and she gazes up at him as though she were begging for a sweet. What a coil we are in," she grumbled. "Charity will come out of this ruined or heartbroken—one of the two, or both."

"Oh, Mama."

"I don't understand," continued her mother testily, "why she accepted Chad's offer in the first place, or why she is hanging on tooth and nail to the idea that marriage to him will satisfy her quite nicely, thank you. It will be almost impossible to release her from her difficulty if she prefers to remain shackled there."

Liza sighed. "I expect it is because of John Weston."

Letitia swung round to stare in surprise.

"Weston? You mean that young man who seems to infest every gathering we've attended for the past several weeks?"

"Yes, I have reason to believe Charity's affections are engaged in that direction."

"Well!" was her mother's only response.

"Indeed. Perfectly ineligible, of course."

"Quite."

The two ladies stood in thoughtful silence for several moments before Liza turned the conversation to an inconsequential subject. On the other side of the Square, Charity and Chad proceeded in an equally meditative manner.

"Chad," said Charity in a tentative voice. "About last night . . ." She trailed off, uncertain as to the path she wished the conversation to take.

Chad's response was not helpful. He merely lifted his brows.

"About last night," she repeated. "I have been meaning to tell you how . . . how grateful I am for your offer of marriage. It saved me from a dreadful situation."

Chad still said nothing, merely regarding her with a sort of melancholy amusement. Charity plodded on. "I mean, I know the whole imbroglio was of my own making. If I had not stolen into the library for what I am sure Mama would say was a most improper meeting with John—"

"Almost an assignation, one might say," interrupted Chad laconically.

Charity flushed. "Yes, I suppose one might. Oh, Chad!" she cried, tears spilling from her great, brown eyes. "I would give anything to have those moments back again. I should never have done it. Particularly"—here a militant sparkle flashed through the tears—"since John behaved in such a perfectly beastly manner. How could he think . . . ?"

Chad grunted in resignation and handed Charity his hand-kerchief.

"Have you considered how you would have responded had the situation been reversed? What if you plunged into a room to discover John sprawled atop a dimpled maiden, her hair all tumbled and her gown rucked up to her knees."

Charity's mouth formed a round, pink *O*.

"I never thought of that. But, if he had an explanation," she continued fiercely, "if he told me . . ."

"And if the maiden were someone with whom John had shown himself to be on extremely friendly terms. And if he spun you a tale about a bat—"

"But it was true!" Charity blew her small nose with great vigor, as though to emphasize her words. "And, of course, I would have believed him. That is . . ." She trailed off again and, a few moments later, sighed. "Yes, I can see where the whole scene was damning in the extreme. But I wish he had trusted me," she concluded miserably.

"And now . . ."

"Yes, to be sure—and now, I've plunged us into the most ghastly bumble bath. Why in the world did you have to offer for me?"

Chad answered with a rueful chuckle. "The words were out before I had quite thought them through. To be honest, I thought you'd refuse me with a disdainful toss of your head."

"I should have done. Oh, Chad, do you suppose I'm really going to have to marry you?"

At her expression of appalled desperation, Chad suppressed a chuckle, and with a merest twitch of his lips assured her that he would do his utmost to prevent that particular catastrophe.

* * *

Three days later, late in the afternoon, any residents of Berkeley Square peering from behind their curtains might have observed an enormous traveling carriage pull up to the door of the town house leased by Chadwick Lockridge. The coach was followed by several smaller vehicles, so that the procession looked as though an ancient behemoth had come to call with its progeny in tow.

Mr. Lockridge was seen emerging from his front door to greet his guests personally, and any watchers still interested would have beheld the stately descent from the carriage of Sir Wilfred Bascombe and his lady.

"Sir Wilfred!" exclaimed Chad, hurrying down the steps toward him. "And Lady Bascombe. We did not expect you so soon. How was your crossing?"

"Smooth as satin," replied Sir Wilfred. His large frame, domed, bald head, and bushy eyebrows gave him the aspect of a benevolent Alp.

His wife, a comfortably plump little woman, sighed in contentment. "I thought we'd *never* get here. It seems as though we've been traveling for a century. How are you, dear boy?" she asked, offering her cheek for a kiss.

"Very pleased to see you, ma'am," he replied, ushering them into the house. Ravi Chand, after exchanging courteous greetings with his master's guests, undertook the supervision of the unloading of their servants and baggage.

Sir Wilfred and his lady were shown immediately to their rooms to wash the dust of their travels from their persons. Later they settled in Chad's spacious drawing room, sipping restoratives, ratafia for Lady B. and brandy for her husband.

There ensued a lively exchange of gossip concerning friends and acquaintances Chad had left in India, as well as persons whom Sir Wilfred and his lady would soon see after their long absence from England. Finally, however, Sir Wilfred, after an extended period of harrumphing, broached the subject that had apparently been weighing heavily on him since his entrance into the house.

"Now tell me," he rumbled, "what is this you wrote me of certain rumors impugning your character? I'll tell you right now, my boy, I won't have it. I simply won't have it!"

Chad grinned. "I can't tell you how I appreciate your saying that, sir, but the situation has been rendered harmless, I believe." He went on to tell him of the Prince Regent's gesture of friendship at Carlton House.

"The Regent did that?" The snowy brows registered a quivering astonishment. "And you sat with him at dinner? Asked for your advice, did he? You must have made a whale of an impression on him in the short time since your return to England."

Chad's lips curved into a wry smile. "I was able to put him in touch with a couple of tips for the ring, and I complimented him on his taste in clothes."

"Ah," said Sir Wilfred, indicating that all was explained.

"Some days after the first rumors surfaced, I mentioned to His Highness that it would do him no good to be seen with me. He was intrigued, and when I explained what was afoot, he took great umbrage."

"Mmmyes, Prinny can display great loyalty, when it doesn't cost him anything."

Chad paused a moment before responding. "I know it is the fashion to poke fun at him, and I'll admit that most of the time he acts like a great, spoiled child—but his small act of friendship meant a great deal to me, and I'm grateful to him."

"Well said, my boy," barked Sir Wilfred jovially.

"As though anyone would believe such arrant nonsense anyway," interposed Lady Bascombe. "But tell us, what else have you been up to since we last saw you?"

"Oh, nothing much, except," he added, his green eyes atwinkle, "that I have become engaged to be married."

"What?" His guests gasped in unison, and it was some moments before their excited comments became coherent.

"But, to whom?" asked Lady Bascombe finally.

"You'll meet her tomorrow night, for the Rushlake ladies have invited us to dinner. They live right next door."

"The Rushlakes?" boomed Sir Wilfred.

"Oh, dear boy," bubbled Lady Bascombe joyfully. "Never tell us that you made up your differences with Lady Elizabeth!"

Chad flushed. "No." He swallowed as though something had caught in his throat. "It is Lady Charity who has agreed to be my wife."

"Oh." The two spoke in unison.

"But . . . Chad," said Lady B. in a quivering voice. "How

old is the child—I mean the young woman? She is some years younger than Lady Elizabeth, I believe?"

"Frances!" said her husband warningly, and now it was her turn to blush.

"That is," she added hastily. "I don't believe I have ever met her."

"You're right, Lady B.," Chad replied with a rueful sigh. "She is little more than a child. She turned eighteen not long ago." He observed with a smile the almost identical expressions of ill-concealed doubt that crossed their faces. "However," he continued, "I am in hopes that the betrothal will come to naught. What I am about to tell you is for your consumption only, but you are my dearest friends in the world, and I would not attempt to gammon you."

He then related to them the tale of the Woodcross musicale, the marauding bat, and his gentlemanly, if somewhat buffleheaded attempt to save Lady Charity Rushlake from ruination.

"How extraordinary!" gasped Lady Bascombe.

"And are you really going to marry the chit?" asked Sir Wilfred in astonishment. "She sounds a complete romp."

"No, no," replied Chad with a chuckle. "She is a very good sort of girl, as you'll see tomorrow evening."

Chapter 14

INDEED, when she was introduced to Sir Wilfred and Lady Bascombe in one of the ground-floor parlors in Rushlake House the following night, Charity was on her best behavior. She curtseyed and dimpled becomingly.

Chad's eyes had flown to Liza as soon as they entered the house, but she would not meet his gaze. Gowned in a robe of celestial blue that created shadowy reflections in her eyes, she extended a hand to her guests, and when Lady Burnsall entered the room a moment later, she made introductions all around. Letitia welcomed the pair delightedly, for she and Frances Bascombe's niece had attended school together.

The next guest to put in an appearance was Sir George Wharburton, who was greeted with a jovial bellow by Sir Wilfred, who recalled that he and Sir George had met many years before when the general, then an up-and-coming junior officer, had been stationed in Bihar. For a few moments the conversation was rife with cheerful talk of India "in the old days," until the sound of the front door opening indicated the arrival of yet another addition to the dinner party.

When Liza's butler ushered the guest into the room, Chad's jaw dropped in outraged astonishment, and his fists curled into balls. Giles Daventry! The unmitigated gall of the bastard to walk into this house, genially sure of his welcome by all who dwelled within.

Well, why wouldn't he? reflected Chad bitterly. Liza had invited him, for God's sake.

Damn!

His thoughts turned to the conversation that had taken place not an hour before in his study between Jem January, Ravi Chand, and himself. Jem, with his ever-present notebook, had presented another report on Daventry's activities, and the picture was growing murky indeed.

"The flow of traffic to and from his lodgings in the wee hours of the night is increasing," said Jem, riffling pages with a flourish. "A week ago, a certain Gyp Mahoney, a gentleman not known to turn down a paying proposition no matter what nastiness might be involved, visited with Mr. D. The next day he hopped a coach at the Bull and Mouth with a ticket to Macclesfield. The day after that"—Jem shot a glance at Chad—"your silk factory burned to the ground."

In a corner of the room near the fireplace, a looming shadow stirred, and Ravi Chand stepped into the light. "It appears to me, my master," he said softly, "that the world would be better off without this person Daven-tree."

A small smile lifted the curve of Chad's mouth. "I tend to agree with you, Ravi Chand. However I must caution you that the laws in this country are fairly stringent about that sort of thing. I should hate to lose you to the hangman's noose. Besides," he added, his voice hardening, "I have plans for Mr. Daventry."

Jem hesitated briefly before putting his notebook down on the table beside him. He pushed himself upright in the small arm chair in which he'd been lounging at his ease, and leaning forward with elbows on knees, gazed with some intensity at Chad.

"Mr. Daventry is in very low water at the moment. You know those family properties he speaks of so airily? The ones that supposedly keep him in funds here in Town? Well, they don't exist."

"What?" Chad's gasp was audible. "I thought he had inherited a respectable competence, in addition to his family estates."

"He did, but he went through it years ago, and the estates were all sold. What he lives on now—and a very precarious existence he maintains—is moneys from a series of fairly profitable and extremely unsavory enterprises. Under another name he owns three fashionable brothels and several decidedly unfashionable ones. He is in silent partnership in a number of gambling establishments—not ones you would care to take your young male relatives to—and he finances several swag operations—that is, the selling of stolen goods," he added as he observed Ravi Chand's uplifted eyebrows. A quick glance at his employer elicited the surprising information that Mr. Lockridge apparently needed no translation. "As well," he continued, "as some other equally shady endeavors. There is even some reliable talk that he participates rather handily in the slave trade. At any rate, due to the current wave of morality in high places, many of his most profitable establishments have been shut down of late. It won't be long before they re-open, but it will be some time before he realizes any profit from them. He lives extravagantly, as you know, and he has been having a bad run at the tables for some time."

Chad wondered at the undertone of bitter satisfaction in Jem's voice as he recited the catalogue of Daventry's current misfortunes.

"My God," he whispered. After a moment, he said, "Would you happen to know if among the gentleman's nocturnal callers there might be one who labors in the firm of Stanhope, Harcourt, and Finch?"

"Investment brokers, aren't they? Let's see." And with more thumbing of pages, Jem murmured to himself until he came to the desired place. "Yes, here it is. A fellow named Joshua Turnbull has been to see him. He's a clerk there. Well, well," he continued in some surprise. "Looks like Giles and Josh have struck up a real friendship, for Turnbull has been a regular visitor to Mr. Daventry's fashionable lodgings in Arlington Street for at least a year."

"A year! Jem, how long have you been watching Giles Daventry. And why?"

"There's lots o' coves in what I'm int'rested, Guv'nor," replied Jem, falling back into his persona of insouciant gutter habitue, and no more could be prised from him.

Returning to the present, Chad bared his teeth in what might have been called a smile and rose from his chair to greet Giles Daventry. He accepted with smiling equanimity Daventry's expressions of felicitation offered to him and Charity.

"No," said Charity in answer to Giles's question. "We have not yet set a date, but we shall do so very soon." She bathed her betrothed in a smile of overpowering radiance.

Over dinner, Chad drifted with a sense of unreality in the current of social chatter that flowed around him. He sat near the foot of the table, with Lady Burnsall on his right and Charity on his left. Thus he was unable to converse with any degree of ease with Liza, who sat at the head of the table. Liza, he noted bitterly, scarcely seemed to notice this unfortunate cir-

cumstance, since she was fully engaged in entertaining Daventry, seated on her right, with sparkling repartee.

Swearing silently, he turned to engage Charity in conversation. As he did so, he noticed for the second or third time that
evening that she was not in spirits. Come to think of it, her
mien had been extraordinarily serious over the last several
days. She was always ready with one of her engaging smiles,
but when she was not actively engaged in conversation, she
tended to droop noticeably. He rather thought he knew the
cause of her malaise. He averted his eyes determinedly from
the golden head at the end of the table and gave himself over
to raising Charity's spirits.

Liza, attempting an intelligent reply to Giles's pleasantries,
felt that the smile she had pinned to her lips earlier in the
evening was in danger of cracking her face. For the first time
since she had known him, the young man's witticisms failed in
their efforts to amuse her. In truth, aside from the uncomfortable intimacy he had forced on her at Woodcross House, he
was boring her to distraction. Why had she invited him
tonight? Her mother's urgings had something to do with it, of
course, but mostly she had only herself to blame for her inabil-
ity to cause pain to an old friend.

When her mother had outlined plans for a dinner party to
welcome the Bascombes on their return to London, Giles had
seemed the most logical choice for the obligatory male guest
needed to even the table. She experienced a fleeting pang at
what Chad would think to find Giles running tame in her
drawing room, but in the next instant, her anger at his recent
insensitive behavior surfaced. The sight of him, bending over
Caroline Poole in a loverlike attitude still lodged in her mind
like a handful of stinging nettles, causing a sudden pricking
when she happened on it unawares.

• She had begun to regret her decision, however, the moment
Giles had been ushered into the front parlor. His attitude of
easy familiarity had returned, and now, as he emphasized a
point, his hand stretched over the table to touch hers. She was
startled at the intensity of the urge she felt to snatch her fingers
away from his. Instead she smiled gently and returned her
hand to her lap.

For an instant a sharp but unreadable expression flashed in
Giles's eyes, but in the next, he withdrew into a cloak of casual affability. He joined in the general conversation, which at

present centered on the financial condition of the East India Company, of which Sir Wilfred was a highly placed member. Giles's knowledge of the Orient was minimal at best, and at the earliest opportunity, he changed the subject.

He leaned forward and looked down the table, catching Chad's eye. "I say, Lockridge," he said, raising his voice slightly so that all at the table ceased their chatter to listen. "How are you progressing on your wager with Liza? Do you think to overcome Lady Liza's Luck, after all?"

"Eh?" Sir Wilfred boomed. "Wager? Chad and Lady Liza?"

Liza flushed, but offered him a calm smile. She explained to Sir Wilfred and his wife the terms of the wager, whereupon the pair replied with suitable expressions of interest and amazement.

Suppressing her irritation that Giles had once more chosen to make public a matter she considered strictly between her and Chad, she continued. "Oh, yes," she said amusedly. "It is a foolish wager, as most are." She explained the details of the stake, concluding with a laugh as she turned to Giles. "I fear you will find Mr. Lockridge closemouthed in the extreme as to his progress, thus, I must hold my own counsel as well."

After several moments of good-natured raillery and advice, the guests turned to other matters and the wager was forgotten. To Liza's dismay, however, it surfaced again later in the evening when the gentlemen joined the ladies after their port and brandy.

"Tell me more about the Queen's Pendant, my dear," said Lady Bascombe. "I've heard it is a masterpiece of the jeweler's art."

"It is exactly that," said Liza. "Although"—she cast a glance toward Chad—"there are those who consider it ugly. Would you like to see it?"

"Surely you don't keep it in the house!" exclaimed Sir Wilfred. "We hear in India that London is a veritable den of crime these days."

"Well, perhaps not quite that bad—and the pendant is heavily insured, but you're right," she replied, laughing. "I've been meaning to put it in the vault at the bank, and plan to do so tomorrow. In the meantime I shall be pleased to give you all a private showing."

She left the room and retrieved the pendant from the cupboard in her study, returning a few moments later with her hands cupped around the wooden box. Opening it, she withdrew the pendant and laid it in Lady Bascombe's lap where it seemed to shoot tongues of flame from its fretwork of jewels.

"Oh, my," breathed Lady Bascombe.

Her sentiments were echoed by all the others in the room, as they gathered to examine the pendant. Each in turn lifted it in reverent hands, turning it in the candlelight until its glow filled the room.

"I had no idea," said Giles, his voice raised barely above a whisper, "that it was so . . . so . . ."

"Big?" interposed Chad. "Yes, my mother always threatened to have it broken up into more manageable pieces—which, according to her, would make up seven or eight reasonable-size pieces of jewelry. The falconer"—he pointed to the central ivory carving—"she said would do very well as a doorstop. Father, of course, turned pale at such heresy. I look forward to returning it to its rightful place in the family, er, bosom."

"Of course," said Liza smoothly. "When I have Brightsprings safely in my possession once more, I may be induced to consider discussing the possibility of selling it to you."

Sir Wilfred poked an elbow at Chad, who sat next to him on a straw-colored satin settee. "Hah!" His laughter boomed around the room. "That pretty much sounds like never to me, my boy."

"But, my God," said Giles, still fascinated by the glittering gems. "You must have paid a small—" He halted abruptly and flushed. "That is . . ." He gave an embarrassed start, knocking over the glass that stood at his elbow on a small sofa table, spilling wine over his sleeve. A footman was summoned, and when he arrived with a cloth, Giles, apparently discomposed by his social gaffe, hurried him from the room, explaining that the servant could better repair the damage to his coat in another part of the house. A small silence greeted this announcement, and when he returned, Liza had restored the pendant to its place in her study. The conversation turned to other topics, and Liza prayed that Giles's inadvertent comment had not led to speculation as to the extent of her wealth.

Later that night Chad paced the floor of his bedchamber, unwilling to seek his bed. Images tormented him of Liza's hand resting on Giles Daventry's arm, her eyes laughing up into his.

It was obvious the fellow virtually ran tame in her house. He had left the room to mop up the wine spilt on his suit with the casual familiarity of a family member. It was equally obvious that Liza had no knowledge of Giles's activities. She had no idea that his "respectable competence" was derived from some of the seamiest establishments in London's unspeakable underside.

Was she actually considering marriage to this filthy piece of scum? He could not let her do that.

Chad moved to the window and looked down into the rear gardens of his house and the one adjoining. His gaze found the stone bench on which Liza had sat in a pool of moonlight, her golden hair turned to silver and her slender body bathed in luminescence. She had seemed a forest nymph carved in marble, but her body against his had been warm and pliant, her mouth moving under his in quivering response.

Well, he certainly did not plan on any more stolen embraces from the lovely Lady Liza. The next moment he uttered a sound in the darkness. Who the devil did he think he was gudgeoning? If Liza were to appear on that bench this very instant, he would be on his way to join her in the next. God, what was the matter with him? What had happened to his hard-won detachment?

He forced his mind away from this intensely bothersome subject and turned it back to Giles Daventry. It appeared that having failed to destroy his reputation through rumor, the bastard was now attempting to ruin him financially. But why? What had he ever done to Daventry to earn such terrible enmity. Of course. Liza. Daventry wanted her, and who could blame him? But, he wondered again, was it merely Liza's delectable person he was after, or her delicious fortune? He rather thought the latter. Daventry had pursued her for years, evidently sure that she would accept him some day. Now, however, the resources necessary for his lavish way of life were nearly depleted. Marriage to an acknowledged heiress would provide a sure and immediate way out of his difficulties. Chad's lip curled. Daventry's eyes had nearly popped from his head when he beheld the Queen's Pendant.

But even if he were wrong; even if Daventry loved Liza with the pure intensity of a flame, the man was a shark and he was not going to have her. He was not, by God, going to have her.

Having settled at least that point to his satisfaction, Chad prepared for bed. He did not summon his valet. Somehow it had become extremely difficult to think of Jem as his valet, and he was loathe to call on him for menial services.

He was musing idly on the mysterious Jem January when a feminine shriek split the night air. He ran to his window as the cry rose again. It had come from Rushlake House! He spun around and ran down the back stairs and out into the garden, and thence to the back door of the neighboring house via the gate he had used those several nights ago. Hearing a noise behind him, he looked over his shoulder to behold Ravi Chand and Jem plunging after him.

The woman screamed again, and now other voices could be heard, raised in querulous surmise. Chad, followed by the two servants, burst into the house without knocking. He made for the main part of the house, only to be brought up short by the sight of a large number of persons in various states of undress gathered in the corridor outside Liza's study. The center of attention was, apparently, a young footman who sat on the floor holding his head and moaning faintly. Over him stood a plump housemaid, the source of the screams and still in good voice. Liza had just joined the group, approaching from the opposite end of the corridor, tying her dressing gown as she ran.

"What is it?" she cried. "What has happened?"

Observing the presence of her mistress, the housemaid swooned, falling in a heap atop the footman.

Bending over the pair, Chad lifted the maid to her feet and handed her over to Liza, who in turn settled the distraught girl into the waiting arms of the housekeeper. He aided the footman to an upright position, recognizing him as the same young man who had assisted Daventry with his wine spill earlier in the evening.

The young man gazed blankly at Chad's trenchant questions, but after a moment he seemed to come to himself. "I dunno, sir," he choked, rubbing the back of his head. "I heard noises coming from Lady Liza's study, and when I went in, it was pitch black. I started to move toward the noise—a sort of scratching noise it was—and something caught me on the back of me head. I didn't know nothing more until I come to just now with Becky standing over me and screeching her hair off."

"My study!" exclaimed Liza, paling.

As one, she and Chad rushed into the room. She lit a candle, after which, in response to the sound of his indrawn breath, she turned to look toward the cupboard that contained the pendant. It did so no longer. To Liza's consternation the candle glow revealed that the door to the cupboard swung wide, and the small strong box in which she kept the pendant was gone.

Chapter 15

IT was some minutes before the crowd of servants could be dispersed. The housekeeper, having quieted the maid, turned her attention to the footman, and with Jem's solicitous assistance, led him off to put a cold compress on the knot that was rapidly swelling at the base of his skull.

Lady Burnsall and Charity had arrived on the scene moments after Chad and Liza entered the study, and now the four of them sat in chairs clustered about Liza's desk. Ravi Chand stood, arms formidably folded, to one side.

"Who could have done this? Was it an intruder? How did he get into the house? Did he take anything else?" The questions tumbled from Charity's lips, remaining almost visible as they hung in the air like so many bothersome insects.

Ravi Chand moved silently to the double doors leading to the outside from the study. When he turned the handle, the door opened easily.

"Did you leave it unlocked the last time you came in?" Chad asked Liza.

"No, that is, I rarely use the door." She flushed remembering that her last foray into the garden had led to her ill-fated meeting with Chad. "Besides, Selkirk, our butler, checks the doors every evening before he retires. He is extremely conscientious."

"Evidently, he failed in his duty tonight, Madame," interposed Ravi Chand. "There is no sign of tampering with the lock." He appropriated a candle and, lifting it high, peered at the ground outside the door. "I do not see any footprints, but it has not rained for some days and the earth is hard."

Liza simply gaped at the man. "You do speak English," she quavered, as though by fastening intently on this irrelevant oddity, she could avoid contemplation of the disaster that had just befallen her. Chad returned to his chair and stared sharply at Liza, who continued to stare dazedly at the Indian servant. "Are you all right?" he asked in a harsh tone of voice.

"What?" She transferred a blind gaze to him. "Oh . . . oh, yes. It's just that—I don't understand how this could have happened." She straightened suddenly, a horrified awareness creeping into her eyes. "Oh, Chad—your pendant. I'm so sorry. We must get it back! We must notify the authorities."

"Yes," he replied, frowning. "I suppose that is the best course."

Liza lifted her brows. "You seem hesitant."

A long moment passed before Chad answered. He was almost sure he knew the identity of the thief, but proving it would be difficult. And how would Liza feel when she discovered that someone so close to her heart had stolen from her? Damn Giles Daventry's black heart!

"No," he said. "It just occurs to me that the magistrate will wonder why the door to your study was left unlocked. They are bound to conclude that the thief was working with someone inside the house."

"But that's impossible!" exclaimed Liza. "No one in the house knew where I kept the pendant. Tonight was the first time it's been out of the cupboard, and no one saw me take it from the cupboard. No one knew—" She stopped suddenly, and Chad returned her startled gaze with a bitter smile.

"No one knew where it was to be found except me," he concluded. "Yes, you did remove it once before, did you not? To show it to me shortly after we agreed to our wager."

"Oh, but Chad . . ." Lady Burnsall lifted her hand as she spoke, and Charity chimed in to join her. "Oh, Chad, none of us would even think—" She stopped abruptly and put her hand to her mouth.

"You do not think me a thief?" Chad's voice was rasping growl. "I was suspected of that and worse not too many years ago."

"Oh Chad, don't be ridiculous. Of course we don't think you stole the pendant. None of us would even consider such a thing." Charity's words spoken in a reassuringly prosaic tone of voice had the effect of a brisk shower of cold water on Chad's inflamed sensibilities. His features relaxed in an appreciative grin. He turned to speak again to Liza, but was interrupted at the entrance of Jem January, whom he introduced to the ladies.

"How is young Stebbins, Mr. er, January?" queried Lady Burnsall.

"Is that his name?" replied Jem. "He will have a pretty fierce headache for a day or so, but he is not seriously damaged." He hesitated for a moment. "He seems very remorseful that he was unable to prevent the entry of your unauthorized visitor, my lady. How long has he been in your service?"

Lady Burnsall looked to Liza, who responded, "You would have to ask Selkirk, our butler, but I believe he has not been with us long—several months, or so."

"I see," said Jem, relapsing into a thoughtful silence.

Chad regarded him curiously, then turned again to Liza.

"If you wish to launch an official investigation into this matter, I'd suggest sending to Bow Street. Jem can set off right now."

"Oh, but could it not wait until morning?" asked Lady Burnsall.

Jem, displaying a marked lack of enthusiasm for the program suggested by his master, expressed mute agreement with the dowager.

"It is my understanding that such an inquiry is best conducted as soon after the fact as possible," said Chad, smiling inwardly. He was struck by the possibility that the pseudo-valet had himself been on the wrong end of more than one Bow Street investigation.

Jem sighed and left the house. Not long afterward, he returned with a portly gentleman dressed in a wide-brimmed hat and coat of fustian, as well as the red waistcoat that proclaimed him to be a Bow Street Runner. He informed the assembled group that his name was George Thurgood, and, pulling a grimy, much-used notebook from one capacious pocket, he interviewed family and staff at some length, with particular attention given to Stebbins, the suffering footman. He eyed Ravi Chand distrustfully, but questioned him only cursorily.

"Ain't much to go on," said the Runner, at the end of his interrogations. He then examined what he described as "the scene," making careful note of the open garden door and the faint scratch marks to be seen on the cupboard lock.

"Mp," he grunted. "Looks like the work of an experienced cracksman. 'Course, if you don't mind me sayin' so, Ma'am, you made his job easy for him. Leavin' the door open was a gracious invitation, you might say. Who knew where the sparkler was kept, besides yerself?"

There was a silence, while a moment of tension settled on the room. Then Chad rose to face the runner. "Lady Elizabeth," he said smoothly, "was kind enough to show me the pendant some weeks ago. Other than that, she tells me no one else was aware of its location."

A glint of suspicion flashed in the runner's eyes, but he said nothing further on the matter, promising only that he would give his entire attention to the theft.

With brisk self-importance, he made his exit, leaving weary family members and servants to seek their beds. Jem and Ravi Chand vanished quietly, and soon only Liza and Chad were left in the elegant little study.

"Thank you for your help," Liza said tiredly. "I really would not have known how to go on." She shook her head. "I feel as though I were still in my bed—that I shall wake up in a moment and find this was all a nightmare."

"Not a pleasant way to end an evening," agreed Chad.

"What about the wager?" Liza's words sounded loud in her ears, dropping into the silence of the room.

"What about it?"

"Well, how can there be a wager when one of the objects staked has vanished?"

"You don't sound as though you have much confidence in the Bow Street magistrate's office. They may surprise you. Perhaps they will apprehend the thief, and you may see the return of your pendant."

"Perhaps." She smiled mistily at him, and he suppressed an urge to gather her in his arms. To his surprise he heard himself ask. "While we're on the subject, why did you go to such a great deal of trouble to acquire the Queen's Pendant in the first place?"

Liza could only stare at him. For, although she had convinced herself that she viewed the purchase of the pendant purely as an investment, she realized with a sudden and blinding insight, that her reason for launching her exhaustive search for it involved her aching desire to present it to Chad. To somehow make up to him for the painful snubbing he had received, and the rumors that had driven him from England. Her only motive had been to make Chad Lockridge happy.

She gasped with the shock of this revelation and realized

that his gaze had intensified, searching hers as though he would look into her soul. The warmth of his hands, still on her shoulders, spread through her body and curled into all her secret places. She swayed toward him, and when his mouth came down on hers, her arms rose involuntarily to clasp him to her. His lips were warm and demanding, and she opened herself to them in a mindless, wondering response. His hands moved over the length of her back, causing her to arch against him, and when they cupped her breasts, a muted cry of longing escaped her.

"Oh, my dear," he whispered against her mouth, "old habits die hard, don't they?"

She drew back to look at him and was dismayed beyond words to discover that he seemed almost angry.

She almost crumpled at the pain his words created in her. Old habits! Not only was she an unpleasant affliction to him, but a bad habit in which he indulged when he was in the mood for dalliance. She moved away from him, her sense of loss almost palpable. What had been a moment of shattering revelation to her had been to him one of simple, basic arousal.

"Yes," she whispered brokenly. "But I am determined to break this one. Please don't do that again, Chad, for I cannot bear it."

She whirled and ran down the corridor toward the main part of the house, leaving him to stare after her. Slowly he turned and made his way back to his own domicile.

Once again he began his bedtime preparations, but it was many more hours before he fell into a fitful sleep.

The next day Liza reported the theft of the pendant to Thomas, who, in turn notified her insurer. This august firm sent its own investigators to the scene, and Liza and her mother spent an unpleasant morning answering questions and allowing dark-suited strangers access to the scene.

By the time they left, Liza indeed felt she was the featured player in one of the early acts of a very bad play. Her mood did not improve during the day, and when she met Chad that evening at a small rout held by Mrs. Colby-Chassins, her answer to his questions regarding the investigation were somewhat snappish.

"The gentlemen from the insurer's office did not seem hopeful. One of them was actually of the opinion that since I kept the pendant in my home instead of in a vault, I am not entitled to recompense for its loss."

"Indeed?"

"Yes, but I soon put him to rights. My contract states merely that the items insured must be kept in a secure place. A locked cupboard in my house is obviously not as secure as one in a bank, but I convinced him that it still fulfilled the spirit of the contract."

Chad smiled. "I can see you driving him from your door with a fiery sword. Did they not come up with any clues as to the one responsible for the theft?"

"No, but they asked a lot of questions." She hesitated a moment, trying to gauge his mood in the meager light of a nearby candelabra. "In fact, I shouldn't be surprised if one or two of them pay a call on you in the near future."

Chad made no reply.

She continued hesitantly. "They asked, of course, who besides myself knew where the pendant was kept, and of course they were most interested when I mentioned you. They also wanted to know who was first on the scene after the robbery occurred. They spoke to Stebbins after that, and they almost visibly pricked up their ears when Stebbins told them that you came bolting into the house through the back door not five minutes after Stebbins was knocked unconscious."

"I see." His tone was so colorless that Liza could not guess what emotion, if any, lay behind it. She sighed. "Chad, I am so sorry. I would not have had this happen for all the jewels in that wretched pendant."

"I know." He sounded inutterably weary, but he reached to take Liza's hand. "You were obliged to tell them the truth, after all."

After that Liza was given little opportunity to reflect on the recent happenings. Letitia greeted her at the breakfast table with the news that they simply *must* see to their social obligations. "For," she said with an emphatic shake of her head, "it has been much too long since we have paid any morning calls. Cat Thurston was delivered of a baby boy last week. Richard, of course, has been puffing off his consequence ever since, and we cannot be remiss in our felicitations. And the Falbourne sisters have been here twice since we last paid a call on them."

Liza had never felt less like engaging in artificial patter, but her mother's martial attitude indicated that no excuses would be brooked or previous engagements begged.

Garbed in a walking dress of lime green twilled silk, topped by a Villager hat whose matching green ribbon was gathered in a bow tucked just beneath one ear, she and Lady Burnsall sallied forth an hour or so later. The dowager, a youthful spring in her step, wore an elegant robe of brown sarcenet, which almost exactly matched the color of her hair. Over this creation lay a cream-colored spencer, with brown braided trim. Her bonnet, too, was cream-colored and adorned with brown plumes that quivered in expressive punctuation for her admiring remarks to the Thurston baby boy and his proud mama and papa, as well as for apologies directed later to the Falbourne sisters.

There were other calls, too, to the Ladies Runstead, Halstead, and Winburton, as well as to Mrs. Gelbert, Mrs. Frey, and the Misses Cashbury. As they emerged from the home of the latter, Liza turned to her mother with a most undutiful expression on her face.

"Mama, I don't care how many dragons of the *ton* we have left unvisited, I am throwing in the hammer. One more cup of tea, and my teeth will begin to float. It is time to go home."

Lady Burnsall nodded in agreement as she sank into the squabs of their carriage. "I couldn't agree with you more, my dear." She sighed and, removing her bonnet, ran her fingers through flattened curls. "It has been a rather tedious afternoon, on the whole, but one must do one's duty, after all."

Liza shot a glance at her mother, then bent to examine the seams on her gloves. "I cannot believe the speed at which gossip travels in this town. At least three people commiserated with me on the theft of the Queen's Pendant."

Her mother sighed. "Yes, I was the recipient of the same sort of thing. I cannot imagine from whom they could have heard of the theft so quickly."

"Nor I." There was a moment's silence before she continued. "Did anyone happen to mention Chad's name in connection with the theft?"

Lady Burnsall sighed again. "Not in so many words. Although that insipid Tina Witherspoon said she heard that Chad was being questioned, along with anyone else who had any knowledge of the pendant."

Liza's fingers clenched in her lap. "Mama, I just can't bear that Chad should again become the target of the same tattle-mongers that drove him from his home six years ago."

"I know, my dear. It is positively monstrous. But, you know, Chad is older now and, I think, much more able to defend himself." She paused for a moment before proceeding delicately. "It is kind of you to be so concerned for the welfare of your future brother-in-law."

Liza's face whitened, but she was saved from having to reply as the town carriage pulled up in front of Rushlake House. Liza descended hurriedly and brushed past a house-maid who was sweeping the front steps. She entered through the open door and divested herself of her bonnet. With a grateful sigh at being again in her own home after a day spent in doing her duty, she opened the door of the little morning room, ushering her mother ahead of her. She then bumped into her from behind as that lady stood stock-still in the doorway.

Liza stared at what she initially perceived as a person standing in the curve of the small grand piano in one corner, and was inutterably shocked when the figure separated into two distinct entities.

"Charity!" gasped Lady Burnsall.

"Mr. Weston!" squeaked Liza.

Chapter 16

CHARITY and John whirled to face the newcomers. Charity made an instinctive attempt to tidy her disarranged hair, and John's hand flew to his cravat, which was sadly askew.

"We . . . we didn't hear you come in," said Charity breathlessly.

"Obviously not," snapped Lady Burnsall. "Charity, how could you? You are betrothed. And as for you young man"—she bent a fearsome scowl on John—"I'll thank you to leave this house and not return."

But the pair did not move. Instead, pale of countenance, John retained Charity's hand in his and faced Liza and Lady Burnsall.

"I apologize for my behavior," he said with quiet intensity, "but I will not make excuses for the fact that I love Charity. And"—he turned to look at the girl who stood with him—"she has assured me that she returns my regard."

"John came to apologize for his misinterpretation of the scene that occurred at the Woodcross Musicale—that is, the bat and all . . . And," she continued hastily, "John has asked me to marry him," said Charity with glowing dignity. "I have told him that I shall be happy to do so."

"Allow me to congratulate you, sister," said Liza flatly, as she and the dowager advanced into the room, closing the door behind them. "You must be the only girl in Mayfair to boast of two fiancés."

"Believe me—*sister*," retorted Charity, her cheeks flushed, "I shall take steps to disengage myself from my other fiancé at the earliest opportunity. You know," she continued pleadingly, "that Chad does not really wish to marry me—and I certainly never wanted to marry him. It would have been the most inconvenient marriage of convenience ever arranged. There have been no contracts signed, no settlements made. I don't see why—"

"Charity," interrupted Liza. "I told you once before that, while John Weston is a fine young man, it is the wish of Mama and myself that you—"

"That I marry some titled idiot for whom I shall never care tuppence!" cried Charity wildly.

Liza turned to look at John. "My dear sir, I have no wish to embarrass you, but you must see that a young woman of Charity's station is obliged to wed for advantage."

"Why?" asked John in a low voice.

"What?" said Liza blankly.

"Where is it written," he continued harshly, "that a young woman must be condemned to marry where she does not love? Lady Liza, Lady Burnsall, I may not be titled, but I can make Charity comfortable. I have a respectable competence, and"— he flushed at Liza's impatient exclamation—"*and,* I have just been hired to manage a vast estate up north."

"What?" repeated Liza, this time in unison with her mother.

"I received an offer from a gentleman who owns an estate in Northumberland. He has heard of my work with crop improvement. He wishes me to incorporate my methods on his estate, and he has offered me what I can only consider a munificent salary to do so."

Liza and the dowager could only gape at the couple. "But—" began Liza, but she was interrupted by the inauspicious entrance of a footman who announced that a visitor had come to call. Mr. Giles Daventry, he said, was waiting in the drawing room to see Lady Liza.

Liza clicked her tongue in annoyance. "Tell him I cannot possibly see him. No," she said hastily after a moment's consideration, "never mind, I shall be up momentarily." She turned back to the others.

"Mr. Weston, I think this is not a good time to continue our discussion." She raised her brows at her mother, who nodded in agreement. "I suggest you leave now, and return tomorrow, when we shall have had time to . . . to consider your proposal."

"Or when you think you have had time to change my mind," cried Charity. "Well, I shan't. You may as well understand that now."

"Your mother and sister are right, Charity," said John, with a smile of such tenderness that Liza felt bathed in its warmth.

"It would be wise to wait until tempers have cooled." He bowed to the ladies and left, promising to see them on the morrow.

Charity said nothing more, but with a minatory glare, swept from the room. Liza and her mother, after an exchange of glances, followed suit.

In the drawing room Giles paced before the long windows that overlooked the square.

"Liza!" He hurried to her as she entered the room, catching her two hands in his own. "I just heard the news of the theft of the Queen's Pendant and felt compelled to offer my condolences."

She smiled and forced a lightness to her tone. "Really Giles, it is only trumpery jewelry. I have not lost a loved one, after all."

Giles drew her to a settee and seated her with great ceremony, and when he had settled himself next to her, he spoke again. "Hardly trumpery, my dear. It must represent a great loss to you. You have notified the authorities, I presume."

She told him of the appearance of the Bow Street Runner and the insurance investigators, and he nodded in satisfaction. "I expect they may wish to talk to me, as well," he said thoughtfully. "And everyone else who attended your little dinner party that night," he added as Liza's brows rose questioningly.

"Oh dear, I hadn't thought of that. Do you think they will bother Sir George? And Sir Wilfred and Lady Bascombe? How very discommoding for them."

"Nonsense." Giles laughed, his fair hair glinting. "I'm sure the questions will be routine and very brief." He rose to stand before the window, staring in apparent fascination at the sight of a carriage stopped before Landsdowne House to disgorge a pair of late afternoon callers. "I wonder," he said tentatively, "if I should mention that Chad had seen the pendant's place of concealment on a previous visit."

Liza contemplated him with a feeling that strongly resembled dislike. "How did you know that I had previously shown the pendant to Chad?" she asked, her tone tinged with acid.

"Why . . . why, I believe he mentioned it to me last night when you brought it out for all of us to view."

"I see. Well, as it happens, Chad has already disclosed that information to Mr. Thurgood, of the Runners."

An expression of relief crossed his well-formed features. "Ah, that's all right, then. I hesitated to divulge information that would surely cast suspicion on him."

"Do you think it would, Giles? Cast suspicion on him?" Her heart thudded unpleasantly as she formed the question, but her face displayed only a calm interest in what he was about to say.

"Well . . . " Giles shrugged uncomfortably. "It's bound to." He drew a deep breath. "To tell you the truth, Liza"—he moved across the room to sit beside her again—"I can't help but think he's behaved in a very havey-cavey manner."

When Liza said nothing, merely staring at him in waiting curiosity, he plunged on in rather a rush. "He was under suspicion the last time the pendant turned up missing. Oh, I know the fact that you were able to buy it from the person who purchased it from Chad's father proved his innocence, but still . . . And now, here he is again, in possession of an apparently comfortable fortune, of which no one seems to know precisely the origin."

Liza still remained silent, but her fingers were beginning to curl tightly in her lap.

"And there's no denying," Giles concluded, disapproving righteousness ringing from every syllable, "that it's extremely odd that he is the only person on the entire planet who knew where the pendant was to be found, besides yourself."

He sat back for a moment, gauging the effect of his words. Liza's demeanor was not promising. Her hands had balled into fists, and in her eyes could be observed flickers of the peculiar shade of blue that can sometimes be seen blazing in white-hot furnaces. And like one of those conflagrations, her eyes were spitting sparks.

"I say this only for your own good, my dear," he added hurriedly. "You know I have championed him for years, but the time has come to look at his activities in a realistic fashion. Now I realize your feeling for him is one of mere friendship, of course. He is betrothed to your sister, after all, but I know how fiercely devoted you can be to those close to you. I would not have you taken advantage of."

At the end of this little speech Liza felt ready to explode. She opened her mouth to demolish Giles and his solicitude, but was silenced as she observed the expression of unhappy concern written plain on his face. She sighed and said stiffly,

"I do thank you, old friend, for your solicitude, but this is, you will understand, a personal matter. And now, since you and I do not stand on ceremony, you will understand that I cannot stay to chat. If you will excuse me, I have urgent matters to which I must attend."

With a regal swish of her skirts, she rose and strode to the door, leaving Giles no alternative but to be ushered from the room and thence from the house.

He stared at the outside of Liza's front door for several moments before strolling to his waiting curricle.

As he did so, he was watched from an upstairs window in the adjoining house, and as his elegant equipage rattled around the Square, turned into Bruton Street, and disappeared from sight, Jem January let the curtain slip back into place and turned to face his employer. Chad sat before the fire in the cheerful little parlor, and Ravi Chand stood, as usual, with arms folded, near the door.

"Well, now," said Jem. "He didn't stay long, at least."

Chad grunted. "Probably just long enough to explain to her that I am the only logical person to suspect of stealing her damned pendant. All with the most sincere regret, of course. If I'm not extraordinarily light on my feet, here, that bastard is going to get me transported. Tell me more of this footman, Stebbins, Jem. It occurs to me that when Daventry heard that Liza planned to take the pendant to the bank the next day, he must have spilled his wine in order to give himself an opportunity for a tête á tête with Stebbins, who apprised him of the pendant's location."

"Mmp—I recognized him as soon as I saw him sitting on the floor, holding his head. He hasn't been acquainted with Daventry long, I think, but he's definitely been one of that gentleman's visitors over the last several months. This is the first I knew of his name or where he plies his trade."

"He looked familiar to me, too," rumbled Chad. "I did not recall until today that he's the same footman who approached Liza with a note from Giles the day she took me into her study to see the pendant. He had an excellent view of the open cupboard and the box from which Liza had just taken the thing."

"He was no doubt in Daventry's employ then," said Jem.

"But Daventry didn't know Liza had the pendant then. Why should he perceive a need to keep an accomplice in Liza's house?"

"Simply to keep tabs on her, I suppose. To be apprised of her social schedule so that he could appear at the same events. To be made aware of who she sees on a regular basis, thus sniffing out any potential rivals."

Chad's only response was an unintelligible growl.

"I have become acquainted with the under-housemaid in the lady's household," interposed Ravi Chand from his corner, "a charming young woman. She tells me that the servants in her household have been expecting what she terms 'an interesting announcement' for these many months. For, she says, the Daventry proposes marriage to her on such a regular basis that he has become somewhat of a joke belowstairs. It seems," he added meditatively, "the Lady Burnsall promotes the match."

Chad ran strong, square fingers through his hair. "Yes, he has them all gudgeoned into thinking he's eminently eligible—the family property up north, and all that. Good God, what if she decides to accept him?" The words caused such a wrenching of his insides that he nearly grunted.

Jem flung himself into an emerald-striped satin armchair by the fire. "Seems as though if she had a *tendre* for him, she'd have accepted him long before now. He's evidently been sniffing after her ever since you left England. On the other hand"—he shot a glance at Chad from under lowered lashes—"perhaps she has her own reasons for keeping him at bay. Him and all the other bucks who've been pursuing her."

Chad caught the glance and returned it sardonically. "You do keep up, don't you, young January?"

"I does me 'umble best, Guv'nor." Jem stood again. "Getting back to the Queen's Pendant. I think we can be fairly sure that it was Stebbins who opened the door for a second accomplice—not Mr. Precious Daventry, of course. He was probably establishing an alibi at White's. I shouldn't be surprised if it were Gyp Mahoney. He has the skill, and as I told you before, it wouldn't have been the first time Daventry's used him for a bit of dirty work." Jem chuckled. "I wonder if Stebbins realized he was going to end up with quite such a lump on the head in order to make the whole thing look realistic."

"But how are we going to prove all this?"

"Perhaps I could arrange a quiet conversation with this Stebbins," said Ravi Chand softly.

Jem chuckled. "I'm sure that after a minute in your company, he'd confess to any crime you'd care to name. That would do us little good, however. He could finger Daventry and catalogue his crimes, but men of Daventry's sort," he continued bitterly, "are adept at turning blame aside. A word to a friend in high places, a guinea or two slipped into the right hand, and such accusations without proof are as snowflakes falling on hot embers." He turned to Chad. "You're going to have to catch him with the goods on his person. Or at least, in his house."

Chad sighed heavily. "And how are we to accomplish that?" His eyes flicked to Ravi Chand, who was clearing his throat purposefully. "No, I have every faith in your ability as a housebreaker, but I hope it won't come to that. Besides, it might only bring danger upon yourself. Giles Daventry appears to have a veritable army of thugs and cutthroats upon whom he can call, and I should imagine he takes care to prevent unauthorized visitors from entering his house."

"I may be able to help," said Jem, after some meditation. "I have a little plan in mind . . ." He stood, smiling. "More of that later, when I have something solid to contribute. Meanwhile"—he turned to Ravi Chand—"shouldn't you be stirring something in the kitchen?"

Ravi Chand answered with great dignity. "All is in readiness. My master's guests will feast royally this evening."

"What about us slaveys belowstairs. Don't we get a taste?"

Ravi Chand did not deign to reply, but swept from the room, allowing the glint in his eye to answer for him.

Jem chuckled. "Are you sure you know what you're letting your guests into?" he asked.

"I have been promising Sir Wilfred and Lady Bascombe a taste of Ravi Chand's cooking since they arrived. I don't know if the Rushlake ladies have ever been treated to an Indian meal before. If not, it should prove an educational experience for them."

"I tried a curry once. Near took the top of my head off."

"And from that, I'm sure you learned the valuable lesson that Indian food must be approached with caution."

"And with a large jug of something very cold and wet in one's hand. Now, esteemed master, it is time for you to dress. Shall I prepare your fireproof cravat?"

When Chad's guests arrived, an hour or so later, his house was redolent with exotic, spicy scents. Charity sniffed appreciatively as she and her mother and her sister, accompanied by Sir George, were shown into the drawing room.

"Mmm," she said, laughing. "What a wonderful idea this is, Chad. I can't wait to sit down at table!"

"You have a treat in store for you, my lady," boomed Sir Wilfred genially. "Ravi Chand is a master of the cookery of most Indian provinces, among a great many other things."

"I hope," interposed Sir George, that he's prepared a good curry. Haven't had one since I left Bengal."

When the group finally entered Chad's dining room, they were not disappointed. Ravi Chand presided over a dazzling assortment of dishes, each of which was proffered in turn.

"Mmm, what is this wonderful creation?" asked Lady Burnsall, waving her fork delicately in the air.

"It is called *rhogan josh,* Memsahib," replied Ravi Chand, his dark face glowing with satisfaction. "It is a Kashmir specialty, made from lamb and a *garam masala,* a special blend of spices that includes cardamom and coriander among other good things."

"Gracious!" she exclaimed. "However did you find cardamom and coriander in London?"

"It is surprising what one can obtain in this vast city, if one knows where to look." Ravi Chand cast a modest look at his shoes.

Chad glanced surreptitiously at Liza, seated near the other end of the table. She had been cordial enough so far this evening, but he placed no reliance on her continued smiles, particularly when he was about to impart to her a news item that would no doubt send her ceilingward.

Charity cleared her throat self-consciously. "John Weston came to see us yesterday," she said to Chad.

Good Lord, the chit must have been reading his mind. Liza's face took on an expression of startled disapproval. She opened her mouth to remonstrate with her sister, but Charity pressed on.

"He had some good news to impart. Someone"—she shot a darkling look at Liza— "has offered him a position based on what he has done."

Sir Wilfred and Lady Bascombe, not being acquainted with John Weston, seemed puzzled at the turn the conversation had taken. Sir George, in Lady Burnsall's confidence, harrumphed into his napkin. Liza's lips tightened in irritation.

"I hardly think—" she began, but was halted by Chad's voice.

"As a matter of fact," he said in a voice of great calm, "I have not had the opportunity to tell you before now, but it was I who offered Mr. Weston the position of estate manager on my place in Northumberland."

He returned to his plate, apparently oblivious of Liza's expression of outraged shock.

"You did what?" she gasped.

"I have been following John's progress for some time, and the young man has a truly remarkable aptitude for his work. I have heard glowing reports of him from several members of the Agricultural Society, and I feel he will be of inestimable value to me."

"Oh, Chad," breathed Charity. Then a stricken look crossed her features. "Oh Chad," she said again, "I have something I must tell you."

"But not now, I think," interrupted Lady Burnsall sharply. She sent a look whose well-bred but unmistakable message was absorbed immediately by her daughters. Charity immediately dropped her gaze to her dinner, while Liza continued to stare in silent, burning reproach at Chad.

"What do you think of Boney's latest escapade?" Sir Wilfred asked in a loud voice. "Have you heard that he is nearing the Belgian border?"

"I don't understand," said Lady Burnsall, "why no one is doing anything about that monster. Apparently he is being allowed to gobble up all the territory that was wrested from him with such suffering and bloodshed, and no one is lifting a finger to stop him."

"Plenty of time for that, my lady," Sir Wilfred answered in a comfortable rumble. "I understand Wellington will be returning to Brussels in a couple of weeks. Then we shall see how Boney larks about."

Chad shifted in his chair. "With half the Peninsular troops gone to fight in America and more sold out, Old Hookey will have the devil of a time scraping together an effective force with which to fight him."

Sir Wilfred swiveled around to gape in astonishment at the younger man. "My boy, you're surely not suggesting that Bonaparte will drive the Allies from the Continent."

"I don't think it will come to that," Chad replied seriously.

"But if the Allies do not stop their eternal bickering, it will be a very near thing."

An uncomfortable silence fell on the group, until Sir George broke the mood in his customary blunt manner. "I want to hear," he barked, "what is to become of the wager between Liza and Chad now that the pendant has been stolen. Nasty business, that," he added with a sympathetic nod to Liza. "Had a visit from a bizarre personage who claims to be a Bow Street runner."

"Oh!" Liza's eyes were wide in startlement. "I'm so sorry you were inconvenienced, Sir George. We thought it best . . ."

"Not at all. Rather enjoyed it, in fact. Never been in on a Bow Street investigation, you know. Queer lot, those fellers, but I understand they're good at what they do."

"Quite," interposed Chad. "It is for that reason that we are in hopes of recovering the pendant. The bet stands. After all, May is almost over, so there is little more than a month to go before "settling day'." He exchanged a glance with Liza that left him feeling as though he'd been shot between the eyes.

At her corner of the table Liza felt she just might burst from the emotions that raged within her. How dare Chad offer John Weston a post, thus enabling that young man to feel he could support a wife? Chad was deliberately promoting a betrothal between John and Charity when he knew that Liza vehemently opposed such a match. All this when he himself was engaged to Charity! The man's bold-faced effrontery was beyond comprehension.

Her racing thoughts stilled suddenly. Yes, altogether past understanding—for why would Chad place himself in the position of fairy godfather to a young man he barely knew? Was this his method of disentangling himself from his betrothal to Charity? Or was he simply amusing himself at the expense of the woman for whom he once proclaimed an undying devotion? Did he derive some twisted pleasure from inserting a spoke into her plans for Charity?

Liza looked up to discover that Ravi Chand was directing the removal of dishes, preparatory to the introduction of the last course. With great ceremony, he ushered in a huge platter, upon which rested a golden, cakelike dish. *"Gajar halva,"* he proclaimed. "Created from carrots and honey and coconuts, among other delicious ingredients. I think you will find it, most honored ladies and gentlemen, a celestial treat."

Chad's guests murmured suitable expressions of delight and anticipation, and at the first taste of the delicacy, declared that Ravi Chand spoke but the truth in his description.

At this point a footman entered the room and spoke quietly to Ravi Chand, who, in turn relayed the message in a whisper to Chad.

"Thomas, here?" asked Chad in surprise. He glanced around at those seated at the table. "Please excuse me for a moment. Someone has come to see me with an urgent message."

Thomas? thought Liza. Thomas Harcourt? What could he have to say to Chad that was of such importance he would travel all the way from the City at dinnertime?

It was some minutes before Chad returned to the dining room, pale-faced. "I'm sorry, but I'm afraid I must leave you all. I have had some very bad news. The mine—that is, I own a mine in Wiltshire, near a village called Hedgemoor. There has been a cave-in. I do not yet know the fate of the workers there, nor any other details. My man is packing for me, and I have ordered my traveling coach brought around. "His questioning gaze traveled to his house guests. "Sir Wilfred and his lady, will, I'm sure, act as my host and hostess for the remainder of the evening."

Amid a chorus of startled condolences, he strode from the room. He paused abruptly as he reached the door. "Liza?" he asked hesitantly, "may I have a word with you before I go?"

Her concern for this latest catastrophe to befall Chad warred with the deep anger that still seethed within her, but almost without volition, she moved toward him.

In the hall Chad took her hand. "I meant to corner you later this evening for a longish discussion of Charity and John and this ridiculous betrothal, but now it seems I shall not have the chance. Please, just let me say that, although I did it to facilitate John's suit with Charity, I meant no hurt to you in offering him a position. I know when you've had time to reflect more, er, even-mindedly on the subject, you'll realize that those two youngsters truly love one another. Charity cannot marry happily elsewhere. And, after all, it is her happiness that you seek, do you not? She will not find it in a title or in a secure position in the *ton*, any more than you have."

For a moment, his green gaze sank into hers. He bent and brushed her cheek lightly with his lips, then turned to greet Jem, who was hurrying down the stairs with a bulging valise.

"No," he said in answer to a question from the valet. "I'm sure you've thought of everything. If not, I'll stop and buy whatever is not at hand."

The next moment he was gone, valise, Jem, and all, and Liza was left standing in the center of the hall, her hand pressed to her cheek.

Chapter 17

IN the days that followed Chad's departure from Berkeley Square, Liza told herself that, though she was, of course, concerned over the disaster at his mine, she did not miss him. She had not known that he owned a mine. Not that there was any reason for him to tell her, but she wondered what other enterprises he was involved in that she knew nothing about.

As she went about her daily routine, Chad's image lodged squarely and firmly in the back of her mind, only too ready to take center stage when she was not actively thinking of something else. Green eyes laughed at her from the oddest places—tea cups and windowpanes and books taken to bed late at night to help one go to sleep. A russet reflection caught in candlelight or a patch of sunshine lying on fine leather sent her thoughts flying to him.

She upbraided herself for her schoolgirl preoccupation. It wasn't as though she had not enough on her mind. Despite the theft of the pendant, she was still determined to win the wager with Chad. She was unaware of Chad's progress, but was satisfied with her own. Nathan Rothschild's advice had proved to be perspicacious, indeed. She had bought several parcels of land outside the little village of Tittlesfield, and had sold them a month later to Horace Pelham for several times the price she had paid for them.

A pleased smile curved Liza's lips as her carriage brought her home from yet another appointment with Thomas. The other investments made with her initial thousand pounds had proved fruitful as well, and as the last weeks of the allotted time fell away, Liza permitted herself a certain confidence in her chances of winning the wager.

And then what? She would have Brightsprings and a pendant she no longer owned—although Chad seemed oddly confident that the jewel would come back to her.

She shook herself briskly. There was a hint of relief in the sigh she expelled as she raised her eyes to discover that her carriage had turned into Berkeley Square. She was much too busy today to consider the problem of the pendant.

She entered her home to find Charity, gowned in a becoming robe of French cambric, waiting for her in the morning parlor. Oh, dear, thought Liza, observing her sister's determined expression and the foot that tapped none too gently beneath a swaying hem of scalloped blond lace.

"Liza," began Charity without preamble, "it has been five days since John was here to ask for my hand, and you have not only refused to see him when he has come to call, but you haven't even had the courtesy to discuss the situation with me."

"I am truly sorry, dearest. I have been . . :"

". . . very busy. Yes, I know. But, you have come home at last, and neither of us, as far as I am aware have any engagements for the rest of the day."

Liza sank down on a settee, and motioned Charity to sit beside her. "You are right," said Liza at last. "I have been avoiding you. Oh, Charity," she continued impulsively, "you know Mama and I have only your best interests at heart."

"I know that, and I appreciate your concern. But, Liza, you have been running things for me all my life. Mama has always deferred to your judgment in everything—even when you were in your teens—perhaps because you are so like Papa—but I have no intention of doing so."

Charity rose and paced the carpet. "My wish to marry John is not a whim, you know. I know my own heart, and . . . and he fills every square inch of it." She stopped directly in front of Liza, her face very pale. "I do not say this to wound you, Liza, nor do I say it to threaten you, but I tell you now, that if you continue to withhold permission for us to wed, we will elope."

"Charity! You would not! You would be ruined."

Charity's mouth curved in a smile that was oddly mature in her piquant little face. "I suppose you're right. But, living in the wilds of Northumberland, I don't suppose I'd notice."

For one of the few times in her life, Liza felt completely at a loss. The brilliant future she had envisioned for her little sister was turning to coal dust before her eyes. Why could not Charity see that a splendid marriage awaited her? Wed to the Viscount Wellbourne, she could become a leader of the *ton*, cherished and secure for the rest of her life.

"What is it that you see in John?" she asked in bewilderment.

Charity paused a moment before answering. "I think it starts with his goodness—and his sincerity. I like his determination, and his intelligence—and his modesty. He's so different from the shallow men I meet at the parties and balls. While I could never be accused of being a bluestocking, I like conversing with him about something other than the cut of his coat, or the hunts he has been with, or how much he won or lost at the tables last night. You know," she concluded, "he reminds me a little of Father."

"Father!" was Liza's startled reply. "Why, Father was one of the most urbane men I've ever known."

"That's true, but when he was in the country . . . I remember him in boots and breeches striding over the land, first at Brightsprings, and later at Chale. He was vitally interested in the productivity of his acres, and he was not too proud to seek the advice of his tenants."

"Yes, that's true, but . . ."

"As for all the wonderful things you have planned for me, Liza—balls and jewels and gowns and the rest—have you never realized that I don't need those things in order to be happy? Have you thought about my having children with a man I don't love? I want to have John's babies!" She ended with a wail.

Liza gazed at her sister, dumbstruck. Her thoughts went back to the words Chad had spoken to her before he left for Wincombe. What if her father had insisted that *she* marry some fashionable fop? Would she have been content with a life of pampered confinement?

She put out a hand to Charity. "My dear," she said softly, "in wanting only your happiness, I never wished to shut you up in a little mold of my own making. I am sorry if I appeared to be doing just that." She smiled at the expression of dawning hope on Charity's features. "On the other hand"—dawn suffered a setback—"you are very young. Are you so sure that your heart has spoken to you in truth?"

Charity's eyes answered for her.

Liza sighed. "Then, you have my blessing, dearest sister. I shall speak to Mama. Oof!" She gasped under the weight of Charity's ecstatic swoop and the jubilant embrace that followed. Liza responded with enthusiasm, but continued in a cautionary tone. "Chad has told me that you may consider yourself released from your betrothal to him, so that aspect of your situation may be resolved with one more announcement in the *Morning Post*. However, I'm not sure you should jump into another formal betrothal right away. It might"—she lifted a hand against Charity's hot rebuttal—"it might be possible to do so if the date for the wedding were set some months in the future. Would you object to a long engagement?"

Charity's face puckered. "Oh, Liza, I don't . . ."

"Perhaps you should talk this over with John," said Liza diplomatically. "And I shall speak to Mama. Then, we can all get together again to sort things out."

"Oh, yes," breathed Charity, the incandescence of her happiness once more shining from every curve of her face. "Oh, Liza, thank you. You are the best of sisters!"

"Yes, I know," replied Liza in amusement. "No, no do not say more. You need not elevate me to sainthood."

Charity bounced to her feet. "I must send a note to John," she trilled. "Perhaps—that is, do you suppose he could come to dinner this evening?"

"I think that would be lovely." Liza laughed aloud as Charity, blowing a kiss, spun about and darted from the room.

Liza listened to the echo of her laughter, a curious sadness settling in her heart. There had been a time when she, too, had glowed with the wonder of first love. Her feet had danced along a petal-strewn path of romantic fantasy. She desperately hoped that Charity would find happiness in her love, instead of the bitterness of rejection that had been her own lot.

Now Chad had returned to take up residence in her life once more. She wished . . .

She wished she didn't miss him so much. And she wished she did not so often feel the sting of unshed tears at the back of her throat when she thought of him. She rose abruptly and hurried from the room. She spent the rest of the time before dinner in profitless surmise as to whether Chad might return to town on the morrow.

John Weston presented himself at Rushlake House shortly before dinner. Liza was on hand to greet him, and when he bowed over her hand, it seemed to her that the young man, behind his very proper demeanor, fairly leaked rays of light, like the beams shining from the cracks of a door closed on a chamber blazing with candles.

Liza had apprised her mother of the change in her attitude toward her sister's betrothal plans, and that lady, always happier in an environment free from strife, smiled sentimentally from her chair at the foot of the table. Liza was pleased for the young couple, but found their haze of happiness rather trying.

Chad did not return the next day, nor, from the level of activity displayed by his house staff, was he expected soon. Nonetheless, when Liza made her entrance into the ballroom at Brentings House the next evening, she flushed in annoyance when she found herself scanning the room for him.

No one watching her, however, would have suspected that she was not in radiant spirits. Afloat in a ravishing confection of apricot satin under a tunic of spangled spider gauze, she laughed and she flirted and she stunned more than one hopeful sprig of the *ton* with her sparkling wit and brilliant beauty. She danced twice with Reggie Hopgood, and allowed Sir George Tomblinson to take her into dinner. Lord Cromarty brought her champagne.

Giles was in attendance, of course. When she caught a glimpse of his silver head bent over the hand of a blushing young deb, she turned away in a conscious effort to avoid him. Later, however, she caught him gazing at her with such an air of despondency that she relented. She was pleased that during the course of the boulanger she granted him, his conversation was brightly unexceptionable. He amused her, as he always had, with tidbits of gossip and the latest *bon mots*. He said nothing that could be construed as personal. By the time he bowed over her hand and saw her into the arms of her next partner, Liza felt herself on a comfortable footing again. After that Giles disappeared into the card room, and did not emerge for the rest of the evening.

Later she found herself standing in conversation with Sir Wilfred and Lady Bascombe.

"Tomorrow?" Liza asked in surprise. "I did not know you planned to abandon us so soon. Where do you go from here?"

"To visit our son and his family in Surrey," replied Lady Bascombe. "We'll stay there a month, and then go to our daughter in Somerset, where we shall admire the granddaughter we have not yet seen."

"After that," interposed Sir Wilfred, "we'll be hopscotching about the country with flying visits to other family and friends. Then back here to London to sponge off Chad once more."

"Nonsense," Liza responded with a laugh. "You know Chad was tickled to death to have you here. He will be disappointed when he returns and finds you gone."

Lady Bascombe's face clouded. "Poor boy. I pray no one lost their lives in the collapse of his mine, but I suppose that is a false hope."

Liza gazed about her at the jeweled throng of dancers. "This seems like another world, does it not?" she murmured. "How can we live so heedlessly amid such wretchedness in so many other corners of our world."

"What somber sentiments on such a festive evening!"

Liza turned to find Chad's friend, Lord Whissenham, at her elbow. "My dance, I believe," he continued as the orchestra began a lively country dance.

"Oh, Jamie. I really do not feel like dancing just now," she said, smiling. "Perhaps we could just sit for a moment. Would that be all right?" She gestured to one of the rout benches lining the ballroom wall.

"Absolutely," he replied with a sweeping bow.

As they moved slowly away from the dance floor, Liza nodded in greeting to Caroline Poole, who was gliding round the floor in the arms of a gentleman known as a certified rake. Caroline's high laugh could be heard as they whirled out of sight.

"Doesn't seem to be missing Chad much, does she?" remarked Jamie contemptuously.

Liza glanced at him, startled. As he settled her onto the rout bench, and took a seat behind her, she began pleating the gauze of her tunic. "Are things quite settled in that quarter, then?" she asked casually.

Jamie's bark of laughter sounded loud in her ears. "Good Lord, no! At least, not as far as anyone knows. It's just that she's such a picture of devotion to him when they're together."

He looked away, and a frown spread across his features. Liza lifted her brows questioningly.

"Have you any news of your pendant?" he asked abruptly.

"No, but Chad seems to think . . ."

"Have you any idea when he will be returning to London?"

She stiffened. "Chad does not consult me on his movements, Jamie. We are not . . ."

"I'm sorry, Liza. It's just that—we've been hearing things—some of them dashed odd."

Liza stilled. "What sort of odd things?"

Jamie squirmed uncomfortably. "That Chad . . . that he's . . ."

"Suspected of having stolen the Queen's Pendant?"

"So you've heard the rumors, too." Jamie expelled a long breath. "Yes, that and more. That Chad is facing financial ruin because he's overextended himself and now, with the disasters that have befallen him . . ."

"And," finished Liza in a voice of dangerous calm, "his desperate straits give him the perfect motive for purloining a valuable jewel from the home of a friend."

"That about sums it up." Jamie nodded his head in glum agreement. "God, Liza, I can't believe this is all starting again."

"Nor I." She swung to him. "You know, Jamie, when he was driven from the country before—because of the rumors— I thought it was one of those inexplicable workings of fate. But now . . . now, I'm beginning to wonder if he is not the victim of some diabolical plot." She smiled painfully. "How melodramatic that sounds."

Jamie shot her a sharp glance. "Perhaps, but I and some of his other friends have been wondering the same thing. Have you anyone in mind?"

"No, of course not. I cannot imagine anyone hating Chad enough to want to ruin him. And I don't know anyone wicked enough to do so." She shook her head. "Perhaps we are talking nonsense. Things like that don't happen outside the covers of novels from the Minerva Press, after all."

Jamie gave her a long look, but said nothing more. In a few moments he returned her to the dance floor, where she was engaged to Ceddie Packwood for a waltz. Ceddie, a young gentleman of serious mien, was full of the subject that was on nearly everyone's lips that evening, Napoleon.

"They say he will soon be ready to march into Belgium. And nothing is being done to stop him. My word, here we are, well into June, and those idiots in Brussels do nothing!"

"There, there, Ceddie," she replied soothingly. "I'm sure the duke has everything well in hand. He has his own problems, you know. I hear he is still trying to draw troops together. Not an easy task, with so many of his Peninsular force gone to fight in America, and more sold out."

"Well, he shouldn't be allowing Bonaparte to frolic all over France, gathering troops as he goes."

"I'm sure you're right, Ceddie, but the music has stopped. Perhaps we might retire to the refreshment room."

Ceddie, flushing to the roots of his hair, profusely begged her pardon and steered her carefully to the chamber adjoining the ballroom, where he procured her a lemonade, proffering it in a worshipful fashion.

The rest of the evening proceeded uneventfully, but her thoughts returned again and again to the conversation with Lord Whissenham. Chad, a victim of someone's spite? No, worse than spite. If what had taken place so long ago, and was happening again now—the undermining of his character, his morals, even his very life—were deliberate, it was an act of wickedness, and of malice so virulent as to border on the criminal.

It was late when Selkirk let her into the house, and she rubbed the spot at the base of her neck where a throbbing ache had begun some hours ago. She prepared to ascend the steps to her room, when her mother's voice reached her from the drawing room.

"Liza? Have you a moment, dear?"

Something in her voice caused Liza to halt with one foot on the staircase.

"Why, Mama, whatever are you doing up at this hour?"

"George just left a few moments ago." She smiled dreamily and beckoned her daughter into the room.

"He asked me to marry him," she said when they were seated in chairs near the fireplace.

"Is that all? Mama, he has been asking you to marry him on a regular basis for a year and a half."

"Yes, but this evening I accepted him."

"Oh, Mama!" was all Liza could say. Then, she jumped up impulsively and dropped to the floor at her mother's knees. "I am so happy for you."

"Are you, dear? I'm glad. I know you like George, but I didn't know how you would feel about having him for your papa-in-law. It isn't," she continued hesitantly. "It is not like it was with your father—nothing ever could be, but George is so . . ."

"Precisely, Mama." Liza squeezed Letitia's hands. "George will make a wonderful life's companion for you, and I wish you both every joy."

Letitia returned the pressure of her daughter's fingers.

"Thank you, Liza. That means a great deal to me. I should hate to live my life alone, you know. I am not a very self-sufficient person. With Charity getting married soon, and you, perhaps as well, eventually . . . Now, that is a possibility," she went on, as Liza lifted a hand in negation. "With Chad having returned to . . ."

"No, Mama," said Liza, rising swiftly. "There is nothing between Chad and me, nor is there any possibility that we will resume the relationship that died six years ago."

"Oh, my dear," replied Lady Burnsall, distressed. "I did not mean . . . Well, perhaps Giles then."

Liza's smile was grim. "I think not, Mama." She forced her expression to a lighter aspect. "Anyway, we are not speaking of me, here. Tell me, have you and Sir George set a date?"

Letitia laughed, her good humor restored. "We have decided to wait until after Charity and John are married. After that . . ."

The two women continued in companionable conversation for some minutes, but at last, good nights were said and each repaired to her bedchamber.

Liza's reflections were bittersweet. She was overjoyed for her mother's happiness, but what about herself? She was sure she would be welcome in Letitia's new household, but she had no wish to play gooseberry to a pair of elderly newlyweds.

It was in some despondency that she allowed her maid to disrobe her and remove the jewelry from her person. Dismissing Prescott, she sat at her dressing table and picked up her hair brush. She brought her hand up and dealt her hair only a few listless strokes before her attention was caught by the sound of masculine laughter.

She swung in the direction of her open window and saw, reflected on the trees outside, light from a room in the house next door. Now she could clearly distinguish the owner of the voice, although the words were unintelligible.

Flinging down her brush, she ran to the window, where she stared into the darkness while she listened helplessly to the thudding of her heart.

Chad was home!

Chapter 18

"I, CHADWICK LOCKRIDGE, do therefore, take thee, Lady Charity Rushlake as my true neighbor and friend from this day forth."

Chad, standing in the center of the drawing room at Rushlake House, bent over Charity's hand and pressed a ceremonious and very noisy kiss on her hand.

"Oh, Chad." Charity giggled. "You are so absurd." Then, she tightened her fingers on his, and her demeanor grew serious. "And you are such a darling man."

"Spare my blushes, you heedless wench," replied Chad, his buccaneer's grin at its most pronounced. "You have already spurned my affection; pray do not compound your cruelty with impudence."

He returned Charity to her seat in a wing chair of straw satin, and lowered himself onto a matching settee next to Lady Burnsall. She beamed on the pair and said to Liza, who was curled on a nearby ottoman, "Now, everything is made right."

Liza smiled a trifle rigidly and said nothing. She had been a little surprised when Chad presented himself on their doorstep only an hour or so after breakfast. He had come, he said, to formally end his betrothal to Charity. Liza's heart had lurched at the sight of him, the morning sun turning that rust-colored head to a blaze of burnished copper.

Within a few minutes he had gracefully relinquished Charity's hand and wished her well in her new, and permanent relationship. Liza's artificial smile faded, and she admonished herself for her less-than-delighted response to this satisfactory conclusion. She was happy, of course, that Charity and Chad were no longer embroiled in a loveless entanglement. And she was tentatively pleased that Charity was to be united in the not-too-distant future to her true love.

But what of her own future? Within a year Charity would be

gone, immersed in rural domesticity in the wilds of Northumberland. Her mother would leave soon afterward to take up residence with her new husband. Liza felt strangely abandoned, and unexpectedly reluctant to face the thought of living alone. She had no doubt of her ability to find a widow or a spinster among her many aunts and cousins to act as her companion, but . . . it would not be the same. She uttered a small sigh and glanced up to find Chad's quizzical gaze on her.

Lord, she was beautiful, Chad thought helplessly to himself. Her lithe body, curved with animal grace on the ottoman, seemed made to fit against his own. His fists formed into knots. Would he ever be able to look at her without wanting to gather her into his arms? Despite his best efforts, he had missed her damnably in the week he had spent in Hedgemoor. He was more than ever determined not to succumb to her charm, for with the rumor machine grinding once more into gear, he was sure that at some point she would turn away from him again. Still, he had hoped for a warmer welcome this morning than the one she offered him. Her mood was extraordinarily pensive, her blue eyes taking on the color of a midnight sky as her gaze seemed to turn inward.

"What?" he asked blankly in response to Charity's question. "The mine? Oh. No, the damage was rather extensive, but not nearly so bad as it might have been. The explosion occurred between shifts, when the day workers were gone and the night workers were just on the way down to replace them."

"But what caused the explosion?" asked Liza. "Surely you maintain strict safety standards in your mine."

He shot her a swift glance. "Yes, I do. As it happens, this particular disaster was arranged."

"No!" gasped Lady Burnsall. "Who would do such a thing? And why?"

"Apparently any number of people would do such a thing for a great deal of money. We were fortunate in that a stranger was spotted in the vicinity of the mine shortly before the explosion, whose description matches a certain felon actively being sought by the authorities for other crimes. His name is Gyp Mahoney."

Liza, suddenly alert, turned to face Chad squarely. "You mean someone was paid to destroy your mine? Good Heavens, hundreds of people might have been killed!"

"Yes," replied Chad in a flat tone. He watched her closely.

"Was the destruction extensive?" Liza asked tentatively. "Will the loss incurred . . . that is . . ."

Chad shook his head. "The loss is negligible—the mill was insured, after all—but the explosion will cause a problem, nevertheless. Production will be halted for some months, and even worse, coupled with the destruction of my silk mill by fire, the impression will be created that I am jinxed, that my enterprises are doomed to failure."

"Oh, that's silly," said Charity.

"Even if that were true, dear boy," chimed in Lady Burnsall, "what difference does it make to you what a parcel of busybodies thinks?"

The two ladies chuckled, but Liza did not join in their amusement.

"It could make a great deal of difference, Mama," she said slowly, her eyes locked with Chad's. "Successful entrepreneurs with money to invest will avoid a seemingly unsuccessful one like the plague. Orders for his goods will dry up if he is considered unreliable, and he will have difficulty hiring skilled employees because they will consider their jobs at risk."

"Oh," said Charity and Lady Burnsall in unison, their eyes round and disturbed.

"And now," continued Liza, "with rumors rampant of . . . oh!"

Her own eyes grew wide in dismay at what she had almost revealed, and she clamped her lips shut.

"And now," Chad finished for her, "with the tale running all over London that I purloined Liza's pendant, my reputation has slipped several notches lower than river muck."

He seemed oddly cheerful as he related these doleful tidings, and Liza eyed him in some puzzlement. He rose from the settee, declaring that, after his week-long absence, he had much to see to at home.

Liza accompanied him into the entry hall, and before allowing Selkirk to see him from the house, he paused to take Liza's hand in his own.

"About the pendant—" he began, but Liza interrupted hurriedly.

"It is not as bad as it sounds, Chad. It is only the same small group of small-minded persons who persist in braying your supposed perfidy about the city."

"Yes," he said, musing aloud. "I believe it to be a very small group indeed, but one that is extraordinarily vociferous." He raised his eyes to Liza's, and something leaped into his gaze that made her suddenly breathless. He made as though to bring her fingers to his lips, but he halted abruptly, and in the next instant, a profound change spread over his features, and he released her hand. "I suppose I should be grateful," he said coolly, "that, so far at least, you are not among their number."

"Chad! As if I would—"

"But why wouldn't you?" His green eyes had taken on their cold, bottle-bottom aspect. "I am, after all, the logical target of all the finger pointing. The last time the rumor-mongers sang their wretched song of my alleged misdoings, you eventually joined their ranks."

Liza whitened, but the blazing retort that sprang to her lips was stilled by the presence of Selkirk. Indeed, Chad had turned on his heel and was gone before she could form a coherent reply. For a moment she stood as though paralyzed, then, instead of returning to the drawing room to rejoin her mother and sister, she fled up the stairs to her room, where she sank down on her bed.

She felt bruised by his words. He might as well have kicked her. How could she have been so stupid as to believe that his feelings for her had warmed? Her childish bid for his attention during that long ago quarrel had been misinterpreted by him, and he would never trust her again. Apparently there was nothing she could do to prove to him that her faith in him had never wavered.

On the other hand, she thought furiously, why should she have to prove herself to him? How could he have thought for an instant that she would forsake him? Or perhaps—and the thought chilled her—he had no desire to rekindle the passionate blaze that had been their first love. He had kissed her, to be sure, but he had made it abundantly clear that his embrace had not been bestowed out of love. "A thorn in his flesh," indeed. Not to mention an old, bad habit. Well, it all meant nothing to her. For if he had repudiated all that had been between them, she had certainly done so as well. Why, until he had turned up on her doorstep three months ago, she had virtually forgotten his existence.

She moved to her window and gazed disconsolately out at the Square, where the June sun cast a Spanish mantilla of dappled lace over the scene. Even if that were true, she reflected, which she was obliged to admit in her heart of hearts it was not, he had, with practically no effort, recaptured the piece of her soul he had claimed in the fragile awakening of her first love. God help her, she was wholly and irretrievably in love with Chad Lockridge.

She felt tears gather as the hopelessness of her situation rose to engulf her. Chad might be attracted to her physically, and Lord knew she wanted him on that level, as well. But the essence of her desire was based on a wanting to share his life—the good times and the bad, the laughter and the pain. And children. She wanted his children. Dear Lord, how she wanted him, all of him.

She slumped against her pillows, but after a few moments she stiffened. Just what was she going to do about it? Dog his steps like a hound out of favor, waiting for a pat on the head? She rather thought not! Make an attempt to snare him with her wiles? She had been told often enough that she was lovely. She turned to view herself in her looking glass. And charming. And witty and intelligent. She sighed. Chad had seen her more than once at her brilliant, beautiful best and had not been impressed.

With a despairing shrug she turned away from the mirror. So be it. She had lived without love for some years now, and could continue doing so. She dashed the tears that threatened to spill from her eyes. She had not cried for Chad Lockridge— or anyone or anything else for six years, and she was damned if she would start repining now. Her life was busy and full, and she had no time for repining over a latter-day pirate with green eyes and brandy-colored hair, and a physique that made her go weak from the neck down. She had urgent matters with which to deal. Projects to oversee. Important undertakings to manage.

Straightening her shoulders, she strode from her room and descended to her study, from whence she was seen no more that morning.

Next door another battle briefing was underway in Chad's study. Ravi Chand was absent, having been called on to settle a minor dispute among the kitchen staff, but Jem, who had accompanied Chad to Hedgemoor, reposed in his usual chair, frayed notebook at the ready.

"Yes, indeed," agreed Jem cheerfully. "Mahoney should not be difficult to apprehend, and when that occurs, he will very

probably sing long and loud about his cozy relationship with
Daventry. If all goes well, we'll have no trouble prosecuting
them both—not only for the mine explosion, but the fire at the
mill as well. To say nothing of the attack on you near Mervale
House."

"And as for the pendant?"

A smile spread over Jem's features. "Ah, yes. I've been
meaning to talk to you about that. I received an interesting
morsel of information late last night. I believe we now have
some promising options to discuss in that direction."

"Aside from allowing Ravi Chand to threaten him with dis-
memberment—which certainly has its appeal—I fail to see
how we're going to connect him with that particular crime.
But proceed. I am all ears."

"That's just the point. I've been all ears, too, and I have had
someone very worthwhile to listen to."

He grinned at the question in Chad's eyes. "I was so impressed with the parade of informers streaming into Daventry's lodgings, that I took a leaf from his book."

His smile widened as comprehension dawned on his master's face. "Yes, some weeks ago I managed to install my own,
er, ally in his household. He serves as a footman, but he has
many other interesting accomplishments, as well. So"—he
rose and bent from the waist in a courtier's bow—"it is with
great pleasure that I inform you that Daventry not only has the
pendant in his possession, but its precise location is known to
us."

Chad, too, leaped to his feet. "My God, Jem! Are you serious?"

"Never more so. We can scoop the thing in as soon as you
say the word."

"No, no—that won't do. It has to be uncovered in the presence of the Runners."

"Nothing simpler. Just notify—what's the name of that
Robin Red Breast?—Thurgood, I think. You can fetch along
Stogumber—that's my inside man—to the magistrate's office,
and with his testimony, you'll have authorization to hurry over
to Daventry's lodgings in Arlington Street and nab the goods."

"My God," breathed Chad. "I can't believe Giles Daventry
is within my grasp at last."

Jem made a sound low in his throat. "And mine."

Chad glanced at him curiously. "Just what is your interest in Daventry, Jem?"

"Perhaps I'll tell you when all this is over. Right now, however"—he rose and stretched his long limbs—"I'd better set a few things in motion. You could do the deed tonight, if you wish."

"No," said Chad sharply. "I do not want to be involved in his capture and arrest." He frowned at Jem's look of puzzlement. "I do not wish to be seen as the instrument of his destruction. At least, not until . . ." He fell silent.

"The Lady Liza is reputed to be quite fond of Giles Daventry."

Chad's tone was frigid. "That is none of your concern."

"Righty-o, yer worship," was Jem's cheerful response. Then, his expression clouded. "But, if you're not going to go to the Runners, who is?" He stared at Chad in dawning suspicion, as that gentleman smiled quietly at him. "Oh no, not Yours Truly. I'm not on what you'd call friendly terms with the people at Bow Street, and I don't want to—"

"Then just think what a large spot of good you'll be doing yourself with them. If you help Thurgood recover the pendant, he'll fall at your feet."

Jem grumbled at some length, but at last agreed to approach the Runner.

"When?" he asked, as though he were ascertaining the date of his own execution.

"Well, I don't believe Daventry is going anywhere, and I don't believe he'll try to sell the pendant—at least in the near future. As far as I can figure, his primary reason for stealing it was to discredit me. Besides, the pendant is well known as a work of art. He'd have a hard time selling it at the moment."

"True."

"I'd like to wait until Gyp Mahoney is apprehended, which should be any time. With the information he can provide, we'll be able to complete our dossier on his more unsavory business activities. We might as well hang him for a sheep *and* for a goat."

"I like your style, guv'nor."

With this Jem waved airily and ambled from the room. Chad shook his head as he watched him out the door, wondering at the background that had produced this extraordinary young man.

He turned back into the room, occupied with his thoughts. What would Liza's response be to Daventry's arrest for theft, and other things? He hoped with all his heart that she did not love the bastard, but even if she did, he could not let her remain unaware of his true character.

There was a good chance he would see Liza tonight. He had somehow allowed himself to be inveigled into taking Caroline to Drury Lane, where Kean was appearing in *Othello*. He sighed heavily.

He had attached himself to the admittedly toothsome Miss Poole shortly after his arrival in England with the unworthy goal of igniting a spark of jealousy in Liza's bosom. He preferred not to contemplate the motives that inspired such a strategy. He knew only that things were getting out of hand. Caroline seemed to be everywhere he turned, and it was getting more and more difficult to avoid her stratagems. It was also getting more and more difficult to listen to her inane chatter and her tuneless laughter. Were Miss Poole's affections truly involved, Chad would have considered his actions to be deplorable, but he was sure that her interest in him lay purely in his monetary worth. Thus it behooved him to take steps to disentangle himself from that beauty's tenacious clutches.

Another thought struck him. Would Liza attend the theater with Giles?

Chad rubbed his neck tiredly and turned to the pile of papers that had accumulated on his desk in his absence.

Liza did not appear with Giles that evening, but her laughing charm was very much in evidence as she chatted with her escort for the evening, the handsome and eminently eligible Lord Francis Meldrun. Charity and John sat slightly behind the couple, completely immersed in each other's company, and Lady Burnsall and Sir George completed the group.

Chad eyed Lord Francis. What did the fellow think he was about, with his arm slung across the back of Liza's chair? And what was Liza thinking of to appear in a public place in that disgraceful décolletage? The fact that the neckline of her simple gown of Italian crepe was of much more modest dimensions that many another lady gracing the theater this evening did not register with him.

"Look, Chad dearest," cooed Caroline. "Is that not Lady Weaveredge waving to you?"

Dearest? When had she taken to calling him that, he wondered, edging his finger round the top of his cravat. He bowed perfunctorily to the dowager in question.

"Are you enjoying Kean's performance?" he asked Caroline abruptly, as her hand stole up to rest on his sleeve.

"Oh, yes," she breathed, though to Chad's knowledge, her eyes had not rested on the stage for more than five minutes during the two acts that had already taken place.

"Are you enjoying Kean's performance?" asked Lord Francis, his head bent solicitously over the sculptured crown into which Liza's curls had been arranged.

"Oh yes," she replied brightly, though to tell the truth, her attention had been less than rapt during the course of the play. "I must say I agree with whoever it was who said that watching Kean act was like reading Shakespeare by lightning flashes."

Lord Francis threw his head back in appreciative laughter, and Liza clenched her teeth at the sound. Someone had evidently told him at some time in his life that he had an engaging laugh, for he loosed it at every opportunity. Tonight his hearty guffaws had given her a splitting headache. Something had, at any rate. Perhaps it was the surreptitious glances she had been casting all evening at Chad Lockridge's box.

He was certainly making a perfect cake of himself over Caroline Poole, and not two days after the termination of his betrothal with Charity. Had the man no sensitivity?

She turned her head away from the romantic scene being enacted before her—and not the one on the stage. Sir George, who made no pretense of liking Shakespeare, was engaging John Weston in a debate over Wellington's tactics in his preparations for the coming engagement with Napoleon.

Liza closed her eyes wearily and prayed for the evening to end.

The news of the coming battle was not to be so easily escaped, however, for two days later, London was brought to fever pitch by the news that Wellington's forces had met those of Napoleon at a tiny hamlet in Belgium called Ligny. The news was not good. British troops had been sighted fleeing the scene in disarray, while word of Blucher's failure at Quatre

Bras added a pall of gloom to the social activities that continued in the capital.

Then, finally, the news arrived that the whole country had feared. Wellington had confronted Napoleon near the village of Waterloo, and the unthinkable had occurred. Wellington was losing!

It was Chad who imparted these appalling tidings to Liza as, once more, they left their respective homes at the same time for appointments in the City. Once more they shared a carriage.

"I find it difficult to credit the rumors," said Chad, adding dryly, "my tolerance quotient for rumors in any form being pretty low at the moment. It seems to me that the persons who are crying the loudest about Wellington's imminent defeat are those who know the least about military matters."

"But if, as you say, the army is running—"

"I did not say that. There is talk of retreat, which as far as I know is still considered a viable strategy under the proper circumstances and does not necessarily imply a rout."

They continued their discussion until the carriage reached Thomas Harcourt's office, where Liza was handed down. She turned to Chad and said tentatively, "Perhaps this is not the time to speak of financial matters, but have you considered the effect the defeat of our forces would have on the Funds."

Chad laughed mirthlessly. "Indeed I have. Such an eventuality will produce a horrendous crash. I believe some are already selling out of the Funds."

"And you?" Liza thought of the wager and Chad's reportedly heavy investment in government securities.

"Yes, I have considered doing so. However, I believe I shall wait until more information trickles through."

"I shall do the same, I suppose. I feel such a traitor at the thought of selling, as though I were somehow betraying my country."

"Nonsense. Leaving your investment to dwindle away will not help the government. Anyway, such drastic action may not be called for."

"Dear God, I hope not," breathed Liza.

The news, however, continued discouraging throughout the day, until when Liza at last returned home late in the afternoon, tales were circulating of wholesale British slaughter. The streets of Brussels, it was said, were red with the blood of the wounded being trundled from the battle in countless wooden carts.

To her displeasure she found a visitor waiting for her in the morning room.

"Giles!" she exclaimed, forcing her voice to a cordiality she did not feel. "I did not expect to see you today."

"I had to talk to you, Liza. You have grown so distant of late . . ."

She was struck with compunction. Her smile was genuine as she interrupted gently. "I am sorry, Giles. Come, I'll have Selkirk bring us something cool, out in the garden."

She took his hand and led him from the rear of the house to the charming bower that had witnessed Chad's embrace with her. Closing her mind to that scene, she gestured Giles to the stone bench and sat down beside him.

He was carrying a small cloth sack, which he kept in his lap. How very handsome he was, thought Liza with some regret, with the sun creating a silvery halo around his head.

"My dear," he began gravely, "I am the bearer of news that is at once very good and very bad."

Liza's eyes searched his in puzzlement. She glanced at the sack.

"Yes," he said, following her gaze. "The object I hold here is the key. You see"—he drew a deep breath—"I know who took your pendant."

Chapter 19

"GILES!" cried Liza in astonished tones.

"As it happens," he continued, "I used to have in my employ a young footman by the name of Francher. I had to let him go, as my staff was becoming too large, but I recommended him to Chad Lockridge, who subsequently hired him."

Liza gestured impatiently. "What can all this have to do with . . . ?"

"Let me finish, my dear. Francher, of course, knew of the theft of your pendant, and through exhaustive discussions in the servants' quarters became familiar with every aspect of the jewel's description. Thus, when he found this"—Giles began to open the sack—"he knew immediately what it was."

With great care Giles drew from the sack a small, empty, wooden box, which he handed to Liza.

Drawing her fingers over the intricate carvings that covered the container, she gasped. "This used to hold the pendant! Where in the world—"

Again Giles interrupted her with great gentleness. "Francher stumbled over it one morning when he drew back the curtains in Chad's study. It was on the floor, tucked behind the drapes. He did not presume to go to the authorities with it himself, so he brought it to me."

Liza gazed, dumbfounded, at the little box around which her numb fingers were curled. She lifted her head to stare at her visitor. "Giles, are you saying that Chad is . . . is the thief?"

Giles's expression was one of profound sadness. "I'm afraid," he said softly, "there can be no other explanation."

"I see." Liza could scarcely speak for the conflicting emotions that raged within her, but her voice remained calm as she spoke. "I wonder why you did not bring this directly to the

Bow Street magistrate, since you seem convinced of Chad's guilt."

He seemed taken aback by her statement. "Why I . . . that is, I thought the news would be better brought to you by a friend than by a minion of the law. I know what a blow the knowledge of his perfidy must be to you."

Liza rose and paced within the confines of the little bower. "I will agree it looks suspicious, but there must be some explanation of how the box came into Chad's house. I refuse to believe he is responsible for the theft."

The change in Giles's expression of regretful sadness to blank astonishment was almost ludicrous. "Liza! You cannot delude yourself. The man is obviously guilty as sin, and the authorities must be notified."

"I agree that the magistrate must be told. But, I tell you this, Giles. Chad Lockridge, whatever his faults, is not a thief. If I were to come upon him in Bond Street with the Queen's Pendant nailed to his forehead, I would still believe in his innocence."

"Your loyalty is to be commended." His voice was flat as he spoke. "However, we shall see how you feel when Lockridge is placed under arrest for the theft." He held out his hand for the box, but she withdrew it from him.

"No, Giles. You are quite correct—the box is evidence against Chad, damning evidence. I shall see that it reaches its proper destination."

Her voice had risen as she spoke, and her words were clearly audible in the garden of the house next door, through which Chad was tramping on his way in from the stables.

He stared, openmouthed, in the direction from whence they had come.

The following day dawned to cloudy skies and an intermittent drizzle. Liza awoke heavy-eyed and unrefreshed, for she had spent the night in fruitless mental convolutions, accompanied by much pillow thumping and twitching of the bed covers. After a hurried breakfast of coffee and toast she sent a message to Chad.

"Thank you for responding so promptly," she said quietly as

she led him into the morning room. "I have something to tell you, and I don't know how to start."

"At the beginning has always worked well for me," responded Chad warily. He subjected her to a closer scrutiny. "You are, as always, a sight to brighten a rainy day, but I have seen you in better looks, my dear."

"I certainly hope so," replied Liza. The corners of her mouth turned up into a tired smile. "Last night was very long. Chad," she continued, waiting for him to be seated on a confidante near the fire, "Giles Daventry came to see me yesterday evening. He seems to believe that it was you who stole the Queen's Pendant."

Chad merely lifted his brows.

Taking a deep breath, Liza continued. "Yes, he feels that the . . . the evidence against you is considerable, and that charges against you may be brought soon."

She raised her eyes anxiously to his. To her surprise a twisted smile played about his lips.

"How very extraordinary," he said. "This evidence, is it something specific?"

The blood drained from her cheeks, but she lifted her chin. "As to that, I cannot say, but—Chad, don't you understand? Giles believes you to be guilty of stealing the pendant!"

Chad's mouth hardened. "Yes, but you see, Mr. Daventry's opinion leaves me unmoved."

"Oh, for Heaven's sake. He as much as told me that he's going to tell the Bow Street magistrate of his suspicions. Don't you understand? You could be arrested!"

Chad sighed. "You know, my dear, I believe we have had this conversation before. Would you have me race to Bow Street and announce to the world at large that I am innocent as a baby's stare. That I did not steal the pendant and I am not a thief?" He took her hand. "Don't you think it would be better to wait until I am accused of something before I charge about making ringing declarations?"

"Yes, but . . ."

"I feel there is nothing I can do at this point, my dear."

"Perhaps you could talk to Giles."

"Why? To persuade him of my innocence?" Chad frowned from beneath lowered brows. "I think not."

"Do you not know what you risk?" Her voice was ragged in her desperation. "What about those who believe you to be on the brink of ruin? They will be only too happy to hear of this latest morsel."

There was a long silence in which an emotion shimmered between them that Liza could not describe. It swirled about her with an intensity that made her feel as though she were being physically assaulted. "Chad," she cried. "He is my friend. He was only trying to spare me."

Chad stared at her. He had never known such agony of spirit. Liza had turned against him yet again. She had not even the grace to admit to him that she planned to take the wooden box to Bow Street—if she had not done so already. He wanted to grasp her by the shoulders and shake her, and tell her that he was not a thief and how could she think he was. And yet, he reflected with numbing sadness, perhaps she was not to blame—any more than she had been the last time. Could she be expected to trust him blindly when all the world branded him a thief and a scoundrel? Probably not, but dear God, he wished she had. Even now, he was conscious of a desire to take her in his arms and kiss her till she was blind.

He stiffened. No, he was damned if he would capitulate to a woman who was in the act of turning her back on him, again. One who, moreover, was apparently in love with another man. He had rid himself of his love for her before, and by God, he could do it again.

Yet, his hand raised without volition to her hair to tuck a stray tendril of gossamer gold that had escaped its confines back into place.

When he spoke, his voice was a harsh growl, at odd variance with the tenderness of his gesture. "I understand your loyalty to your . . . friend, Liza, but I must do as I think appropriate."

"Which is nothing at all."

"At the moment, yes."

Liza knew a desire to scream her frustration at him. Was he going to allow history to repeat itself? Would he let himself be driven from his home yet again, all through his stupid pride? This time it would go beyond rumor. This time he would likely find himself under a warrant of arrest and he would have to flee, literally, like a thief in the night. It was not to be borne! And, apparently, there was nothing she could do. Last time she had pled with him, to no avail. She was not in the habit of repeating her mistakes. She rose abruptly.

"Then there is no more to be said." Her voice was icy as she prepared to leave the room. She halted at the doorway. "By the by, our wager, in case it escaped your notice, will be up in less than a week. I have instructed Thomas to prepare a record of my investments. Shall we agree to meet in his office at, say, eleven o'clock on the twenty-fifth?"

Chad merely nodded as he picked up hat, gloves, and walking stick preparatory to making his exit from Liza's home. She walked silently with him to the front door, and as she stepped aside for him to pass, she glanced up at him. She intercepted a gaze of such bleak despondency that something in her twisted, and she almost put out a hand to him. She let it drop to her side, however, and, bidding him a cool farewell, she closed the door behind him.

The rest of the day limped along as dismally as the weather that accompanied it. Liza ventured into the rain for a brief trip into the City only to discover that the banks and exchanges had turned into madhouses, and she was hard put not to cover her ears against the din of frantic voices calling out sell orders and desperate announcements of more bad news from the front.

In truth after months of frivolous indifference, London was reeling with an unprecedented sense of defeat. In countless drawing rooms ladies whispered of imminent invasion by hordes of lust-crazed Frenchmen. In the clubs gentlemen gathered to shake their heads at the disaster they had foreseen all along.

The Rushlake ladies, sending regrets to a card party at which they had promised to appear, spent a quiet evening at home. John Weston, who had become a household fixture, came to call on Charity, and later in the evening, Sir George dropped by for a cozy tête-à-tête with his intended. Liza smiled to see her mother blushing like a young girl at his heartily proffered compliments.

Having little inclination to play gooseberry, she retired to her study, where, ignoring the rain that beat a cheerless rhythm against the windows, she pondered the day's events. It all seemed too much to comprehend. Chad's straits seemed so dire as to be almost beyond comprehension. The thought of his imminent arrest for theft was . . . well, unthinkable. How could he maintain such a calm facade in the teeth of such a disaster?

She did not know the extent of his financial holdings, but surely an upheaval of this sort would ruin him. With a start she considered his promise to hire John Weston at his Northumberland estate. Would he be able to hold that offer open?

And what of the wager between Chad and herself? If he were facing ruin, she was unprepared to wrest Brightsprings from him, assuming that she were to win. And how could she lose, if Chad had sunk his thousand pounds in government securities? It certainly did not speak well for his business acumen to have done so, she reflected. With the news of Wellington's defeat ringing throughout the country, Consols would be at a cataclysmically low ebb. She wondered if he had sold out of the Funds today.

She turned and addressed herself to the small pile of papers that had accumulated during recent days. It was high time, she told herself firmly, that she thrust her personal problems to the back of her mind and caught up with her business interests. In a few moments, however, her pen hovered over the papers, unguided, as her gaze lifted to stare unseeing into the dancing flames in the fireplace.

She frowned as her thoughts swung to Giles. For how many years had he been her friend? Almost since childhood. She had taken it for granted that she would always be fond of him, even when she was most irritated at his importunate proposals of marriage. She had always enjoyed his company and looked forward to their time spent together. Of late, however, she had found herself growing distant from him. She was vaguely aware that her change in feeling had something to do with Chad. For so long Giles had championed Chad in his difficulties. Now he had done a complete about-face. Yet his distrust of Chad had begun, she felt, long before his erstwhile footman had presented him with that empty box. In fact the suspicion was beginning to creep over her that Giles, despite his protestations of good will, had never been one of Chad's well-wishers. The tale of his former footman and the wooden box was, come to think of it, full of improbable coincidence.

She shivered a little, though it was not cold in the room, and turned back to her papers. She was thus occupied some hours later when she looked up in surprise to note that her working candles were guttering in their sockets. She glanced at the little ormolu clock on her desk. Good Heavens, it was nearly midnight! Charity and Lady Burnsall had popped their heads in the door hours ago to bid her good night. She laid aside her paperwork and rose, stretching.

She had just reached the hall and set her foot on the first stair when she was startled by the sound of a peremptory knock on the front door. Realizing that the servants had long since retired, she hurried to answer it. She stared in astonishment at the bulky figure that stood, dripping wet, before her.

"Why, Mr. Rothschild! Whatever are you . . . ? That is, do come in."

"Goot eefening, Lady Elizabet." Nathan Rothschild entered and shook himself like a large dog, causing a spray of water to rise in a cloud about him. "I know it iss an odd time to be payink a call, but I haf news I must impart to you."

"Certainly," she replied in great mystification. "But here, let me take your coat—and your hat."

"No, no," he protested. "I am much too vet to enter your home, chust let me—"

"Nonsense." She drew his sodden coat from his shoulders and led him into the morning parlor, seating him in a chair before the banked fire.

"May I ring for some tea for you?" she asked solicitously. "Or, perhaps a hot drink—a toddy?"

"Nein, nein—t'ank you, my dear, but my stay vill be brief." He waved a plump hand. "Sit, pleese."

Obediently she perched on the chair opposite and gazed at him expectantly.

His expression became serious. "Lady Elizabet, I must ask you to keep vat I am about to tell you in absolute confidence. No, vait . . ." He lifted a finger in admonition as she opened her mouth to assure him. "Dis is not an easy t'ing dat I ask, for I haf news to impart to you dat vill rock de City to its foundations. If you say you vill keep silent on de matter, I vill trust you, because I know you to be honorable—and discreet."

Liza's returning gaze was skeptical, but she was aware that Nathan Rothschild was not known for speaking wildly. She hesitated, then nodded solemnly.

"Very well, I give you my word that I will say nothing to anyone about what you are to tell me—unless, of course," she added with a wary smile, "it involves something criminal."

"Nein, it is nottink uf de kind." He shifted his bulk portentously. "I haf chust returned from de Continent."

"What!" gasped Liza. She could not have been more astonished if he had informed her that he had just flown down from the moon. "But, it's the middle of the night, and it's pouring rain!"

"Yes, it vass an interesting journey. My lady, I haf spent de last t'ree days in Belgium."

Liza's eyes grew even more round, but she said nothing.

"Und," he continued with a broad smile, "I am most happy to inform you dat yesterday eefening, de Duke uf Vellinkton defeated Napoleon Bonaparte near de village of Vaterloo."

Liza simply sat and let the room rock around her.

"Defeated!" she cried at last. "Napoleon? But we heard . . ."

"I know vat you heard, but I am tellink you vat is true. At about nine o'clock last night, the great emperor left his headquarters at a farmhouse south of Vaterloo and went skulking off into de night toward Paris."

"I cannot believe this!" Her great relief and joy made her voice a mere squeak of emotion. "Are you sure, Mr. Rothschild? You were really there? That is, pray forgive me, but—"

"Ja, ja, I understand. Yes, I vas dere, und I tell you, dat is vat happened. It vas a bloody business, but Vellinkton carried de day."

"But this is wonderful news! Why in the world do you wish to keep it a—oh!", she cried, in sudden comprehension.

Rothschild's eyes twinkled. "I see you haf it figured out. Haf you sold your government securities, like all de odder vitless, sky-fallink chickens in de City?"

"No, I had considered it, and probably would have tomorrow," she confessed, "but I just couldn't bring myself to do so." She laughed aloud. "Instead I shall now instruct my broker to buy all the government stock he can lay his hands on."

"Goot."

"Who else have you told of this?" she asked hesitantly.

"I haf not said a vord to anyvun but you, Lady Elizabet." He stood and moved to take her hand. "You did me a great service once, my dear lady, and Nat'an Rothschild does not forget such t'ings."

As she rose to smile in gratitude, a sudden thought struck her, and for several moments, her mind was busy with this new channel. As she accompanied the bulky financier from the room, she made up her mind, and in the hall, she turned to face him.

"Mr. Rothschild, with your permission, I would like to tell one other person of your news." She continued hurriedly as he gazed at her in consternation. "I will vouch for his discretion and his honor, and I can assure you that he will be circumspect in his dealings."

"Nein!" He shouted the word, his face darkening. "You gafe your vord!"

She laid an anxious hand on his arm.

"I know, and I will not break my promise. I told you I would speak only with your permission." She took a deep breath. "I wish to relate to Chad Lockridge what you have told me. Perhaps you have heard of him. For reasons I cannot go into, I feel—that is, I would like him to know what has happened. It's . . . it's rather a matter of honor."

"I know vat it iss!" exclaimed Rothschild. "It's dot stupid vager, is it not?"

Liza nodded in wordless astonishment. "But, how could you possibly . . . ?"

He fluttered sausagelike fingers in irritation tinged with amusement. "I am a successful man. How do you t'ink I got dat vay? I know everyt'ink!" He swept his arm in a grandiloquent gesture. "Are you tellink me he put his whole stake in de Funds? Vat a *schafkopf*! But vy should you tell him uf dis? It may vell ruin your chances uf winning de bet?" He stared at her assessingly, and a look of surprise came over his features. "So dot's how it is, is it?" He sighed heavily. "I know Meester Lockridge by reputation. He is, as you say, an honorable man.

Ferry vell, my lady, tell your young man not to sell his government bonds. Tell him, England vas fictorious at Vaterloo. But"—he wagged an admonishing hand—"no more tellink. I didn't risk my neck sloggink across the Channel on a rainy night chust to hear my information called from de housetops."

Shrugging into his coat, he plunged through the open door and into his waiting carriage.

Slowly Liza began her interrupted journey up the stairs, but halfway up, she halted. Running back down, she sought out a heavy cloak and ran out into the rain.

Chapter 20

"**B**UT this is incredible!" Chad gripped Liza's shoulders as they stood in the center of the entrance hall in his home. "Are you sure?"

"Yes!" Liza explained breathlessly. "The rumors of disaster were all wrong. Wellington has defeated Napoleon! Oh, Chad, we've won!" Speechless, Chad led her to his study, where a fire still blazed brightly in the hearth.

"You are working late tonight," she said, glancing at the disorder on his desk.

"Yes," he said briefly. Jem and Ravi Chand had left the room only seconds before Liza had appeared at his front door. Plans for the downfall of Mr. Giles Daventry were reaching fulfillment. Gyp Mahoney had been apprehended late the evening before and had squealed like a frightened pig. By this time tomorrow, if all went well, Daventry would be less than dust beneath the feet of his ill-wishers. "Now tell me," he continued. "Just what did Rothschild say?"

Once more, Liza related the incredible tale of Nathan Rothschild's stormy Channel voyage, and the information that he had brought with him.

"I don't know the details, but he said that Napoleon is headed back to Paris with his tail between his legs. He also said," she recounted with sadness, "that there were many casualties. I fear our victory came at a great cost."

"Lord," said Chad, pacing the floor as he mused. "What a hullabaloo there will be tomorrow."

"Yes, but probably not until late in the day. Mr. Rothschild said that it will probably take that long for the news to reach this country through the normal channels. Chad, do you know what that means?"

Chad's answer came slowly. "It means that for the next

eighteen to twenty hours no one else in the country will know of the victory, if we keep your promise to Rothschild." He swung to face Liza again. "Did you sell out today?"

"My government securities? No. Did you?"

"No, I have been extremely reluctant to do so. You see, I found it extremely difficult to believe in the word of defeat that was being bandied about so carelessly. There just didn't seem to be enough information to justify that conclusion. However recent reports were beginning to carry quite an authentic ring to them. I planned to go into the City tomorrow to give Thomas a sell order. Naturally," he continued, glancing at her sharply, "I shall abide by your promise. I shall say nothing until the news comes in some sort of official statement."

By now he had settled Liza in a chair by the fire and poured glasses of sherry for both of them. He seated himself nearby and scrutinized her carefully.

Liza became aware of the silence about them. The wine, she thought, had gone to her head rather quickly, for, gazing into the emerald depths of his eyes, she felt dizzy and breathless. When he reached to touch her hand, the pressure of his fingers seemed to warm her, as though a spark from the fire had leaped to consume her.

"Liza . . ." His voice was low and uncharacteristically hesitant. "Why did you come to tell me this?"

She knew the heat that sprang to her cheeks did not come from the hearth, and she made as though to remove her hand from Chad's grasp. He only gripped her fingers tighter, and she dropped her eyes.

"I have heard that much, if not all, of the thousand pounds you staked against the Queen's Pendant was put into government securities." She shot a glance upward and read a number of conflicting emotions in his eyes—surprise, amusement, and even a certain sheepishness, she thought. "I would not like to win our wager," she continued, swallowing hard, "knowing that I withheld information that could have affected the outcome." She looked at him as straightly as she was able. "I considered it a matter of honor."

"I see."

For a moment Chad was struck speechless by the sense of wonder and dawning hope that enveloped him like a shining beneficence. That Liza would do this for him! That she would jeopardize her own chance of winning the wager by giving him this information! Brightsprings meant everything to her, yet she was willing to give it up for him.

Involuntarily he drew nearer to her, and Liza breathed in the scent of him—pleasantly musky, she noted with an odd detachment, and holding a hint of spice.

He lifted a hand to trace the curve of her cheek, and her heart pounded in such a tumultuous response that she felt he must feel it in his own pulse. His breath was warm against her skin as he bent his head closer. She lifted hers, mindlessly offering her lips.

Suddenly the door to the study was flung open, and the two sprang apart like guilty school children.

"I say," said Jem. "I forgot—oh!" His startled gaze encompassed the pair seated by the fireplace. "I'm terribly sorry, sir, I didn't know you had a, ah, a visitor." He withdrew the head he had thrust into the room, but Chad stood abruptly.

"No, no, it's all right, Jem."

Liza, too, had risen hurriedly, placing herself several feet away from her host. "Yes, I . . . I was just leaving. I had a message of, um, some urgency to deliver and . . ." Distractedly, she searched for the cloak and bonnet she had discarded upon her entry into the study. Springing into action, Jem plucked the garments from their resting place on Chad's desk and with valetlike precision assisted his master's harried guest in donning them.

No more was said between Chad and Liza until they reached the hall. With one hand on the latch, he adjusted the bonnet that had been tied so hastily.

"Perhaps we could drive into the City together tomorrow?" he asked.

Shaken, she merely nodded.

"And tomorrow evening—the celebrations should begin by then. Will you be out and about to enjoy them?"

"Yes, I suppose—oh!" She had gone a little pale. "I have an engagement that I . . . that is, we have been invited to Vauxhall—Charity and Mama have been looking forward to it. And since . . . that is, they cannot very well go without me."

"Oh?" Chad's tone was courteous, but rather distant.

"Yes, you see," said Liza in a failing voice. "The invitation is from Giles."

"I see." The icy rain that dashed into their faces as Chad escorted Liza to her door was no more chill than his reply. "I shall bid you good night, then, Lady Liza. And, I thank you for the information you brought."

Having handed her into her house, he turned on his heel and made his way back to his own.

Miserably Liza began the ascent to her room, unladylike epithets exploding in small bursts with each step. Damn that peculiar valet for his untimely intrusion! Damn her own idiocy in allowing Giles Daventry's name to come between her and Chad in that last intimate moment. And damn Giles Daventry himself. She reached her room, and, disinclined to endure the presence of her maid, began disrobing.

She had no desire to see Giles the next evening. If it weren't for Mama and Charity, she would have sent a note of regret. All the world and his wife would be at Vauxhall tomorrow, she supposed, for by then news of Wellington's victory would have been trumpeted across the country. She could not deprive her mother and sister of their pleasure.

She would instead, she determined, use the opportunity to impress upon Giles that she no longer considered him her companion and confidante, and that he would no longer be allowed to run tame in her household.

With these thoughts clutched firmly to her breast, she fell at last into a troubled sleep.

Next door Chad was experiencing the same difficulty in finding repose. Giles Daventry again! Liza certainly gave every evidence of preferring the company of that toad to his own. Yet, he was sure the fire that had plunged through his veins at her touch this evening had been matched by her own. If his blasted valet had not interrupted them . . . He had been prepared to forget—at least for that one, precious moment—that Liza believed him to be a thief. For, surely, would she have hastened to tell him of Wellington's victory, obviously against Rothschild's wishes, if she did not feel something for him? She spoke of honor, but he could have sworn there was something more involved. He hugged the knowledge to him, as a man caught out in freezing weather would warm himself with a glowing ember.

There would, he reflected with mixed emotions, be no meeting between Liza and Daventry at Vauxhall tomorrow evening, for if all went according to plan, Daventry would by then be under arrest for thievery and a number of other crimes. All was arranged with the magistrate for Jem and Ravi Chand to meet with the Runner, George Thurgood, at Daventry's lodgings late in the afternoon. At that point the pendant would be revealed in its hiding place, and Giles Daventry's nefarious activities would be put to an end.

Chad, meanwhile, was to repair to Liza's side, ready to apprise her of these dramatic events. He preferred not to dwell on what her reaction would be, but he would be there to cushion her shock and to comfort her—if she would allow him that privilege.

Everyone agreed that the day could not have been more perfect for an occasion of celebration. Liza had been right in her expectations, for the crowd that jostled and pushed about the Great Walk at Vauxhall Gardens was the largest she had ever seen. From their vantage point in the box Giles had hired, overlooking the concert pavilion, the press of merrymakers was so great that the waiters carrying trays of the famous burnt-wine punch and ham shavings to the tables that lined the walk were barely able to complete their rounds.

As Nathan Rothschild had predicted, the news of the British victory at Waterloo had not reached the public until very late in the afternoon. Earlier in the day she and Chad had made their way into the City in a ride that had been silent and uncomfortable.

"You want to do what?" Thomas had exclaimed, openmouthed, when they had explained their mission. "Good God, I've been doing nothing for the past two days but selling for my clients, and you want me to buy?" He had expostulated at some length, but in the end was forced to do their bidding. They went home immediately, and the carriage ride home seemed interminable.

Then, as the sun had begun to sink behind the chimney pots of the metropolis, and as the gentlemen in the clubs in St. James's Street were discussing the disaster that had befallen them, one of them looked out into street and saw to his astonishment a carriage wending its way from the Palace bearing several captured French Eagles. Shortly after that official word came from the War Office, and it was not long before word had spread from the City to Hampstead to Hackney to Greenwich to Lambeth, and from the exalted heights of Mayfair to the stews of Seven Dials. Soon all of London was ablaze with excitement. Huzzahs from thousands of throats filled the streets, and the sound of firecrackers and pistol shots could be heard everywhere.

Giles seemed to have been particularly affected, mused Liza. He had arrived at Rushlake House at the appointed time, his hazel eyes sparkling with an almost fevered animation. He had chattered incessantly during the drive to the river, where he had provided not only a scull for their transportation to the Vauxhall steps, but had arranged for a boat of violins and flutes to accompany them on their short journey.

Now he sat at Liza's side, his arm draped across the back of her chair. Twice he had allowed his fingers to slide along her shoulder, bare except for the zephyr scarf that she had chosen to wear over her gown of deep pink silk. She had shivered in distaste at his touch, and he had glanced at her in surprise, his eyes narrowing. Liza noted with some curiosity that several times during the evening, Giles consulted a small watch that hung from his waistcoat pocket.

The crowd roared as the band swung into a series of patriotic selections, phasing gradually into more popular songs of the day. When, in honor of Britain's Prussian allies, a vigorous German polka commenced, John Weston declared that he could contain himself no longer, and whisked Charity from the box to join the couples who had taken up the dance with a great stamping of feet and fluttering of skirts.

"Shall we join them, my dear?" asked Giles, his lips close to Liza's ear.

She withdrew slightly. "In this crowd? We shall be crushed to bits. Let us just enjoy the sight from here, shall we?"

"Nonsense." He rose and grasped her fingers. "This is a night for merriment!" he cried gaily, "and the more to share it with, the better. Come." Without giving her time to protest, he pulled her to her feet and hurried her from the box onto the Great Walk.

Once there Liza found herself buffeted unmercifully by the press of the other dancers, and after a few moments, even Giles's enthusiasm began to flag. He led her to one of the walks leading from the Pavilion, where the throng of concert-goers began to thin considerably.

"Whew!" exclaimed Giles, shrugging his disarranged coat into place. "You were right. I think we barely escaped with our lives." He replaced Liza's shawl about her, from where it now trailed to the ground, and lifting his hand, he tucked a wispy curl back into place. Liza had never resented these small intimacies from him before, but now she stiffened involuntarily. Apparently oblivious, Giles grasped her elbow.

He was oddly pale as he turned to speak to her. "Would you care to walk along the path before returning to the fray? I fear it may be some time before we can return to our box."

This plan of action suited Liza, for she had been looking all evening for an opportunity to speak quietly with Giles. She turned to accompany him, but was stayed for an instant as she caught a glimpse of a coppery head in the midst of the group of whirling dancers they had just left.

Chad! What in the world was he doing here? She craned her head for a glimpse of Caroline, but could see no sign of the beauty. The next instant Chad had disappeared, and Liza wondered if she had really seen him at all. With a smile she allowed herself to be led by Giles down the shadowed walk that led to one of the Gardens' picturesque groves.

Where the devil was she? thought Chad frantically. He pushed his way through the crowd of merrymakers toward the box where he had seen Lady Burnsall and Sir George a few minutes before, but it was still empty save for that amiable couple. He had seen Charity and John, flushed with laughter and love as they spun about the walkway directly before the pavilion. But of Liza, who was presumably with Daventry, there was no sign.

Dear God, what else could go wrong? The plan, so meticulously brought forward to bring Giles Daventry to justice, had developed into an unmitigated disaster. Jem had set out with Ravi Chand some hours earlier to meet George Thurgood at Daventry's lodging. They had returned not long afterward with the gloomy tidings that they had been met at the door by Jem's "inside man," who was fairly dancing in frustration. Their prey, he said, had left not five minutes earlier, and he had taken the pendant with him!

A search of Daventry's regular haunts failed to produce any

trace of him, and in desperation, Chad had come to Vauxhall in hopes of intercepting him here. God knew he had no wish to confront the bastard in front of Liza, but he now saw no other choice. Jem had stayed behind in Arlington Street, and Ravi Chand was also scouring the pleasure garden. He and Chad had persuaded Thurgood to join them. They had separated, but Chad had caught a glimpse of the Runner earlier, looking a great deal as though he would rather be someplace else.

Liza walked quietly in step with Giles. From time to time she cast a surreptitious glance at him, wondering at the aura of suppressed tension that surrounded him. She had, during the course of the day, composed several graceful little speeches, one of which she now pulled to the front of her mind.

"Giles," she began, but she got no further. They had reached a secluded glade near one wall of the Gardens, and here Giles halted abruptly.

"Liza," he said simultaneously. They both laughed awkwardly, and Giles drew her to a convenient bench near a small door in the wall.

"Liza." He repeated the word in a firm tone of voice. "There has been a rift between us of late, which I wish very much to heal. Pray tell me, most dear to my heart, what have I done to offend you."

Liza schooled her expression to one of compassion and turned to him. "You have done nothing in particular to offend me, Giles. It merely seems to me that of late you and I—that is, your values are different from mine. We apparently see things in different lights, and these—"

"No! Do not say so. You know I would do anything for you. You speak of Chad Lockridge, do you not? Liza, for years I have kept my knowledge of his villainy to myself to spare you. Now, when I begin to reveal the truth to you—you turn away from me."

She tried once more. "Giles, I do not know what it is you think you know, but I will not hear—"

"Then hear this." Giles leaped from the bench and plunged himself to one knee at Liza's feet. "My dearest girl, I know one thing beyond a shadow of a doubt. In the chaos of our misunderstandings, my love for you is like a star on the horizon. You must know that I worship you, and want nothing

more than to make you my own—so that I may protect you
forever from men such as Chad Lockridge."

"Giles!" Liza was so taken aback that, despite her anger at
his accusations, she almost laughed aloud at the absurd
grandiloquence of his words. She tried without success to
wrest herself from his grasping fingers. She looked about the
little grove and discovered to her dismay that she and Giles
were quite alone there. Embarrassed, and not a little alarmed
by Giles's wild fervor, she struggled to her feet. "Giles, you
have said quite enough, and," she continued in a sharp voice,
"you are being quite ridiculous."

He rose and stood very still.

"Am I?" he asked softly, and with infinite sadness. For a
moment Liza knew a deep regret at the course their friendship
has taken. An apology rose to her lips, but the next moment
Giles had grasped her gently by her shoulders.

"Oh, Liza, why could you not have loved me?" He bent his
head to hers and placed a gentle kiss on her lips. Liza made no
protest, but stood within his embrace, stiff and unresponsive.

He released her after a moment, and stood back to gaze at
her, his hair an almost luminescent silver in the moonlight fil-
tering through the nearby tree branches. His eyes glowed
oddly.

"And that, I suppose, is that." Liza caught a hint of rueful
amusement in his tone. "I shall return you to your family now,
but there is something I must show you first."

To Liza's surprise he began to lead her toward the small
door she had observed earlier.

Feeling extremely uncomfortable, she demurred awkwardly.
"Giles, please, let us go back."

"I'm afraid I must insist, my dear."

To Liza's astonishment, he continued to propel her toward
the door in the wall.

She opened her mouth to utter a more vehement protest, but
she was interrupted by a hard, cool voice speaking from the
shadows.

"The lady said she would rather not, Daventry. Perhaps she
has an aversion to being abducted."

Giles and Liza whirled in unison.

"Chad!" gasped Liza.

"That being the case," continued Chad, as though she had

not spoken, "I think it would be wise to take your filthy hands from her."

"What the devil do you think you're about, Lockridge?" snapped Giles, thrusting Liza behind him. "You have interrupted a private conversation, and you—"

"I know what I have interrupted, Daventry, and it is the last kidnapping in which you will ever be involved." Chad's voice rang with a tone Liza had never heard.

"What are you talking about, Chad?" she asked, bewildered. "Abduction? Kidnapping?"

"I think he has gone mad," snarled Giles. "Perhaps his financial difficulties, combined with guilt over his criminal affairs have given him a brain fever."

"Giles!" Liza could only stare at him, dumbfounded.

"But it's all true." Giles's voice rose. "I went to Bow Street today, Lockridge, and told them of the box containing Liza's pendant. I told them where it was found. I expect that when you return home tonight, you will find the Runners waiting for you."

Chad's voice was chilled steel as he spoke quietly. "I'm afraid it is with you they wish to speak—of the pendant—and piracy—and the slave trade among other things. If you—"

"Stop!" Liza raised her voice in anguish. "I don't know what is going on here, but I intend to find out. Let us all go to Rushlake House where we can—"

"I think not," Giles answered with brittle laughter. "I have no interest in sitting down at Rushlake House or anywhere else with Chad Lockridge."

Still holding Liza in his grip, he strode to the little door, which to Liza's surprise, proved to be unlocked. Giles flung it open. "If you won't leave," he said to Chad, "I shall escort Lady Liza home in my own conveyance."

Liza gave a small cry of protest as Giles began to bundle her through the door ahead of him, and with the speed of a striking panther, Chad sprang. He plunged one balled fist into the pit of Giles's stomach, and caught him squarely on the chin with the other. Giles crumpled to the ground, and in one fluid movement, Chad was atop him, his fingers wrapped around the other man's throat.

"I know," he said with great precision, "that you have the

pendant concealed somewhere on your slimy person, Daventry. Tell me where it is before I choke the life out of you."

Chad was not even breathing hard, and his words were spoken with a quiet calm that chilled Liza. She looked up suddenly, to discover that Ravi Chand had arrived on the scene. Moving silently as one with the shadows that surrounded them, he bent over Chad and Giles. In his hand, Liza caught the gleam of a knife blade raised purposefully.

"No!" she screamed.

"Do not concern yourself, lady," Ravi Chand said with what he no doubt considered calm reassurance. He gestured with the dagger. "A precaution merely."

He cast his eyes down to where Giles writhed in Chad's grip.

"Tell me what I want to know," Chad repeated as Giles pulled desperately at his fingers. Giles's muffled cries were growing faint when Ravi Chand prodded Chad gently with the tip of his evil-looking blade.

"Pardon, master. It appears the piece of dung"—he nudged Giles ungently with one large foot—"wishes to speak. Perhaps it is of no account, but he seems on the verge of expiring."

With a sudden movement Chad released his victim and sprang to his feet. He spoke in a soft growl as Ravi Chand hauled Giles to his feet. "Fetch it out, Daventry. Now."

"I don't know what you're talking about," croaked Giles. Chad took a menacing step toward him as Ravi Chand sighed meditatively. The knife blade gleamed once more and came to rest just above the top button of Giles's waistcoat.

Giles made a strangled sound and fumbled in his coat pocket. When he withdrew his hand, Liza cried out as she glimpsed the glitter of red and green fire blazing from between his fingers.

"The pendant!" she breathed. "The Queen's Pendant. Dear God, Giles . . ." She advanced on him, moving without volition until she stood directly before him. "Why, Giles?" Her voice broke. *"Why?"*

Dumbly he extended his hands to her, and she brought hers up to receive the pendant. He stepped back from her.

"You'd never understand in a million years," he said with an air of great weariness. "You with your comfortable fortune, and your tiresome ability to make money whenever you turn your hand to it."

"Which"—Chad's cool voice interrupted—"no doubt explains your plans to whisk Liza away for a clandestine marriage."

Liza whirled to face him. "Clandestine marriage?" she whispered in bewilderment.

Chapter 21

IT seemed to Liza that the world was slowly dropping away from her piece by piece. This scene could not be taking place. She looked at Giles and saw a stranger. "Clandestine marriage?" she repeated through stiff lips.

"You have led us a merry chase today, Daventry," Chad continued conversationally. "It took us all of a very long afternoon to discover your plans. After we discovered you had removed the pendant from its hiding place in your bedchamber, it was several hours before we were able to learn that you had hired a traveling coach whose destination was to be Dover. Let me guess—the pendant, being extremely well known, had proved to be impossible to sell in this country, so you determined to peddle it on the Continent."

"What nonsense," snorted Giles.

"But," Chad continued smoothly, "the thought must have struck you immediately—why travel alone? Liza was proving unresponsive to your ardent declarations of love, and you were growing more and more desperate to get your hands on that comfortable fortune."

A sound escaped Liza, and for the first time since his silent glance a few moments before, Chad looked directly at her. In the darkened confines of the little bower it was hard to read his expression, but Liza thought she could detect concern and a certain wariness, and something else she could not define.

For a moment it looked as though Giles would continue his posture of outraged bluster, but then he slumped and expelled a sobbing breath. "Yes, it is true, but Liza, I have loved you for so long—I would have made you my queen! You could have chosen no other man who would—"

"The slave trade, Giles." Liza's voice cut through his impassioned words like a shard of ice. "Tell me about the slave trade."

Giles slumped onto the stone bench, defeat written in every line of his body.

"And tell her about the brothels, Daventry, and all the young women you have plucked off the streets, or from home and family to work in them."

"Oh my God, Giles . . ."

Her voice trailed off as footsteps could be heard approaching the little glade, and, with a strangled curse, a man thrust himself into their midst. He was short and portly and in a foul temper.

He peered around him and heaved an irritated grunt. "So here you are. I've been swanning about this benighted place fer an hour or more lookin' for ye. Had me face slapped twice and got me arse kicked as well, beggin' yer pardon, my lady."

George Thurgood looked quickly at Chad, then bent a baleful stare on Giles. "This the miscreant, is it? Sorry lookin' sight, ain't 'e?"

Giles scarcely seemed to notice when the Runner approached him and began reading in a singsong voice the charges against him. Mr. Thurgood had barely finished his litany when Charity and John Weston, followed closely by Lady Burnsall and Sir George, burst into the now-crowded shady nook.

"Liza?" chirped Lady Burnsall. "Chad? And Giles, for Heavens sake. We have been looking all over for you. What are you all doing hiding away here?"

"Liza!" This time it was Charity, raising her voice in astonishment. "Your pendant! It is returned to you. Who . . . ?" Once again an excited babble broke out accompanied by confused exclamations issuing from several throats. After several moments silence fell, as all present turned to contemplate Giles Daventry and his revealed iniquity.

"Good God," rumbled Sir George. "Who would have believed it?" Which seemed to sum up everyone's feelings.

"Mr. Daventry, sir?" The voice came from a young man who stood at the open doorway in the wall. "It's well beyond the hour you told me to have the coach ready. Is everything . . ." His words trailed off in a gurgle as he noticed the bulky figure hovering nearby, wearing the distinctive red waistcoat of a Bow Street Runner. Hastily he began to back through the door.

"Stebbins!" Liza, who had thought the evening could conain no more thunderbolts, fairly squeaked in her astonishment. "What are you doing here? Have you been—"

"Don't let him get away!" shouted Chad as the man prepared to distance himself from the scene with all possible speed. John Weston, who stood nearest to the wall, stepped forward, and surprised himself as well as the rest of the company, by flooring Lady Liza's erstwhile footman with a single blow to the chin.

"Oh, John," breathed Charity in starry-eyed wonderment.

"Well done!" Chad laughed. "I didn't realize you had a punishing left among your other talents." He moved toward Liza, and, observing the shock in her wide eyes, he motioned to the Runner, who began to haul Giles to his feet with the assistance of Ravi Chand. The Sikh had scooped up the unfortunate footman with one hand and now had him tucked under one arm, looking rather like a farmer's wife taking a pig to market.

A small disturbance took place, then, as Jem January strode into the shady enclosure. He looked somewhat the worse for wear, and inside his jacket a packet bulged conspicuously.

"Ah, Mr. Daventry," he said, a devil-light glinting in his eyes. "I see you are already in custody. I'm sorry to have missed the main event, but your minions in Arlington Street took exception to the removal of some papers I coveted. However I look forward to a comfortable coze with you"—he looked around—"in more private quarters."

Giles stared at him in blank astonishment. "I don't know you," he said plaintively. He gazed at the group surrounding him. "I don't know this man," he repeated, as though that fact somehow provided a measure of exoneration.

"Jem January, at your service, sir," responded that gentleman silkily. "And yes, you do know me, although it's been some time since we met."

Giles turned away, and with one last agonized glance at Liza, allowed himself to be led away by George Thurgood and Ravi Chand.

It was some hours later before all the questions had been dealt with to everyone's satisfaction. After the removal of Giles and the footman, Stebbins, from the scene, the rest of the party had adjourned to Chad's house, where he launched on an explanation of the stirring events of the evening.

"And I must not," he concluded with a burst of laughter,

"forget to thank the ally whom Providence thrust into my life at a most opportune moment."

All eyes turned to Jem, who rose and bowed. Despite his rather dilapidated appearance, he gave every appearance of one who was at home to a peg in a gentleman's drawing room.

Chad described the attack on him near Mervale house. Liza whitened, and Chad never took his eyes from her face as he told of the evidence that pointed to Giles's responsibility for the burning of his mill and the explosion at his mine.

"Dear God," she whispered. It was as though Chad spoke of someone she had never known—a vicious stranger who had for no reason set upon a maniacal course of destruction. With an effort she turned her attention back to Chad.

". . . who, by the way, has promised us an explanation of his dogged interest in Mr. Daventry's activities. Mr., ah, January?"

Jem turned to the faces interestedly tilted toward his. He smiled. "No, not January, as you have no doubt surmised by now. I took the name from the month I arrived in London for the first time." He drew in a deep breath. "I must apologize to you Mr. Lockridge, and to all the rest of you, I suppose, for entering your life under false pretenses. My name is Jeremy Standish, and my home is in Gloucestershire."

"Standish," repeated Chad thoughtfully. "I once knew a family of that name. My father used to buy horses from a Charles Standish. He was one of the best breeders in the country."

A smile sprang to lighten Jem's gray eyes. "Yes, Charles was my father."

"But"—Chad spoke slowly—"he wasn't Mr. Charles Standish; he was Lord Glenraven, was he not?"

Jem shuffled awkwardly. "Yes, that's true. My father was heir to a modest barony in Gloucestershire where my family and I lived happily until, through a piece of blackest perfidy, our home was taken from us. I won't burden you with details—suffice it to say that we were destroyed with the assistance of Giles Daventry. Because of him, and one other, I found myself alone in the world and cast upon the unkind streets of London at the tender age of fourteen years. I fared unexpectedly well in the tender environment of Seven Dials . . ."

"My God," muttered Chad, and the others in the group murmured like comments among themselves.

". . . and," continued Jem, "amassed a considerable amount of money—some of it by not very lawful means, I must confess—as well as an extensive network of, er, assistants, among them, skilled informants."

"But, here, I say," interposed Sir George. "If your father is dead, then . . . by Godfrey, you must be Lord Glenraven!"

"Well," said Jem shrugging his shoulders sheepishly, "yes, I am Lord Glenraven, though the title sounds much grander than circumstances warrant." He waited for the astonished gasps of his listeners to subside before continuing.

"The intention grew within me to right the wrong inflicted on my family, and in order to accomplish this, it was necessary for me to compile a complete dossier on the activities of Mr. Daventry." He turned to Chad with a grin. "It was my pursuit of Daventry, of course, that hurled me into your orbit so unexpectedly, and that is the one thing for which I owe him a debt of gratitude." He slipped into a thick Cockney voice. "It's been a pleasure to have the servin' of such a gentleman, yer worship. However," he continued with insouciance, "I fear I must hand in my resignation. It is time . . ." He paused, and concluded in a choked voice. "It is time for me to go home."

Chad rose to shake his hand. "Jem—or, rather, my lord, it's been one of the great pleasures of my life to know you. And if there is anything I can do in that other matter, you have but to ask."

"I should like to second that," interposed Liza. "I have a great deal for which to thank you, as well."

Jem raised his hand in a gesture resembling a salute. "I'm pleased to have assisted in the return of your property, my lady, and may I offer my good wishes for your future, er, enterprises."

"I suppose," said Chad, eyeing the thick packet of papers Jem still clutched to his chest, "you'll be heading for Gloucestershire immediately?"

"Yes, just as soon as I can arrange to talk to Daventry. There are still some things I must know that only he can tell me. And now"—Jem turned to address the group that was still hanging on his every word. "If you all will excuse me, it's been a hard day, and"—he gestured with the papers—"I have some reading to do."

Those remaining in the room spent some minutes in astonished speculation about the young man who had just absented himself. Then, Lady Burnsall stood to give her hand to Sir George.

"It is getting late, and, as that extraordinary young person just said, this has been a most fatiguing day. Do take me home, my dear. Charity, it is time you were in your bed, as well."

Charity rose and turned to John, who arranged her scarf gently over her shoulders. Liza, too, stood, and reached for her own belongings, but Chad laid his hand on her arm. "I wonder if I might have a word with you, Liza."

"Oh, but . . ." began Lady Burnsall. Then, eyeing her older daughter, she said simply. "Don't stay too long, my dear."

In a few moments Chad and Liza were alone in the elegant drawing room. Chad took her hands in his own. "I am so very sorry about all this," he said in a low voice.

"About Giles?"

"Yes. I . . . I know how you felt about him—and I truly regret causing you pain by . . . bringing him down. But, Liza, I was so afraid you would marry him, not knowing what he was like. I couldn't let you."

"Chad." Liza's voice was gentle. "The things you told me about Giles tonight—and the things he revealed about himself—came as a painful shock, but I had already become uncomfortable with him. I had begun to suspect that it was he who was responsible for the flow of rumors that nearly drew you under." She shook her head dazedly. "I thought him my friend. How could I have been so wrong about him?"

Chad said nothing, but his clasp on her fingers tightened. As always this created a sense of breathless anticipation within her, and she did not withdraw from him. She raised her eyes shyly to his. "I'm glad you asked me to stay, for I have something I wish to discuss with you, as well."

Chad studied her for a moment before saying, "And what is that?"

"Our wager will be up in two days," she began hesitantly.

"Yes," he answered in a low voice. What was she up to now, he wondered.

"I know that by this time tomorrow, the government securities you purchased with your wager stake will have increased many times in value. And perhaps that will enable you to win the wager, but, I don't want to wait that long. I wish to concede."

This was the last thing he had expected to hear her say, and he gaped at her unbelievingly.

"But . . . Why?"

"Because . . ." She fell silent, then continued on in a rush. "Because it was a stupid wager in the first place, and I only agreed to it because I . . . I have always wished for you to have the Queen's Pendant."

For one of the few times in his life, Chad felt bereft of speech.

"I don't understand," he said stupidly.

Liza sighed. "I'm not sure I do either, but I felt I owed it to you. I was so wretched when you left England, and, despite the fact that I hated you for leaving me, I felt somehow responsible for all that happened to you afterwards—your hasty flight, and the sly whisperings about your possible theft of the pendant. I was determined that I would recover it and prove the rumors false." She uttered a small, self-deprecating laugh. "You will think me a complete widgeon, but I had visions of bestowing the pendant on you . . . just so." She placed the jewel in his hands in a formal gesture. "Accompanied by a noble speech of the most exquisite sensibility, whereupon you would fall at my feet in gratitude. And then . . ." She bit her lips on the words she nearly uttered without thought—*and then I thought you might love me again.* Lord, she had almost made a complete fool of herself.

Chad felt as though he stood frozen in the center of a maelstrom of his own conflicting emotions. Grasping the pendant as he would a sword hilt, he fixed on the single most shattering of her utterances.

"*I*—left *you*? How can you possibly . . . ? If you will recall, Lady Liza, it was you who literally turned away from me, with words to the effect—as *I* recall—that you should have listened to your friends long before, implying that the tattle-mongers had been right all along." All the hurt and rage and disillusionment that had engulfed him on beholding her slender form so resolutely turned away from him, her hair falling down her back in a river of gold, rose to pierce him anew.

"I trusted you—I loved you. You were my rock in the ocean of slander in which I was drowning. And in the end, you, too, betrayed me." His gaze, which burned into hers like shafts of dark green fire, dropped to the pendant. "I thank you for your gesture—a truly generous one, but the Queen's Pendant is much too valuable to be used merely to assuage your conscience. I am, however, perfectly willing to call off the wager, and I shall be happy to purchase the bauble at market value."

He dropped the pendant in her lap and rose, moving to the window, where he stood looking out into the darkness. Liza stared at him aghast. Dear God, how could things have gone so wrong, and how could he possibly think that . . . ? She took a deep breath and schooled herself to the frigid calm she had developed with such great effort.

"Perhaps," she said stiffly, "you will be good enough to do the same for me in regard to Brightsprings."

Chad said nothing for several moments, then he turned to face her. "Sell Brightsprings to you?" He said at last, an odd tremor in his voice. "I'm afraid I cannot do that, for I have already sold it."

Liza went rigid with shock. She could not have heard correctly! Did he hate her so much that he would dangle Brightsprings before her only to toss it to someone else? But he could not have done so! How could he sell property that he had put up as a stake in a wager? Only a complete scoundrel would do such a thing, and Chad was not . . . She looked up to find him standing directly in front of her.

"Come," he said shortly. Dazedly Liza rose and followed him from the room. He led her down a short corridor to a chamber that evidently served him as a study. Numb with grief and humiliation, she watched as he withdrew from a drawer in his desk a piece of paper. Beckoning her into the room, he held the paper out to her.

"This is the title to Brightsprings," he said.

"But . . . I thought you said you . . ."

"I did sell it, but the deed has not yet been transferred. Would you like to know the identity of the buyer?"

Was this to be the final outrage, she wondered. Swallowing the hot words that sprang from her lips, she snatched the title from him. Her gaze traveled quickly over paragraphs of legal jargon until she came to a single line at the bottom, labeled PURCHASER. There, in flowing script was written—her own name! She lifted her eyes to Chad.

"I don't understand. How . . ."

"I prevailed upon Thomas to act in your behalf. You have

purchased Brightsprings for the sum of one guinea. The transaction was completed on the same day that our wager was sealed. I acted in much the same manner as you did with the pendant—and for much the same reasons. I invested in the Funds because I chose not to win the wager."

A trembling started deep within Liza's body and found its way into her voice. "And were you also hoping for gratitude, Mr. Lockridge? If so, I fear you will be sadly disappointed, for—oh, damn!"

To her horror the tears that had been welling in her throat, seemingly since Chad's return from India, chose that moment to burst from her.

"Liza!" cried Chad. "My God, don't do that." In a softer voice, he continued. "I've never seen you cry."

The tears, once started, would not be stopped. "That's because I haven't—that is, I never do—as a general r-rule. Please, p-pay me no attention. Oh, how I hate watering p-pots!" she choked, as a veritable freshet streamed down her cheeks. "P-pray excuse me. I . . . I have to g-go now."

She whirled blindly and would have run from the room, but Chad grasped her shoulders and turned her face into his shoulder.

"Liza, what is it? I thought you would be pleased."

"And I thought you would be p-pleased to have the Queen's Pendant returned to you, but . . . Oh, for Heaven's sake—have you a handkerchief about you?"

From his waistcoat pocket, Chad produced the desired article and Liza blew her streaming nose and mopped her cheeks. She pushed away from him.

"I don't know what made me do that. Please forgive me."

"I hurt you, Liza. I'm sorry for that."

"You hurt me before, too, and you were not in the least sorry about that." The tears started again, and Liza dabbed furiously at her eyes. "How could you say that I turned against you? I may have said some things—and I may have—well, yes, I did turn my back. But you hadn't had two words to say to me in weeks—I wanted you to . . . *talk* to me." She could barely speak for the sobs that shook her. "I know it was s-stupid, but I was trying to goad you into some reaction. I thought you would t-take me in your arms and . . . But you d-didn't. You just . . . Ohhh!" she wailed, weeping as she had done six years ago, huddled behind the door Chad had closed against her. What was the matter with her? Why couldn't she stop this stupid blubbering? She would be dissolving his carpet pretty soon. What must he think of her?

Whirling, she ran from him. She plunged pell-mell down the corridor, out of his house and into her own. She did not stop until she reached the sanctuary of her study. She flew to her desk and sank into a chair, discovering only then that Chad had followed her.

"What are you doing here?" she cried, her tears flowing unabated. "I w-wish to be alone!" She fumbled blindly in one of the drawers of her desk, searching for another handkerchief. Her furious rummaging caused a small wooden box to be expelled from its place, and it fell with a thump to the floor.

Chad did not answer, but, unthinking, bent to scoop up the box, his attention concentrated on Liza. It was only when he moved to set it on the desk that he glanced at it—and then looked again.

He turned it in his hands. "Isn't this the box made to hold the pendant?" he asked, an odd tone in his voice.

"Yes," she replied, still rummaging for something with which to stanch the seemingly bottomless well of her tears.

"But, didn't you take it to the magistrate?"

"The magi . . . no, of course not. Oh!" She glared at him suspiciously. "How did you know . . . ?"

"I overheard part of your chat with Giles in the garden the other day. It was my understanding that you planned to race over to Bow Street at the earliest opportunity to—"

"Chad Lockridge, you are the stupidest man I ever knew!" Her eyes were by now so swollen, she could barely see him, and she dashed her hand over them in an irritated attempt to clear her vision. "Do you really think I would simply hand over a piece of damning evidence against you? I knew you were innocent, after all—why would I go out of my way to cast suspicion on you?"

For a long moment Chad could only stare at her. He felt as though an incandescent flare had exploded inside him, illuminating dark corners that had festered within him for years. He gathered Liza to him. She made no resistance, but continued to murmur in damp, incomprehensible periods against his shoulder. She grew still, finally, except for a few convulsive aftersobs, but did not lift her head.

"How could I have been so stupid, Liza?" He lifted her chin

and smiled down into the drowned pools that were her eyes. "For that matter, how could you have been so stupid? What a pair we were—so full of misplaced pride that we could let fifteen minutes' worth of spiteful conversation ruin our lives? Or, at least, it almost ruined our lives."

Taking the handkerchief from her fingers, he wiped the last of her tears away. "You look like the very devil," he said tenderly, at which Liza uttered a watery chuckle.

"You certainly know how to cozen a lady, you silver-tongued rascal."

"It's a gift," he replied, his lips against her hair. He withdrew a little, so that he could look down into her face once more. "Do you think—that is—can we go back, Liza? I never stopped loving you, and I know now that I never will."

"Chad, I don't think we can ever go back, but we can go forward, because I love you, too. So very much."

She might have had more to say on the subject, but she was momentarily silenced as Chad's mouth came down on hers. She melted against him and gave herself up to the dizzying wonder of his embrace.

"Oh, Chad, my darling," she murmured some moments later, as, disheveled and breathless, she rested her head on his shoulder once more. "Perhaps I was wrong about not going back, for you make me feel like a young girl in love again."

"Instead of the ape leader you have become?" he asked solicitously. To stifle any protest she might utter against such calumny, he bent his head once again. After a very long while, Liza pushed herself gently away from him.

"I think," she said, with a shaky laugh, "that you had better take yourself off, Mr. Lockridge, before my reputation is irretrievably ruined."

"Oh, that's all right," replied Chad, pulling her to him once more. "Much is allowed engaged persons, after all."

"Ah. Are we engaged then?"

"My good woman." He bent a reproachful glance on her. "Have you been toying with my affections all this time? Or—no, you're right. I knew there was something that had escaped my attention. Lady Elizabeth, will you do me the inestimable honor of becoming my wife? At the first possible opportunity?"

For an answer she cupped his face in her hands and, pulling

it close to her own, pressed her lips against his once more. This time it was Chad who ended the embrace.

"You're right," he said in a husky growl. "It's time for me to go home—now."

They walked in silence through the silent house. She paused as a thought struck her. "Will the value of your newly purchased government stock be enough to offset the damage Giles caused to your financial efforts?"

He smiled down at her in the darkness.

"There is one other thing that slipped my mind. The losses I suffered were inconsequential. Liza, my dearest love, I have a confession to make to you. I am a very wealthy man."

"Oh," said Liza, snuggling into his shoulder, uncaring. They began walking again. "We shall have to inform Thomas first thing in the morning," she said, the happiness that surged through her creating an almost visible glow.

"Yes, he'll be pleased—and probably pretty self-congratulatory. I think he has rather fancied himself as matchmaker over the last three months."

"And here I thought it was all due to my famous luck," she replied, her laughter bright.

"No," said her beloved softly as he bent to her once more. "I rather think it was mine."